ot
hj
e. ...mber. New books
mont'
s

Critical Approaches to Children's Literature

Series Editors
Kerry Mallan
Cultural & Language Studies
Queensland University of Technology
Brisbane, QLD, Australia

Clare Bradford
Deakin University
Burwood, VIC, Australia

This timely new series brings innovative perspectives to research on children's literature. It offers accessible but sophisticated accounts of contemporary critical approaches and applies them to the study of a diverse range of children's texts - literature, film and multimedia. Critical Approaches to Children's Literature includes monographs from both internationally recognised and emerging scholars. It demonstrates how new voices, new combinations of theories, and new shifts in the scholarship of literary and cultural studies illuminate the study of children's texts.

More information about this series at
http://www.palgrave.com/gp/series/14930

Elisabeth Rose Gruner

Constructing the Adolescent Reader in Contemporary Young Adult Fiction

palgrave
macmillan

2019

Children's Books, Hist. of 1749

Elisabeth Rose Gruner
Richmond, VA, USA

Critical Approaches to Children's Literature
ISBN 978-1-137-53923-6   ISBN 978-1-137-53924-3   (eBook)
https://doi.org/10.1057/978-1-137-53924-3

© The Editor(s) (if applicable) and The Author(s) 2019
The author(s) has/have asserted their right(s) to be identified as the author(s) of this work in accordance with the Copyright, Designs and Patents Act 1988.
This work is subject to copyright. All rights are solely and exclusively licensed by the Publisher, whether the whole or part of the material is concerned, specifically the rights of translation, reprinting, reuse of illustrations, recitation, broadcasting, reproduction on microfilms or in any other physical way, and transmission or information storage and retrieval, electronic adaptation, computer software, or by similar or dissimilar methodology now known or hereafter developed.
The use of general descriptive names, registered names, trademarks, service marks, etc. in this publication does not imply, even in the absence of a specific statement, that such names are exempt from the relevant protective laws and regulations and therefore free for general use.
The publisher, the authors and the editors are safe to assume that the advice and information in this book are believed to be true and accurate at the date of publication. Neither the publisher nor the authors or the editors give a warranty, expressed or implied, with respect to the material contained herein or for any errors or omissions that may have been made. The publisher remains neutral with regard to jurisdictional claims in published maps and institutional affiliations.

Cover illustration: Westend61 Getty Images

This Palgrave Macmillan imprint is published by the registered company Springer Nature Limited
The registered company address is: The Campus, 4 Crinan Street, London, N1 9XW, United Kingdom

LONDON
2 9 JUL 2019
LIBRARY

To my Mother and Father

Acknowledgements

Sometime early in my academic career, in one of those conversations about families that are mostly meant to build sympathy for the speaker, I mentioned to a friend that my mother had read my dissertation and returned it with the typos marked. "Hold up," my friend responded. "Your mother *read* your dissertation?"

Well, yes. And before she did, she read the novels that I'd written about so that she'd understand it. If I didn't know it then, I know now what an act of love that was.

My mother made me a reader. She read voraciously and nearly indiscriminately, introducing me to Jane Austen and Georgette Heyer, Alcott and Twain, Burnett and Streatfeild, mixing genres and modes with an abandon that I have never fully discarded. While I now specialize in the one genre that I never found in her bookshelves, I like to think she'd approve of YA's place betwixt and between, like her favorite popular romances (see Chapter 3). While she didn't live to see this project finished and didn't have the chance to read this batch of books, I am taking this opportunity to thank her now for the great gift of her attention, her reading: a gift I am learning to value more and more every day.

This project was supported by grants from the University of Richmond's Arts & Sciences Faculty Research Committee, whose summer grant program gave me the freedom to research and write through two long summers on either side of my sabbatical. The A&S Dean's Office supported my most recent sabbatical, giving me the freedom to take a full year away from teaching and service simply to write.

My thanks go especially to former Dean Kathleen Skerrett, in whose office I worked for three years and who modeled a commitment to ongoing scholarship that inspired me to restart this project when it had stalled, as well as to Dean Patrice Rankine, whose support for my sabbatical enabled me to finish the project (almost) on schedule. I spent a good deal of that sabbatical writing in my kitchen, where Lu Bukach's impeccable design sense and craftsmanship created an environment equally conducive to baking and writing—sometimes at the same time—so I thank him here as well. The staff of Boatwright Memorial Library, particularly Carol Wittig, Head of Research & Instruction; Marcia Whitehead, Humanities Librarian; the Interlibrary Loan Office; and especially my friend Lucretia McCulley, Head of Scholarly Communication, has been indefatigable in support of both my research and my teaching for my entire career at Richmond, and these thanks are nowhere near enough.

Portions of Chapter 3 first appeared in my 2011 book chapter, "Telling Old Tales Newly: Intertextuality in Young Adult Fiction for Girls," in *Telling Children's Stories: Narrative Theory and Children's Literature*, ed. Michael Cadden. Lincoln, NE: University of Nebraska Press, 3–21. Chapter 5 is based in part on my 2011 article, "Wrestling with Religion: Pullman, Pratchett, and the Uses of Story," *Children's Literature Association Quarterly* 36:3, 276–295, which was later revised and republished as "Leading Through Reading in Contemporary Young Adult Fantasy by Philip Pullman and Terry Pratchett" in *Frontiers in Spiritual Leadership: Discovering the Better Angels of Our Nature*, ed. Allison, Scott; Kocher, Craig; and Goethals, Al. 2016. Palgrave Macmillan, 127–146. And speaking of Palgrave, I have had nothing but support and encouragement from a series of editors there, and most especially from Vicky Bates, to whom my profound thanks.

The Children's Literature Association has been my academic support network for many years now, offering me the colleagues and mentorship that a small department cannot provide. Conference goers over the years have asked great questions, suggested books I hadn't heard of, and offered thought-provoking talks that inspired me, and I cannot begin to express my gratitude. Phil Nel, Roberta Seelinger Trites, Richard Flynn, Lynne Vallone, Lissa Paul, Michelle Martin, and the late June Cummins are only a few among the many ChLA members who welcomed me early on, and whose friendship and support have been central to my development as a scholar and critic of children's and YA literature. Teya Rosenberg and Naomi Wood, as well as Lee Talley and Karin Westman, have included me in a number of generative conference panels, urging me to put words together before I was quite ready and thereby jump-starting sections of this book at key moments. Lee is also a subtle and encouraging reader of some of the worst first drafts ever and has cheered me on when revision seemed impossible. Julie Pfeiffer has championed this work from the start; I'm eternally grateful for her support and friendship.

Patricia Herrera was my accountability buddy at the start of this project, and Stephanie Cobb served the same indispensable function over the course of my sabbatical: thank you both. Early in this project, I spent productive hours with a writing group that included, at various times, Abigail Cheever, Laura Browder, Carol Summers, and Sydney Watts, all of whom made insightful and incisive comments on drafts of material that eventually made its way into the book. My departmental wise women, Abigail Cheever, Monika Siebert, and Elizabeth Outka, have offered support, guidance, fried chickpeas, books I kept too long, and medical advice above and beyond the call of duty; your friendship enriches my life. My weird sisters, Kristy Sánchez Carter and Roxanne Eberle, have been there since the beginning; Roxanne shared her book proposal with me and encouraged me to write about Twilight, and Kristy introduced me to Kiese Laymon's work. I love you both. My birthday buddies, Jane Berry and Yvonne Howell, had nothing to do with this book but I want to thank them anyway.

Rebecca Steinitz has read every word of this book in some form or other and offered guidance on its composition from the start all the way through to the finish line. While I am solely responsible for its failings, she has helped bring its argument forward in ways large and small, and my gratitude for her friendship is one of the best good things I will ever record.

And to my family: Given our adolescent history, my brothers, Mike and Larry, have been surprisingly supportive; my sister, Caroline, knows just how hard this work is and has been a cheerleader all along. My love and gratitude for all three of you are endless.

During the writing of this book, my young adult children have been transforming themselves before my eyes into some of the most excellent humans I know. For all the times I've nodded and smiled without really paying attention because I was thinking about the book, my apologies. And for all the books you've recommended or critiqued, and for your willingness to talk about them with me, my thanks. Mariah and Rose, you are the future I've been waiting for—but no pressure.

I kept this book away from Mark while I was writing it because he reads too carefully and I was afraid of what he'd find, afraid he'd suggest revisions I wasn't up to. I'm still a little afraid of that but it's too late now, so, Mark, read away. All those conversations over breakfast, or dinner, or whenever, have made their way into this and have made the book deeper and richer, just as you have enriched my life in all ways. Thank you.

If my mother made me a reader, she and my dad between them made me a writer. It was my mom who told me, on the days when I said I was bored and had nothing to read, that I could write something myself. And it was my dad who told me stories without endings and asked me to dream them up myself. He's the most disciplined writer I know, and the most productive, and if I have utterly failed to follow in his footsteps I have nonetheless learned from him more than I can possibly say. This book is dedicated to them both, with thanks for the books, the stories, and the love.

CONTENTS

CHAPTER 1

Introduction: Young Adults, Reading, and Young Adult Reading

This book begins in my classrooms, in three specific, ongoing, and related student concerns about teen readers and their reading. First, confronted with young adult literature that they deem "bad"—by which they usually mean of poor literary quality—college students often defend it for their imagined child and adolescent readers, on the grounds that "at least they're reading." I've heard this defense offered up for books as disparate as the *Baby-Sitters Club*, the *Twilight* Saga, and the Harry Potter series, all of which seemed to be subject to professorial disapproval. The students are afraid—or even sure—that the books they are championing are too popular to be literary, but they value them nonetheless. Their baseline assumption that all reading is good, however, quickly runs up against its own limits and the second concern. When confronted with literature they deem "bad"—in this case usually for controversial or challenging content rather than literary quality—those same students may challenge its "appropriateness" and argue for restricting its readership. Books as disparate as *The Adventures of Huckleberry Finn* (race), *Weetzie Bat* (sex/sexuality), and *The Giver* (death/eugenics), among others, have raised these challenges over the years, and I'm sure my colleagues can name many others. Is reading an unalloyed good, then, as the first comment suggests, or is it not? This seemingly naïve question has proved, in my classrooms at least, one of the most difficult to answer.

© The Author(s) 2019

E. R. Gruner, *Constructing the Adolescent Reader in Contemporary Young Adult Fiction*, Critical Approaches to Children's Literature, https://doi.org/10.1057/978-1-137-53924-3_1

The third concern is closely related to the second. Certain characters, students often find, are either good or poor role models for the readers they imagine encountering them. A book's appropriateness for young readers, then, might be determined not simply by a specific kind of content, but by the presence or absence of positive role models within the text. Students in my fairy-tale classes, for example, frequently end up debating whether or not to continue reading "Cinderella" to children, given the perceived antifeminist qualities of its heroine. Readers of the *Twilight* saga similarly debate Bella Swan's status as a role model, given how passively she accepts her vampire lover's rules for her behavior. Role model criticism, while rarely practiced by professionals, still has great currency in the classroom, if only because it is so often the first move of a beginner critic.[1]

In thinking about these questions and the relationships between them, I too began to look for role models—specifically, of readers. If reading is as important as we think it is, surely writers are finding a way to signal that importance. Who is reading in the books my students were reading? Who are the imagined readers for these books? And what kind of reading are they modeling for their readers? That search led to this book. What I found is that contemporary YA novels depict reading as neither an unalloyed good nor a dangerous ploy, but rather an essential, occasionally fraught, by turns escapist and instrumental, deeply pleasurable and highly contentious activity that has value far beyond the classroom skills or the specific content it conveys. As I will argue, books for teens depict teen readers as doers and suggest that their ability to read deeply, critically, and communally is crucial to the development of adolescent agency.

In the rest of this introduction, I focus first on the relevance of this claim: why does it matter what is happening in young adult fiction? I next focus more closely on the claim itself, clarifying terms that are often used interchangeably and exploring the implications of various approaches to

---

[1] In my article, "Cinderella, Marie Antoinette, and Sara: Roles and Role Models in *A Little Princess*," I argue for a more nuanced understanding of the value of role modeling. In brief, it seems to me that novels depicting readers, especially, speak to their own readers about the value of reading in ways that we should pay attention to. While we cannot posit a one-to-one relationship between character and reader, such novels "nurture the narrative imagination," expanding the opportunities to think about how reading works (Gruner 1998, 180).

reading. I then outline my interpretive methods, after which I provide a brief map of the book's organization. At a time when YA fiction's popularity seems to be ever-increasing despite widespread anxiety about reading's diminishing importance,[2] it seems critical to be clear-eyed about what reading does, why it is valuable, and how to promote it in a rising generation. This book is my contribution to that effort.

Why YA?

Why focus on teen readers and YA literature? For several interrelated reasons. First, as my students have intuited with their first concern, there is a widespread language of crisis around teen reading. Starting in the early 2000s, the National Endowment for the Arts published a series of reports on the status of reading in the USA that raised concerns about both the amount and quality of teen reading that continue to this day. In 2007, NEA Chair Dana Gioia introduced the second of these reports, "To Read or Not to Read," with the dire news that "Although there has been measurable progress in recent years in reading ability at the elementary school level, all progress appears to halt as children enter their teenage years" ("To Read" 2007, 5). Not only reading ability, but reading quantity also seemed to have fallen in the early twenty-first century (see, e.g., the reports on "Kids & Family Reading" issued roughly biennially by the Scholastic Corporation since 2006). Such findings date back at least to the end of the twentieth century: the National Education Association reports, for example, that "between 1984 and 1996 ...the percentage of 12th grade students reporting that they 'never' or 'hardly ever' read for fun increased from 9 percent to 16 percent" ("Reading at Risk" 2004).[3]

While the overwhelming evidence of these reports suggested a widespread crisis, not all analysts agreed. In 2011, Hannah Withers and Lauren Ross claimed that "Worldwide, young adults are the most

---

[2] See below for a fuller discussion of both of these claims.

[3] This number seems only to have grown in several more recent surveys. In 2004, 33% of Scottish pupils and 29% of UK pupils overall responded that they never or hardly ever read for pleasure (UK National Literacy Trust 2006, 11). In several recent Scholastic surveys, 18–21% of 15–17-year-olds said "I do not like [reading] at all" (2010, 44; 2015, 95; 2017, 103). While quantity and ability are of course different, and reading for pleasure may be an activity divorced from ability, many studies link them. For my purposes, reports on all three issues contribute to the larger sense of "crisis" that surrounds child and adolescent reading.

literate demographic" (Withers and Ross 2011). Going on to cite "a 2008 UNESCO report of literacy rates in 2000," they write: "96.8 percent of young adults in North America, ages 15–24, are literate and in the world, 87.6 percent of the same age group (959 million kids) can read (worldwide, only 82.4 percent of adults—people older than fifteen—are literate)" (Withers and Ross 2011). And while the National Endowment for the Arts proclaimed a crisis in reports from 2004 to 2007, their 2009 report was optimistically titled "Reading on the Rise: A New Chapter in American Literacy." In this report, chairman Dana Gioia announced that "After decades of declining trends, there has been a decisive and unambiguous increase among virtually every group measured in this comprehensive national survey" ("Reading on the Rise" 2009, preface).

But bad news travels further, faster, than good news, and my students—like many of us—are more attuned to the story of decline. Furthermore, a closer look at the data reveals that ability and amount, quality and quantity, are so frequently confused in the reports that it is hard, indeed, for a non-specialist to determine what the status of teen reading is at any given time. What is clear, however, is that people looking for bad news about reading often find it in the teen years, when reading becomes a complex set of interrelated skills. If the first stage of reading is decoding ("learning to read") and the second, beginning in about third grade or at about age eight, is functional literacy ("reading to learn"), adolescent literacy[4] encompasses a wide variety of skills, including "analysis, synthesis, organization, and evaluation," (Jacobs 2008, 15, quoting NCTE 2006, 5), or "engaging with complex ideas and information through interaction with written documents" and "using texts as vehicles for learning, critiquing, and extrapolating from

---

[4]In her recent *Tales of Literacy for the 21st Century*, Maryanne Wolf notes that the terms "literacy" and "reading" frequently substitute for each other; she distinguishes them as follows: "*literacy* refers to the attainment by an individual or a society of the full panoply of reading and writing skills. *Reading* refers more specifically to the multiple perceptual, cognitive, linguistic, affective, and physiological processes involved in the act of decoding and comprehending written language" (Wolf and Gottwald 2016, 2–3). In this work, I focus especially on reading, most often on reading books: books for young adults, perhaps unsurprisingly, are particularly likely to endorse book reading, and to depict book reading as an activity that will change readers' lives. As I will go on to argue, however, we will also see other kinds of reading, and indeed, the development of a broad array of literacy skills, as essential to civic agency in the twenty-first century.

extant knowledge" (Ippolito et al. 2008, 1–2).[5] Adolescence, in other words, is where children's reading branches out into a range of opportunities and meanings—or, as the crisis narrative suggests, fails to do so. As such, it focuses us on the importance and meaning of reading itself.

Second, my focus on young adult literature reflects its importance and popularity as well as its engagement with adolescent readers. While adolescent readers do not limit themselves to any one genre of literature, YA literature is of course the only genre that directly targets them. YA literature has been one of the most popular genres of the last twenty years, and it is within roughly the same time span that it has drawn serious attention from literary scholars.[6] While there have certainly been novels for and about young people for as long as there have been novels, the term "young adult" as applied to books for teenagers seems to date to the mid-twentieth century.[7] YA literature's generic status may be almost as vexed as the reading abilities and propensities of its audience. Lee Talley suggests that it can be tempting to see YA literature as "challeng[ing] the status quo," but the history of the genre tells a more complex story (Talley 2011, 228).[8] For Roberta Seelinger Trites, defining the genre cuts across both form and content—while most adolescent novels are, as she says, concerned like children's fiction with issues of growth, they also "tend to interrogate social constructions, foregrounding the relationship between the society and the individual rather than focusing on Self and self-discovery as children's literature does" (Trites 2000, 20). Trites argues for

---

[5] Jacobs synthesizes earlier research in noting that adolescent literacy requires enhanced reasoning skills in addition to the decoding skills of early reading (Jacobs 2008, 11–12 and 15–16). She is also, I believe, unique in suggesting that the issues of adolescent literacy begin to manifest as early as third or fourth grade. I also find Nilsen and Donelson's model of stages of literary appreciation helpful; they identify the teen years as a time of "finding oneself in literature" and "venturing beyond the self" (Nilsen and Donelson 2009, 11).

[6] See Withers and Ross (2011) and Hunt (1996).

[7] Cart (2011) has the most generous timeline of the many historians of YA literature, tracing its origins from 1868 with the publication of *Ragged Dick* and *Little Women*, but dating its contemporary manifestation from Maureen Daly's *Seventeenth Summer* (1942). Others locate its origins later, with novels such as *The Catcher in the Rye* (Salinger 1951) and *The Outsiders* (Hinton 1967) (see Chapter 2).

[8] See Coats (2011), Cart (2011), and Trites (2000) for fuller discussions of YA literature's origins and history, theoretical approaches to it, and its importance in the history of literature. As recently as 2011, Karen Coats noted that few critical works theorize YA fiction "as distinctive from literature for either children or adults" (Coats 2011, 317).

focusing on continued, rather than achieved, growth as a hallmark of adolescent literature; this suggests a formal definition of the genre in terms of a certain lack of closure, or openness to possibility, that is less characteristic of children's fiction. Of course, as Michael Cart notes, YA literature is also free—some might say compelled—to take up content issues that are far less visible in children's literature, including sexuality and sexual experience, drugs and other consciousness-altering experimentation, death, and suicide, etc. In both form and content, then, YA literature can stand in opposition to certain core values of contemporary society—the desire to "know" and to come to closure, and the desire to protect youth from the harsh realities of life. As Trites notes, however, in depicting adolescents' struggles with institutional power, the genre also constitutes its readers as social agents, incorporating them into the institutions it seems to challenge (Trites 2000, 27). This seems to me particularly true when we look at the way literacy functions in the genre: it is both the mode of entry into the form and a contested value within it. Reading is necessary—but dangerous; pleasurable—but painful; useful—but entertaining; girlish—but powerful; a right and a privilege.[9]

This book's purview is the very recent past: books published from the turn of the twentieth/twenty-first century forward. I am particularly interested in what's been happening since, for example, the USA adopted a national testing program for public schools (2002), *The New York Times* separated children's and young adult books from the adult best-seller list (2000), the 9/11 terror attacks created a seismic shift in the US and world politics (2001), and more generally, women and people of color became an increasingly important (if never valued enough) part of the political, literary, and cultural scene. Young people have been a part of all of these developments—as children in schools subject to standardized testing, as readers of best-selling novels, as migrants and refugees displaced by never-ending wars, as victims of race- and gender-based violence and activists against it, for example. Others have written eloquently on these topics, and I cannot pretend to do justice to them all; here, I simply note that we are in a historical moment

---

[9] In selecting texts for inclusion in this study, I have included some texts that might typically be considered "middle-grade" rather than "young adult," including Jacqueline Woodson's *Brown Girl Dreaming* and the Harry Potter series of novels. I have done so deliberately, because of their engagement with reading and their refusal to come to easy closure. I will address generic considerations more fully in the individual chapters that follow.

when teenagers are at the center of many of our most important cultural events. Their reading reflects that importance, I argue, by depicting young readers whose reading itself has shifted, and shifted in such a way as to help them develop their agency in an often hostile world. In the texts I examine, young readers who learn to read deeply and communally are able to make their worlds better.

In looking for depictions of reading and readers, I have focused especially on metafictions: novels that call attention to their own fictionality by thematizing reading itself. According to Joe Sutliff Sanders, the "mode of metafiction ... that documents the relationship between books and their readers" is "uniquely popular in children's literature," but it certainly has its place in young adult literature as well (Sanders 2009, 351).[10] As both Sanders and Claudia Nelson note, children's (and YA) metafiction reveals, among other things, adult concerns about children's and teen reading; it therefore provides a lens into the adolescent literacy crisis. YA fiction rarely escapes didacticism, however buried; one task of the YA metafiction, then, is to teach its reader how to read.[11] In doing so, it provides both reasons for reading and representations of reading; it often, however, also provides (perhaps inadvertent) cautionary tales about the dangers or limits of reading. In their ambivalent didacticism, YA metafictions encourage their readers to deepen their reading even as they recognize and depict its limits as a liberatory practice.

What is Reading Now?

While the language of crisis surrounding adolescent reading may be overblown or misplaced, many researchers still believe that reading itself is fundamentally changing in the twenty-first century, and not for the better. In her recent *Reader, Come Home*, reading researcher and

[10]My own use of the term "metafiction" tracks closely with Sanders's. Claudia Nelson distinguishes between novels which feature "bookworms," all of which might be said to be metafictional in that they call attention to reading, and subsets of that larger category, such as "intrusion fantasies" (one of which, *A Breath of Eyre*, I discuss in Chapter 3) and works about storytelling, many of which are included in this study (Nelson 2006, 223). Geoff Moss more restrictively claims that "metafiction ... denies that language is invisible and prevents total absorption in or identification with a book" (Moss 1990, 14).

[11]Trites writes: "In a literature often about growth, it is the rare author who can resist the impulse to moralize about how people grow" (Trites 2000, 73). Here, I focus on young people's growth as readers.

cognitive scientist Maryanne Wolf focuses on the effect of digital devices on reading, arguing that many readers now "scan" rather than reading deeply. Her analysis, furthermore, has implications for the economic and political prospects of both the readers themselves and the larger community of which they are a part:

> The complexity of argument and thought is being lost, "so that the end of deep reading—which is critical analysis, empathy, and ultimately a contemplative look at the truth—doesn't happen." The result in the past, she added, has been demagoguery. "If we in the twenty-first century are to preserve a vital collective conscience, we must ensure that all members of our society are able to read and think both deeply and well". (MacNeil 2018)

Of course, the digital revolution is not the only context for twenty-first-century reading. We also now read in an economic context ("the knowledge economy") that names reading a central requirement of economic viability; a cultural and political context that has expanded the literary canon over the last fifty years (though perhaps not as much as it might have), which may reflect an effort to expand readerly empathy; and a post-9/11 context that names some texts and readers "good" and others "bad" without significantly engaging them. That is, reading is at the center of many of our most recalcitrant recent political and social issues, and teen reading engages them all.

Economic Viability

Vicki Jacobs notes that the language of crisis is often a response to changes in what educators and policy-makers demand of readers, reflecting the development of a new model for reading rather than an actual decline in reading ability (Jacobs 2008, 16–21). That is, with the decline in factory work and other blue-collar trades, and the concomitant development of the "information" or "knowledge" economy, the demand for reading skills in the workplace has risen.[12]

[12] See *Reading Next* (2004, 1), Heller (n.d., n.p.), Fiester (2013, 9). But see also Moore et al., who make a similar point about future literacy needs in their position statement on adolescent literacy: "Adolescents entering the adult world in the 21st century will read and write more than at any other time in human history. They will need advanced levels of literacy to perform their jobs, run their households, act as citizens, and conduct their personal lives. They will need literacy to cope with the flood of information they will find

In the preface to "To Read or Not to Read," Gioia writes, "poor reading skills correlate with lower levels of financial and job success," ("To Read" 2007, 4). Similarly, focusing specifically on adolescent literacy, Ernest B. Fleishman's report for the Scholastic Corporation, "Adolescent Literacy: A National Reading Crisis," notes that:

> The societal implications of widespread adolescent illiteracy are sobering. Today's young adults who either graduate with low literacy skills or drop out of school have little chance for employment, even in low-paying jobs, and are more likely to end up on public assistance. Those who do find work are often stuck in minimum wage jobs that pay too little to support a family in today's society. (Fleishman, n.d., 2)[13]

As I noted above, literacy has long been associated with economic viability. Indeed, Maryanne Wolf, taking us deep into prehistory, attributes the development of reading and writing themselves (limited as they may have been) with the need to keep track of trade transactions.[14] Thus, as Steven Fischer and others claim, reading is an economic necessity of modern life:

> The development of a market economy of course favors those who can read and write. ... [A]bove all, it was the ability to read that created the Modern Human, and it was no coincidence that its emergence occurred at the intersect of the most-frequented land, river and sea routes that bore printed books and other reading material: widespread literacy is everywhere foremost a geo-economic occurrence. (Fischer 2003, 254)

Widespread literacy, then, developed alongside a modern market economy.

---

everywhere they turn. They will need literacy to feed their imaginations so they can create the world of the future. In a complex and sometimes even dangerous world, their ability to read will be crucial" (Moore et al. 1999, 99).

[13] See also: "American youth need strong literacy skills to succeed in school and in life. Students who do not acquire these skills find themselves at a serious disadvantage in social settings, as civil participants, and in the working world" (*Reading Next* 2004, 3).

[14] In *Proust and the Squid*, Wolf notes the origins of writing in clay "tokens" used to record "the number of goods bought or sold, such as sheep, goats, or bottles of wine. A lovely irony of our species' cognitive growth is that the world of letters may have begun as an envelope for the world of numbers" (Wolf 2007, 27).

Career readiness often involves what we might call "useful" or "informational" literacy, which is the first step in "reading to learn," the childhood precursor to adolescent literacy (see Jacobs 2008, 12).[15] Yet the modern knowledge economy requires a different kind of reading. These larger concerns about developing literacy beyond simple decoding lie behind the movement toward "standards-based" reading education. For example, the authors of "Ready or Not: Creating a High School Diploma That Counts" (the report that launched the effort to develop the US standards now known as the Common Core) preface their report with quotations from unnamed employers such as: "We cannot employ people here who cannot articulate clearly, cannot think clearly, who do not have the ability to absorb data, read effectively, write effectively … " (American Diploma Project 2004, iv). The verbs this unnamed executive deploys reflect those usually employed by adolescent reading researchers to describe that stage of literacy development (see above) and suggest a more nuanced set of skills than simple decoding: to "articulate," "think," and "absorb" is to be able to reflect on one's reading, not simply to pull data out of it. Yet while imaginative literature such as fiction demands these higher-order skills, characters who read in many YA novels may focus especially on informational literacy, suggesting an odd mismatch between the actions of the implied reader and the reader in the text. I discuss this issue more fully in Chapter 2.

Empathy

Empathy, or the ability to "feel with" another intelligence, is also an important outcome of reading, and failures of reading may be seen as failures of empathy.[16] Cognitive psychologist Maryanne Wolf and critic Lisa

---

[15] See Resnick and Resnick (1989, 186–187), for elaborations of these nearly self-evident categories. "Useful" literacy includes anything the reader can use immediately: recipes and user guides, for example. "Informational" literacy involves reading to develop a body of knowledge. Resnick and Resnick are careful to note that these are not properties of texts themselves, but of the reader's interaction with the text. That is, the cookbook reader who is making dinner is involved in a useful literacy transaction, while the cookbook reader who wants to gain an appreciation for how sourdough bread is made is engaged in an informational (or perhaps even a pleasurable, depending on her motives) literacy transaction. Both are, of course, essential to many kinds of employment.

[16] See Chapter 3 for a particularly gendered version of this argument. While some researchers may distinguish "theory of mind" from "empathy," others use them nearly interchangeably. For my purposes in this work, their similarities—the ability to recognize another's humanity—are more important than their differences. See Ann Jurecic for an especially

Zunshine, among others, focus on how reading (especially reading imaginative literature) helps develop a "theory of mind," or an ability to recognize the other as human. Wolf, for example, claims that "through stories and books [the child] is beginning to learn a repertoire of emotions...At work here is a reciprocal relationship between emotional development and reading" (Wolf 2007, 85). Such claims, however, long predate the development of cognitive neuroscience. Seth Lerer documents readers and writers from Augustine to the authors of the New England Primer, to cite some of his earliest examples, who thought of reading books as writing on the minds or souls of the reader, developing, for example, fellow feeling or fear—both, of course, components of empathy.[17] Wolf herself develops her argument for empathy as much from children's literature as from the evidence of cognitive neuroscience: reading, she writes, "is where we first learn to roam without abandon through Middle Earth, Lilliput, and Narnia. It is the place we first tried on the experiences of those we would never meet: princes and paupers, dragons and damsels, !Kung warriors, and a German-Jewish girl hiding in a Dutch attic from Nazi soldiers" (Wolf 2007, 7). For Elaine Scarry, the value of literature is its "capacity... to exercise and reinforce our recognition that there *are* other points of view in the world, and to make this recognition a powerful mental habit" (Scarry 2014, 42, emphasis in original).

For cognitive psychologist/novelist Keith Oatley, self-knowledge is the form of empathy most importantly developed through reading. Oatley argues that "that fiction is a kind of simulation of the social world. Stories were the very first simulations, designed to run on minds thousands of years before computers were invented. If we are right, then just as pilots' skills dealing with unanticipated events improve when they spend time in a flight simulator, so people's skills understanding

thoughtful analysis of the contributions and limitations of an empathy-based literary criticism. Suzanne Keen helpfully distinguishes between empathy as "cognitive perspective taking" and "affective empathy," a "vicarious, spontaneous sharing of affect" (Keen 2007, 4, 9).

[17] See Lerer (2006, 632–635). One of the most instructive of his anecdotes comes from Augustine's *Confessions*, in which he writes of his overwhelming sympathy for the *Aeneid*'s Dido—a sympathy he decries for taking his attention from God: "I learned to lament the death of Dido, who killed herself for love, while all the time, in the midst of these things, I was dying, separated from you, my God and my Life, and I shed no tears for my own plight" (*Aeneid* 1.13, Lerer 2006, 632). Note that for Augustine, unlike contemporary defenders of reading, such sympathy leads to sin.

themselves and others should improve when they spend time reading fiction" (Oatley 2011).[18] Half the children and teens surveyed in the Scholastic 2010 survey agreed that reading can "help you figure out who you are and who you could become as you grow older" ("Kids and Family" 2010, 21).[19] Oatley's studies of changes in attitude after reading fiction seem to support this claim.

Furthermore, Oatley and others' work on the positive outcomes of reading fiction forms the premises of movements like the #WeNeedDiverseBooks movement. Discussed more fully in Chapter 4, the movement proceeds from the premise that reading can develop both empathy for the other and validation for the self, qualities that demand a more diverse assortment of books for all readers. They are also, not incidentally, qualities that are frequently cited as twenty-first-century career skills.

While some researchers may focus on failures of empathy when teens *don't* read, others emphasize the dangers of empathy with what they *do* read. For example Ewan Morrison, writing in the *Guardian*, argues against reading YA dystopian fiction on the grounds that readers might identify with its anti-government thrust and thus may be susceptible to right-wing conspiracy theories (Morrison 2014). Meghan Cox Gurdon, in a frequently cited article in the *Wall Street Journal*, lamented the emphasis on "abuse, violence, and depravity" in YA literature, focusing especially how "dark" YA literature negatively affects readers' "happiness, moral development and tenderness of heart" (Gurdon 2011). Two years later, Tanith Carey wrote a similar piece, taking issue with what she called "Sick Lit" for the way it encourages identification with characters who self-harm, commit suicide, or spend their last days worrying about such trivialities as makeup and hair when they are dying (Carey 2013). While it is easy to dismantle this argument,[20] it is nonetheless common among those who would more closely curate, if not censor, teens' reading. As my own students suggest with their occasional desire to restrict teens' reading, dystopian fiction,

---

[18] Oatley's argument logically extends beyond fictional texts, of course, to all kinds of storytelling and storymaking, though his and my focus remains primarily on novels.

[19] While Scholastic's survey is biennial, the questions and the format for reporting the responses have not remained consistent over the years. This question does not seem to have been asked in more recent surveys.

[20] Michelle Pauli in the *Guardian* did so almost immediately, repeating the more common argument that teens—and others—"read to explore and experience other lives and thoughts and situations in a safe way" (Pauli 2013).

"problem novels," and the depiction of sex, drugs, and death in YA literature all raise concerns among (certain) commentators,[21] and complicate the position that simply increasing teens' reading will increase their economic and/or social skills.[22] This dilemma is further complicated when we consider the relationship between reading and citizenship.

Citizenship

Literacy and democracy have long been associated; from John Dewey to Paulo Freire, Thomas Jefferson to W.E.B. DuBois, theorists of both democracy and literacy connect the two. Widespread participation in democracy has, of course, not always seemed desirable, and literacy's association with democracy has not always been recognized as a social good. As Ana-Isabel Aliaga-Buchenau writes, "British nineteenth-century writers "criticized mass literacy as a cause of social dissolution," whereas French and American authors "were torn between applauding literacy as a tool of social advancement and socialization and criticizing it as dangerous to both the character and society as a whole" (Aliaga-Buchenau 2004, xi). Modern Western democracies, however, assume literate citizens who can read ballots, take written information on candidates and issues into account, and make informed judgments based on their reading.[23] Steven Wolk, in "Reading for a Better World," takes the association of citizenship and reading as a given: "Living in a democracy poses specific obligations for reading. While a nation of workers requires a country that *can* read, a democracy requires people that *do* read, read widely, and think and act in response to their reading" (Wolk 2000, 665, emphasis in original). Similarly, Bennett, Rhine, and Flickinger summarize earlier writers and reformers from the Massachusetts Bay Colony to "citizenship theorists of the early twentieth century," who "believed that literacy was a *sine qua non* for effective participation in public affairs"

---

[21] Perhaps the best indicators of the issues that most raise anxieties among parents and other gatekeepers are the ALA's annual lists of most banned and challenged books.

[22] My students frequently enter their Children's/YA literature class proclaiming that what's most important is simply that children read. But many of our class discussions are given over to the "appropriateness" (their word) of one book or another for the designated age group—even if the target readers are adolescents only a few years younger than themselves.

[23] Failures of democracy, in this narrative, thus correlate closely with failures in reading. I treat this issue more fully in Chapter 6.

(Bennett et al. 2000, 167). Jacy Ippolito and co-authors concur: "literacy liberates us from dependence on received wisdom and allows us to find and weigh the evidence ourselves. Simply put, literacy is a cornerstone of our freedom" (Ippolito et al. 2008, 1). Empirical evidence confirms that "the more Americans read, the more active they are in political arena" (Bennett et al. 2000, 180). Further, "spending time reading … enhances" tolerance, or the ability to "'put up with' … unpopular ideas" (Bennett et al. 2000, 182). Such tolerance, Bennet and his co-authors claim, is "a key facet of citizenship in an increasingly pluralistic society" (Bennett et al. 2000, 182). This claim associates citizenship with empathy, of course—it may also underlie at least one of the arguments associating literacy's empathy-creating qualities with career readiness: "Ready or Not," for example, associates the ability to tolerate ambiguity and to understand moral dilemmas in literature with workplace skills (American Diploma Project 2004, 30).

As with the argument linking reading and empathy, however, the argument that citizenship requires literacy may not be universally accepted. For example, a recent lawsuit charges the Michigan Department of Education with denying citizens a constitutional right by not teaching them to read. The plaintiffs' argument rests on the premise that literacy is a necessary precondition for the other rights enumerated in the Constitution; the judge overseeing the case, however, dismissed it on the grounds that the right to literacy is not guaranteed.[24] At the time of this writing, the case remains unresolved, with the plaintiffs planning to appeal the judge's decision.

While literacy writ large clearly has an association with citizenship, the specific correlation of adolescent literacy with civic engagement, as with both economic viability and empathy, is one primarily of futurity: that is, if literacy is required to make good citizens, adolescence is the time when this will (or won't) happen. While "the young adult text can be seen as a means of guiding youth through the social processes that lead to culturally determined maturity as well as a means of socializing youth," it may also "be seen as 'a series of inspired exercises in iconoclasm—of taboo busting, of shibboleth shattering'" (Pattee 2004, 244–245, 245 [citing Cart 1996]).

---

[24]Educational theorists dating back to the early republic debated whether public education should focus on basic work-related skills or "enrichment"—this dispute seems to be replicating that early debate (see Neem 2017, Chapter 3). Again, the argument is more complex than I can develop here; see Wong (2018) for a more thorough discussion.

If YA fiction may seem by turns to indoctrinate or to challenge,[25] it is the interaction with the text rather than the text itself that determines both the extent and the quality of a reader's political engagement. Thus, we turn to the reader.

METHODS: READING "READING"—AND READERS

I have taken an interdisciplinary approach in this book, recognizing that excellent work on reading has come from a variety of arenas—most helpfully, education, cognitive studies, literacy studies, and literary studies. Each of these disciplines has its own methods and approaches, and at times, they may seem to work at cross-purposes. In reports produced by Scholastic and the National Endowment for the Arts, as well as the studies done by cognitive neuroscientists and sociologists of reading, readers can be quantified, described, even individually named. Their readers are what we might call concrete readers—readers who are available for empirical analysis. In this study, however, "readers" are also characters—not only characters in the novels I discuss, but characters called forth by them. Reader-response theory suggests that while each reader's encounter with a text is unique, there are also certain expectations of a reader set up by a text. The reader imagined by the text—a "function of the work, even though it is not represented in the work"—is known as the "implied reader" (Schmid 2014, 2). While concrete readers may—indeed, often will—respond to texts as implied readers are assumed to, it is the latter rather than the former that we can derive from the text.[26] According to Robyn McCallum, commenting on theories of implied readers, "The idea that the 'best' readings are produced through strategies of identification places limitations on both reading strategies and narrative techniques" (McCallum 1999, 16). In the chapters that follow, then, I look at the readers represented within YA fiction, the implied

---

[25]Trites suggests that it does both at the same time. See especially "the paradox of rebelling to conform," a characteristic she finds especially in school stories, but which could be said to characterize much of YA literature more generally (Trites 2000, 34).

[26]See Schmid (2014): "The co-creative activity of the recipient can take on a degree and pursue a direction that is not provided in the work. Readings that fail to achieve or that even deliberately resist a reception designed in the work may well broaden the work's meaning. However, it must be conceded that every work contains, to a greater or lesser degree of ambiguity, signs pointing to its ideal reading" (10).

readers called forth by the novels and the limits within which both operate. If the character-as-reader is the protagonist of this study, the implied reader is their constant companion, the target of these role models, and the hope for the future that these novels embody.

I use the word "companion" deliberately, to indicate the sense of shared mission that these novels ultimately endorse. Reading, for centuries depicted most often as a solitary practice, becomes at its best in these novels a shared enterprise, a communal act.[27] When readers read together, they become civic agents, or develop the capacity to do so; when reading remains solitary or is utterly denied, so too is agency. Thus, these novels move beyond a simple "preaching to the choir"—representing reading as good to their own, presumably already converted, readers—or reinscribing of the authors' own likely history as readers, to begin, however tentatively, to develop new models of reading for a new era.

Jonathan Alexander's recent *Writing Youth: Young Adult Fiction as Literacy Sponsorship* suggests that YA literature's focus on literacy has recently taken "a peculiarly *neoliberal* form in its insistence that young people take responsibility for themselves and not rely on social structures for support" (Alexander 2017, 20). While I agree that we see an individualized instrumentalizing of literacy in some of the YA novels I will discuss, I analyze a countervailing impulse to create a communal reading practice that works against the individualist model.[28] We often start with the individual reader, however, in the character-driven novels that focus, among other things, on the development of reading skills and competencies of their protagonists. We might call these novels "literacy narratives." The term "literacy narrative" comes from Janet Carey Eldred and Peter Mortensen, who adapt it from literacy studies to literary studies, distinguishing literacy narratives from coming of age novels or novels of education,[29] though there are, of course, significant overlaps between them. A "literacy narrative" tells the story of a character's "ongoing, social process of language acquisition" (Eldred and Mortensen 1992, 512).

---

[27] See Long (1993) and Chapter 6, below.

[28] Alexander also examines what he calls a move toward "collaboration and collectivity" in works by some YA lit authors. Such efforts lie primarily in youth-developed media rather than the collaborative reading practices I analyze in the chapters that follow.

[29] Literacy narratives can also be distinguished from the school stories treated in Chapter 2, which focus more on the content and purpose of their protagonists' reading than on their acquisition of skills.

"Language acquisition," here, may go far beyond the basics of learning to speak, incorporating all the varieties of literacies—oral, written, and cultural—that a character may acquire in the course of that character's narrative. Literacy narratives also raise questions, such as: "What happens if speaking a new language means cultural displacement? What happens if speaking a new language means losing self? … What happens when literacy is too narrowly defined as mere 'skills'?" (Eldred and Mortensen 1992, 515). These are, of course, particularly important questions when thinking about the ways reading is taught and tested, the skills we value in readers, and the ways literacy is marked and measured. While we may assume that more literacy and more agency are *a priori* goods, such may not always seem to be the case for young readers, depending on their contexts. In the analyses that follow, adolescent protagonists acquire literacy skills sufficient to their contexts—to school, to their gendered or raced socialization, their religious or magical affiliations, or, finally, their status as citizens.

Reader-response theory, the literacy narrative, metafiction, and the contributions of the empiricists all influence my work, but I have not consulted teen readers directly. Caroline Hunt laments this tendency: "In a field where nearly every serious essay considers the nature of the constructed reader and comments on the fact that almost all books for children and adolescents are written by adults, why are we not communicating more with actual teens?" (Hunt 2017, 215). While I recognize Hunt's concern, I am less troubled by it than she is, as I am a critic of fiction, not of teenagers. To be slightly less blithe, my training as a literary critic teaches me to focus on meaning inherent in texts—both the novels I engage with here and the extraliterary texts that surround them, which do indeed focus on concrete readers from time to time. Moreover, as Deirdre Shauna Lynch and Evelyne Ender have written of the reader in the novel, "Mysteriously, almost miraculously, this genre can enable us to read as though we were someone else—to apprehend, even as we ourselves read, how words on a page or screen put that other mind in motion too" (Lynch and Ender 2018, 1074).[30]

---

[30] Lynch and Ender's comment comes in the introduction to a PMLA special issue on "Cultures of Reading"—an issue containing no articles at all on reading in children's or young adult literature. Given that reading develops most in those early years, this seems to me a striking omission.

Finally, my memories of myself as reader, while certainly not substitutive for contemporary concrete readers, constitute my intervention into reading-as-practice, beyond reading-as-representation. While this book is not a history of my own reading, nor an account of any particular readers, I nonetheless ground it in my experience of reading, prefacing each chapter with a brief recollection. Reading has been a constant in my life from my earliest memories; I literally cannot recall myself as other than a reader, and my adolescent reading was formative in ways I have become increasingly aware of as I wrote this book. It was how I connected to others (if also how I was, at times, set apart); it was how I made sense of what often seemed senseless. I read for inclusion and escape, for mirrors and windows, for raw truths and flights of fancy. My first fictional role models were Bilbo Baggins and Laura Ingalls; the first novel that ever made me cry was *Gone with the Wind*. While I still love the humor, the adventure, and the rebellion that I found in those books, it took me years to try to unlearn the stories about race relations and gender roles that I imbibed from them—years and many other, better stories. This is not a book about those books, but about their power, and the power of books like them.

ORGANIZATION

This book unfolds in six chapters and a brief epilogue. In Chapter 2, I explore contemporary school stories. In novels set in school, characters depicted as readers may resist required reading but embrace what they discover on their own, resist the way they are being taught, or develop their own idiosyncratic ways of reading. Written against the backdrop of a new emphasis on standards-based learning, these texts are less focused on testing than we might have expected; rather, the novels provide a "shadow syllabus" for their implied readers, suggesting that through reading (especially reading these "syllabi"), they may develop power and agency. Braiding a commentary on reading within the literature provided in an educational setting provides a metacritical opportunity for the implied readers of these novels to reflect on their own literacy. Centering school as the site of reading, however, ultimately reinforces the values of the institution in which students' literacy is being produced, thus limiting their agency.

Many theorists of adolescent literacy focus specifically on gendered reading, finding both higher literacy rates and higher engagement in literature among girls than boys. While these data may certainly be challenged—and while they are usually used to focus on efforts to increase readership among boys—I argue in Chapter 3 that reading's association with girls raises a number of related problems. In texts structured by or in conversation with the romance tradition (both fairy-tales and novels), YA novels for girls are designed to generate empathy in their implied readers. These novels mount an implicit argument for reading's value that lies especially in a traditional, and traditionally gendered, literary canon: reading connects us, it makes us better, it "humanizes" us. Ultimately, however, these novels may provide a cautionary tale for the humanist defense of reading. Equating reading with humanization often comes in a package of conservative assumptions about gender and reading that threatens to undo the very claims that humanists are making.

In Chapter 4, I look specifically at the relationship between literacy and minoritized youth. In a climate informed by the #WeNeedDiverseBooks movement—though far from fully responsive to it—it is not surprising to find texts focusing specifically on adolescent literacy among underrepresented teens. Literacy and minoritized communities have a vexed relationship in the USA, from the denial of literacy to enslaved peoples to the literacy tests used to deny voting rights. The readers I examine in this chapter do not take their literacy for granted, but they are also under no illusion that reading alone will make them either whole or free. Economic power and political engagement take a backseat to empathy in novels that strive to reimagine the literary tradition. As both fictional characters and implied readers engage with the White canon, they must also craft their own—and the novels themselves may become the stories their characters seek out.

In Chapter 5, I take up how teen readers approach sacred or prophetic texts within both realistic and fantasy novels. It can be dangerous to read, these novels suggest, and perhaps especially dangerous to take on the task of interpretation—a task with little economic benefit and some risk. Such reading, however, empowers the young protagonists of these novels and may provide a model for deep reading that, crucially, involves developing a community of readers. These books challenge our perception of reading as a solitary act, providing a new method for reading both against and within the community.

Chapter 6 continues the exploration of power and agency by focusing specifically on reading and citizenship. As this introduction has already made clear, one of the primary benefits of reading, both for the

individual reader and for the *polis*, is the development of civic engagement. In a variety of disparate works—from historical fiction to dystopian literature, high fantasy to contemporary fantasy—literacy is central
to political agency. These novels reflect contemporary anxieties about
surveillance, totalitarianism, racial oppression, and other forms of civic
disempowerment. The stakes of adolescent literacy are high, these novels
suggest, because it is so critical to a particular kind of political engagement: both critically aware and empathic. While reading becomes part
of a system of resistance to oppression, not all YA authors are equally
sanguine about its potential: empathy, critical analysis, or political awareness may and often do fail, singly or together. Reading is the necessary
but not sufficient precondition, these novels suggest, for an engaged
citizenry.

Finally, in the epilogue, I turn to the most popular books for young
readers of the last several decades to ask: where are the readers in,
rather than of, the Harry Potter series? In *Harry Potter and the Deathly
Hallows*, Harry and his friends are finally required to grapple with all the
elements of literacy sketched out in this study. From reading in school
to gendered reading, reading for political engagement and across racial
(or species) divides, the characters in this final novel in the Harry Potter
series learn to read against the fundamentalist grain of their earlier
efforts. They develop a collaborative communal reading that provides a
model for their implied readers and a happy ending for the series. Yet
that happy ending rests on earlier compromises; reading remains both
indispensable and limited in the happy outcome. The book concludes,
then, with both a celebration and a caveat: adolescent reading is alive
and well, and changing before our eyes. The books for adolescents that
I have studied here model, at their best, a deep and communal reading
that contributes indispensably to the future of youth civic agency.

Works Cited

Alexander, Jonathan. 2017. *Writing Youth: Young Adult Fiction as Literacy
    Sponsorship*. Lanham, MD: Lexington Books.
Aliaga-Buchenau, Ana-Isabel. 2004. *The "Dangerous" Potential of Reading: Readers
    and the Negotiation of Power in Nineteenth-Century Narratives*. London:
    Routledge.
The American Diploma Project. 2004. *Ready or Not: Creating a High School Diploma
    That Counts*. Achieve, Inc. https://www.achieve.org/files/ReadyorNot.pdf.

Bennett, Stephen Earl, Staci L. Rhine, and Richard S. Flickinger. 2000. Reading's Impact on Democratic Citizenship in America. *Political Behavior* 22 (3): 167–195.

Carey, Tanith. 2013. The 'Sick-Lit' Books Aimed at Children: It's a Disturbing Phenomenon. Tales of Teenage Cancer, Self-Harm and Suicide.... *Daily Mail*, January 2. http://www.dailymail.co.uk/femail/article-2256356/The-sick-lit-books-aimed-children-Its-disturbing-phenomenon-Tales-teenage-cancer-self-harm-suicide-.html?ito=feeds-newsxml.

Cart, Michael. 2011. *Young Adult Literature: From Romance to Realism.* Chicago: ALA.

Christie, Frances, and Alyson Simpson (eds.). 2010. *Literacy and Social Responsibility: Multiple Perspectives.* London: Equinox.

Coats, Karen. 2011. Young Adult Literature: Growing Up, in Theory. In *Handbook of Research on Children's and Young Adult Literature*, ed. Shelby A. Wolf, Karen Coats, Patricia Enciso, and Christine A. Jenkins, 315–329. New York: Routledge.

DuCharme, Jamie. 2018. A Third of Teenagers Don't Read Books for Pleasure Anymore. *TIME*, August 20. http://time.com/5371053/teenagers-books-social-media/.

Eagleton, Terry. 1983, rev. 1996. *Literary Theory: An Introduction.* Minneapolis, MN: University of Minnesota Press.

Eldred, Janet Carey, and Peter Mortensen. 1992. Reading Literacy Narratives. *College English* 54 (5): 512–539.

Fiester, Leila. 2013. Early Warning Confirmed: A Research Update on Third Grade Reading. The Annie E. Casey Foundation. https://www.aecf.org/resources/early-warning-confirmed/.

Fischer, Steven Roger. 2003. *A History of Reading.* London: Reaktion Books.

Fleishman, Ernest B. n.d. Adolescent Literacy: A National Reading Crisis. Scholastic Professional Paper. https://www.scholastic.com/dodea/pdfs/Paper_Literacy_Crisis.pdf.

Freire, Paulo, and Donaldo Macedo. 1987. *Literacy: Reading the Word and the World.* Westport, CT: Bergin & Garvey.

Graff, Harvey J. 2011. *Literacy Myths, Legacies, and Lessons: New Studies on Literacy.* New Brunswick, NJ: Transaction Publishers.

Gruner, Elisabeth Rose. 1998. Cinderella, Marie Antoinette, and Sara: Roles and Role Models in *A Little Princess. The Lion and the Unicorn* 22 (2): 163–187.

Gurdon, Meghan Cox. 2011. Darkness Too Visible; Contemporary Fiction for Teens Is Rife with Explicit Abuse, Violence and Depravity. Why Is This Considered a Good Idea? *Wall Street Journal*, June 4. http://newman.richmond.edu:2048/login?url=https://search.proquest.com/docview/870051663?accountid=14731. Last updated November 18, 2017.

Hateley, Erica. 2012. 'In the Hands of the Receivers': The Politics of Literacy in *The Savage* by David Almond and Dave McKean. *Children's Literature in Education* 43: 170–180.

Heller, Rafael. n.d. The Scope of the Adolescent Literacy Crisis. *AdLit 101*. http://www.adlit.org/adlit_101/scope_of_the_adolescent_literacy_crisis/.

Hunt, Caroline. 1996. Young Adult Literature Evades the Theorists. *Children's Literature Association Quarterly* 21 (1): 4–11.

Hunt, Caroline. 2017. Forum: New Issues, New Responses in Young Adult Literature Criticism: Theory Rises, Maginot Line Endures. *Children's Literature Association Quarterly* 42 (2): 205–217.

Ippolito, Jacy, Jennifer L. Steele, and Jennifer F. Samson. 2008. Introduction: Why Adolescent Literacy Matters Now. *Harvard Educational Review* 78 (1): 1–6.

Jacobs, Vicki A. 2008. Adolescent Literacy: Putting the Crisis in Context. *Harvard Educational Review* 78 (1): 7–39.

Jurecic, Ann. 2011. Empathy and the Critic. *College English* 74 (1): 10–27.

Keen, Suzanne. 2007. *Empathy and the Novel*. New York: Oxford University Press.

Lee, Paula Young. 2016. The Power of Pop Literature: Why We Need Diverse Books More Than Ever. Salon.com, September 30. http://www.salon.com/2016/09/30/the-power-of-pop-literature-why-we-need-diverse-ya-books-more-than-ever/.

Lerer, Seth. 2006. "Thy Life to Mend, This Book Attend": Reading and Healing in the Arc of Children's Literature. *New Literary History* 37 (3): 631–642.

Long, Elizabeth. 1993. Textual Interpretation as Collective Action. In *The Ethnography of Reading*, ed. Jonathan Boyarin, 180–211. Berkeley: University of California Press.

Lord, Audre. 1983. The Master's Tools Will Never Dismantle the Master's House. In *This Bridge Called My Back: Writings by Radical Women of Color*, ed. Cherríe Moraga and Gloria Anzaldúa, 94–101. New York: Kitchen Table Press.

Lynch, Deirdre Shauna, and Evelyn Ender. 2018. Time for Reading. *PMLA* 133 (8): 1073–1082.

MacNeil, Taylor. 2018. Slow Down, Reader. *Tufts Now*, August 6.

McCallum, Robyn. 1999. *Ideologies of Identity in Adolescent Fiction: The Dialogic Construction of Subjectivity*. New York and London: Garland.

Moore, David W., Thomas W. Bean, Deanna Birdyshaw, and James A. Rycik. 1999. Adolescent Literacy: A Position Statement. *Journal of Adolescent & Adult Literacy* 43 (1): 97–112.

Morrison, Ewan. 2014. YA Dystopias Teach Children to Submit to the Free Market, not Fight Authority. *The Guardian*. September 1. https://www.theguardian.com/books/2014/sep/01/ya-dystopias-children-free-market-hunger-games-the-giver-divergent.

Moss, Geoff. 1990. Metafiction and the Poetics of Children's Literature. *Children's Literature Association Quarterly* 15 (2): 50–52.

Neem, Johann M. 2017. *Democracy's Schools: The Rise of Public Education in America*. Baltimore: Johns Hopkins University Press.

Nelson, Claudia. 2006. Writing the Reader: The Literary Child in and Beyond the Book. *Children's Literature Association Quarterly* 31 (3): 222–236.

Nilsen, Alleen Pace, and Kenneth L. Donelson. 2009. *Literature for Today's Young Adults*, 8th ed. Boston: Pearson.

Oatley, Keith. 2011. Why Fiction is Good for You. *Literary Review of Canada*, July/August. https://reviewcanada.ca/magazine/2011/07/why-fiction-is-good-for-you/.

Pattee, Amy S. 2004. Disturbing the Peace: The Function of Young Adult Literature and the Case of Catherine Atkins' *When Jeff Comes Home*. *Children's Literature in Education* 35 (3): 241–255.

Pauli, Michelle. 2013. 'Sick-lit'? Evidently Young Adult Fiction Is Too Complex for the Daily Mail. *The Guardian*, January 4. http://www.guardian.co.uk/books/2013/jan/04/sick-lit-young-adult-fiction-mail.

Price, Leah. 2012. *How to Do Things With Books in Victorian Britain*. Princeton: Princeton University Press.

"Reading at Risk: A Survey of Literary Reading in America." 2004. NEA Research Report #46. June. https://www.arts.gov/sites/default/files/RaRExec.pdf.

Reading Next—A Vision for Action and Research in Middle and High School Literacy: A Report to the Carnegie Corporation of New York. 2004. Alliance for Excellent Education. https://www.carnegie.org/media/filer_public/b7/5f/b75fba81-16cb-422d-ab59-373a6a07eb74/ccny_report_2004_reading.pdf.

"Reading on the Rise: A New Chapter in American Literacy." 2009. NEA Research Report, January. https://www.arts.gov/sites/default/files/ReadingonRise.pdf.

Resnick, Daniel P., and Lauren B. Resnick. 1989. Varieties of Literacy. In *Social History and Issues in Human Consciousness: Some Interdisciplinary Connections*, ed. Andrew E. Barnes and Peter N. Stearns, 171–196. New York: New York University Press.

Sanders, Joe Sutliff. 2009. The Critical Reader in Children's Metafiction. *The Lion and the Unicorn* 33 (3): 349–361.

Scarry, Elaine. 2014. Poetry, Injury, and the Ethics of Reading. In *The Humanities and Public Life*, ed. Peter Brooks and Hilary Jewett. New York: Fordham University Press.

Schmid, Wolf. 2014. Implied Reader. In *The Living Handbook of Narratology*, ed. Peter Hühn et al. Hamburg: Hamburg University.

Scholastic Kids & Family Reading Report. 2006.

———. 2008. *Reading in the 21st Century: Turning the Page with Technology*.

———. 2010. *Turning the Page in the Digital Age*. http://mediaroom.scholastic.com/files/KFRR_2010.pdf.

———. 2013. http://mediaroom.scholastic.com/files/kfrr2013-wappendix.pdf.

———. 2015. http://www.scholastic.com/readingreport/Scholastic-KidsAndFamilyReadingReport-5thEdition.pdf?v=100.

———. 2017. http://www.scholastic.com/readingreport/files/Scholastic-KFRR-6ed-2017.pdf.

Smith, Dinitia. 2000. The Times Plans a Children's Best-Seller List. *The New York Times*, June 24. https://www.nytimes.com/2000/06/24/books/the-times-plans-a-children-s-best-seller-list.html.

Stephens, John, and Robyn MacCallum. 1998. *Retelling Stories, Framing Culture: Traditional Story and Metanarratives in Children's Literature*. New York: Routledge.

Talley, Lee A. 2011. *Young Adult: Keywords for Children's Literature*, ed. Philip Nel and Lissa Paul. New York: New York University Press.

"To Read or Not to Read: A Question of National Consequence." 2007. NEA Research Report #47, November. https://www.arts.gov/sites/default/files/ToRead.pdf.

Tribunella, Eric L. 2007. Institutionalizing *The Outsiders*: YA Literature, Social Class, and the American Faith in Education. *Children's Literature in Education* 38: 87–101.

Trites, Roberta Seelinger. 2000. *Disturbing the Universe: Power and Repression in Adolescent Literature*. Iowa City: University of Iowa Press.

UK National Literacy Trust. 2006. *Reading for Pleasure: A Research Overview*. November. https://literacytrust.org.uk/research-services/research-reports/reading-pleasure-research-overview/.

U.S. National Education Association. n.d. Facts About Children's Literacy: Children Who Are Read to at Home Have a Higher Success Rate in School. http://www.nea.org/grants/facts-about-childrens-literacy.html.

Withers, Hannah, and Lauren Ross. 2011. Young People are Reading More Than You. *McSweeney's Internet Tendency*, February 8. https://www.mcsweeneys.net/articles/young-people-are-reading-more-than-you.

Wolf, Maryanne. 2007. *Proust and the Squid: The Story and Science of the Reading Brain*. New York: HarperPerennial.

———. 2018. *Reader, Come Home: The Reading Brain in a Digital World*. New York: HarperCollins.

Wolf, Maryanne, and Stephanie Gottwald. 2016. *Tales of Literacy for the 21st Century*. Oxford: Oxford University Press.

Wolk, Steven. 2000. Reading for a Better World: Teaching for Social Responsibility With Young Adult Literature. *Journal of Adolescent and Adult Literacy* 52 (8): 664–673.

Wong, Alia. 2018. Students in Detroit Are Suing the State Because They Weren't Taught to Read. *The Atlantic*, July 6. https://www.theatlantic.com/education/archive/2018/07/no-right-become-literate/564545/.

Zunshine, Lisa. 2006. *Why We Read Fiction: Theory of Mind and the Novel*. Columbus: Ohio State University Press.

CHAPTER 2

Reading in School

Next to my high school yearbook photo is a series of quotations taken from an eclectic group of sources: a play I'd read in my AP English class, my Classics teacher, a piece my chamber choir had sung, and Jane Austen. The quotations, interspersed with thanks to friends and teachers, were intended to signal aspects of my identity—my favorite people, courses, activities, authors. The Austen quotation—"I do not wish to think alike. I wish to have my own opinions"—was, I thought, my manifesto against the conformity of high school life. I prided myself on my independence of thought as well as my erudition—the quotation came not from one of the six canonical novels (only one of which, *Pride and Prejudice* we'd read in English class the year before) but from an unfinished novel, *The Watsons*, which I'd read on my own.[1]

A bookish teen, I used my reading to signal both inclusion and exclusion. But my desire to extend my reading beyond the prescribed curriculum, to make it my own, demonstrates exactly how enmeshed I was in the values of that curriculum, which was—at least in part—to teach me how to read for myself. And while I cast myself as an independent thinker, the kind of independence I here demonstrated—reading more

---

[1] Or maybe not. My recent attempts to trace the quotations have been fruitless, and I now believe that these particular lines may in fact have been written by a later "editor" who wrote a continuation of Austen's unfinished novel. If so, the edition from which I extracted the text is now out of print and unavailable.

© The Author(s) 2019   25
E. R. Gruner, *Constructing the Adolescent Reader in Contemporary Young Adult Fiction*, Critical Approaches to Children's Literature,
https://doi.org/10.1057/978-1-137-53924-3_2

than was assigned, using my reading to shape my opinions—was certainly compatible with what I was being taught to develop. We could say, then, that I here demonstrate what Roberta Seelinger Trites calls "the paradox of rebelling to conform" (Trites 2000, 34).

I begin with myself as a teen reader, a reader in school, because it is at least in part through my own experience that I read the characters in contemporary YA novels set in school. Like me, the characters I discuss in this chapter find themselves in books, at least partially; they connect through reading, they rebel and conform. Like me as well, they start out in school.

Reading is central to secondary school, most obviously in the formal curriculum of English (or language arts), History (or social studies), and foreign languages, though of course in every subject with a textbook. This book therefore begins in school, with literature written for young adults that engages with the high school curriculum in a variety of ways. As many critics have noted, school stories are a central part of the children's and YA literary canon. Early school stories such as Thomas Hughes's *Tom Brown's School-Days* (1857) "focus … on the initiation, conflicts, and eventual successes of a new student," often with the emphasis outside rather than inside the classroom, and this pattern continues in many contemporary school stories as well (Reimer 2009, 213). While most critics thus focus on the ways that school stories depict the construction of the citizen, regardless of school curricula, I am here especially interested in the relatively rare cases in which novels set in school actually depict interactions with the curriculum (34).[2] In its deep enmeshment in the educational process, recent YA literature set in school enters into the ongoing conversation about reading, posing questions such as: What is the value of reading? Why study literature? Does fiction matter in an information age? The answers they provide are sometimes tentative and often surprising: more often than not, contemporary school stories demonstrate a skepticism about reading that belies their implied readers' interests. Yet, as I will argue, their readerly protagonists engage in communal interpretive practices that extend their reading experiences: reading moves out beyond the curriculum, the school, and even the book, and they engage the word and the world as developing agents.

---

[2] Hughes writes, in the voice of the headmaster: "The object of all schools is not to ram Latin and Greek into boys, but to make them good English boys, good future citizens" (63). Most literary critics seem to agree; see Trites, 32; Reimer (2009, 222–224); and Rollin (2001) (where this passage is quoted).

The Catcher in the Rye and *The Outsiders* represent one branch of YA literature's origins, both in flight from and deeply engaged with school.[3] While neither Holden Caulfield of *The Catcher in the Rye* (Salinger 1951) nor Ponyboy of *The Outsiders* (Hinton 1967) spends much time in school within the pages of their respective novels, both are thoroughly implicated in the curricula of their times and our own. Holden famously misreads the Robert Burns poem, "Comin' Thro' the Rye," to give his novel its title, while *The Outsiders'* memorable tagline, "Stay gold, Ponyboy," references the Robert Frost poem, "Nothing gold can stay." Not only are both novels then tied to canonical poems, both represent themselves, in part (in the case of *The Catcher in the Rye*) or in full (in the case of *The Outsiders*) as the product of a class assignment. Finally, each has itself become a part of the high school canon—both are frequently found on summer reading lists or the syllabi of American high school English classes. Readers of the novels can thus share the fictional plane with characters in the novels in more than one way: students reading a novel can find themselves sharing a reading list with a protagonist, reading a novel as an assignment in which characters read other novels for assignments, or, perhaps most confusingly, reading a novel in which characters have "written" part of the novel as their own assignment.[4]

These are not simply coincidences. This threefold connection: representing reading within the text, representing [a portion of] the text itself as the product of an educational assignment, and finally becoming an educational product, is common to many young adult novels, especially those set in, around, or even in flight from school.[5] The braiding of a commentary on education within the literature provided in the educational setting provides a metacritical opportunity for students to reflect

[3]As noted in Chapter 1, YA literature has many origins. Its presence in the school curriculum, however, often originates in the social realism of teen novels such as *The Outsiders*, *The Catcher in the Rye*, as well, frequently appears on school reading lists and is often retrospectively classed among YA fiction. See Tribunella (2007) for a fuller discussion of that novel's place in the history of YA literature and the high school canon.

[4]See the epilogue for a more extended discussion of this kind of sharing of fictional planes in *Harry Potter and the Deathly Hallows* and *The Tales of Beedle the Bard*.

[5]These novels, though set in school, may not conform to the generic expectations of the school story, which almost always include, among other things, the incorporation of a new student (the protagonist) into a school community. While this is true for some of the novels I discuss, as we shall see below, it is not true of, for example, *The Outsiders*, *The Catcher in the Rye*, or *King Dork*.

on their own literacy, but ultimately reinforces the values of the institu-tion in which their literacy is being produced.[6] Novels like *The Catcher in the Rye* and more recent YA "classics" such as *Speak* (Anderson 1999), *Looking for Alaska* (Green 2005), *King Dork* (Portman 2006), and *The Disreputable History of Frankie Landau-Banks* (Lockhart 2008) all engage with the high school curriculum, present portions of the text as if they were assignments, and have now become the stuff of high school reading lists themselves. Unlike the earlier novels, however, the nov-els from the 1990s and 2000s that I focus on in this chapter take place within, rather than outside of, a high school campus. Even more fully implicated than their predecessors in the educational institutions they often appear to oppose, these novels play with reading, with the ways reading is taught, assigned, and experienced, metafictionally commenting on the experience their own implied readers are also undergoing, reas-suring them of its value and purpose, and modeling deeper and more experimental ways of playing with texts that may expand their readerly repertoires.

This chapter focuses first on where adolescents read. While the pro-tagonists of the foundational texts of YA literature, *The Catcher in the Rye* and *The Outsiders*, spend most of their time outside of school—even when, as noted above, their stories are deeply embedded in the educa-tional context—the novels of the 1990s and 2000s I discuss here revisit the school story, remaking it for a new generation. Thus even in *Speak* and *King Dork*, whose protagonists mostly define themselves in opposi-tion to school, the institution nonetheless remains a dominant setting for the text. This is not surprising: indeed, the students I teach in college are

---

[6] Eric Tribunella's reading of *The Outsiders* provides the template for my argument here, though he focuses broadly on the high school curriculum rather than specifically on read-ing, as I do. In his article, he reminds us that despite the fact that the novel takes place primarily outside of school, "as the novel ends we learn that Ponyboy is submitting it as make-up work for his English class. Hence, the book refers to itself as the product of an instructional assignment" (Tribunella 2007, 89). Tribunella argues convincingly that the novel becomes "effectively an endorsement of American education," and a celebration of the reader as a participant in a "common culture"—rather than, for example, a more sys-tematic analysis of class politics (Tribunella 2007, 99). Thus Tribunella emphasizes the ways in which the novel folds its readers, like its characters, into the institutions of school and social class, despite its seemingly radical depiction of class conflict in the body of the text. Tribunella does not really discuss the implications, either, of the novel that Ponyboy reads. It seems to me that the choice of *Gone with the Wind* may make his case even more fully.

likely to find themselves somewhat surprised by texts from earlier generations, in which children and young adults seem to spend days unsupervised. This is unlike their own experience, which far more closely tracks what we see in more recent novels: if they do not experience outright surveillance, they at least expect some daily contact with institutional authority. While in later chapters, we will explore reading that goes far afield, here we start where many students also start: in school, with curricular reading.

The "where" of reading also often determines the "what": for many adolescents, a great deal if not most of reading they do is assigned, curricular reading. In the novels I discuss here, the informational literacy transactions[7] of curricular reading form the groundwork for other, often more complex, literacy transactions. While not all readers develop into what Latrobe and Drury call "deep readers," the protagonists of the novels discussed here use assigned texts to connect with each other, with their own pasts, and with a larger community of readers in order to make meaning out of their experience both in and outside of school (Latrobe and Drury 2009, 5; see below for a more extended discussion of "deep reading" and of literacy transactions).

The "what" then connects us to the "how," which is the central focus of this chapter. The characters in these novels develop power and agency through the development of higher-order literacy skills. They misread and appropriate canonical texts, reject assigned texts in favor of pleasure reading, and move from solitary reading to communal interpretation, all the while developing deeper reading practices than their assignments demand. In modeling these skills for their adolescent readers, the texts implicitly reassure them of the value of the activity they are undertaking—and of the educational institution they may otherwise seem to oppose. The novels finally demonstrate a deeply paradoxical stance toward school, one that is familiar to any deep reader: opposing its authoritarian tendencies while celebrating the curriculum that can, even unintentionally, help adolescents along the way to developing agency.[8]

[7] As noted in the introduction, I take this term from Daniel P., and Lauren B. Resnick's work in "Varieties of literacy," though Luke and Freebody's "four resources model" might term it "meaning making" (see Brenner 2012, 42 for more on the "four resources model").

[8] Vicki Carrington, in her Bourdieuian reading of school literacy practices, reverses the emphasis here: "The legitimate linguistic habitus is objectified in the artifacts of school literacy instruction. Reference and textbooks, audiovisual and computer software, instructional texts, and the majority of children's literature, objectify and represent the legitimacy

WHERE: THE SCHOOL STORY

It's not surprising that YA literature would take place in school. As Roberta Trites notes, "the concept of school as a social institution is omnipresent in adolescent literature" (Trites 2000, 31). This is so, of course, at least in part because school is omnipresent in adolescent life, at least since the advent of compulsory education. While the school-leaving age is legally 16 in both the UK and the USA, where most of the novels I treat in this book are set, middle-class adolescents in both countries who expect to go to college (the target audience for most of the novels as well as the class that comprises the protagonists of the novels discussed in this chapter) usually graduate from high school at around age 18. Even Walter Dean Myers' *Monster*, whose central character is in jail, actually conforms to this pattern: a large part of the drama of the novel lies in his seeming departure from the expectations of his teachers and his family that he will finish high school and go to college. Trites focuses on the ways school functions as an institution against which adolescents may rebel in ways that set up later conformity; my emphasis here, however, is on the specific details of the school's literary curriculum rather than on the larger structures of power.

For Miles (Pudge) Halter and Frankie Landau-Banks, protagonists of the two boarding school novels *Looking for Alaska* and *The Disreputable History of Frankie Landau-Banks*, school involve a choice, and the choice is connected with reading. Miles leaves his public school in Florida to attend his father's alma mater, Culver Academy, in order to "seek a Great Perhaps" (Green 2005, 5). Miles gleans this language from a biography of François Rabelais, a book he has read primarily in order to find out Rabelais' last words. Frankie Landau-Banks, similarly attending her father's alma mater, is at Alabaster "for the connections" according to her father (Lockhart 2008, 20). Frankie herself, like Miles, is centrally connected with reading throughout the novel, from her reading of

---

of the official code. As much as they might convey and construe a liberatory ideology, these artifacts are self-limiting in that they portray the practices expected of the ideal literate citizen, and furthermore, present these practices as the consequence of literacy learning rather than as its precondition" (Carrington 2001, 277–278). While I find much of her argument compelling, my focus in this chapter is on the ways adolescents are able to evade official stories and write their own.

Dorothy Parker to her attraction to her first boyfriend for "his messy dorm room stacked with piles of paperbacks" (Lockhart 2008, 5, 30). While we see both characters first as extracurricular readers, however, it is their curricular reading that shapes both novels: the reading in Miles's World Religions class and the reading from Foucault that Frankie is introduced to in her course on Cities. The same is true of *King Dork*, in which a readerly protagonist—Tom Henderson introduces himself as a "kid who reads too much" (Portman 2006, 5)—nonetheless engages most deeply with an assigned text, *The Catcher in the Rye*, almost in spite of himself. Even in *Speak*, whose protagonist is not much of a reader, curricular reading such as *The Scarlet Letter* threads through the novel in significant ways and helps Melinda develop the agency that is the novel's focus.

Most reading done in school is what we might term either a "useful" or an "informational literacy transaction." The first is "when a reader uses a text to negotiate a particular, practical, here-and-now situation" (Resnick and Resnick 1989, 179), such as looking for a specific mathematical formula or recipe. The second, informational reading, is "meant to give the reader new knowledge and understanding, but not necessarily to help negotiate any specific situation" (Resnick and Resnick 1989, 186). Thinking of texts in this way focuses on an interaction with a text rather than its implicit purpose: when Pratchett's Tiffany Aching uses *The Goode Childe's Booke of Faerie Tales* to ascertain what kind of monster has arisen from the river, for example, she is engaging in a useful literacy transaction, even if most often one reads fairy-tales for pleasure (Pratchett 2003, 13–14). Similarly, when Melinda reads about suffragettes for her social studies paper, or Tom is assigned vocabulary words from *The Catcher in the Rye*, their teachers are engaging them in informational literacy transactions (*Speak, King Dork*).

But, of course, literacy continues to develop in adolescence.[9] Moving beyond the basic decoding and analytical skills that most readers develop in childhood, adolescent readers are developing the foundations for what Latrobe and Drury term "deep reading"—reading that, among other things, recognizes the possibility of approaching a text through a number of different conceptual frameworks. Deep readers may approach the text through the consideration of text, author, reader, and context

---

[9] See Jacobs (2008) and Ippolito et al. (2008), for an extended discussion of literacy in adolescence.

(Latrobe and Drury 2009, 5)—thus, adolescent readers' approach to a text should ideally not be unitary but multiple, contextual, and relational. Rather than "decoding" for literal meaning or even for "deeper" meaning or symbolism, adolescent readers should, according to Latrobe and Drury, be learning to recognize that texts can have different meanings for different readers and in different contexts, and can have different meanings depending on the reader's awareness of the author as a person or the text as a construct. The transactional readings often prescribed by the curriculum should ideally give way, then, as readers develop other frameworks for deep reading.

The standard secondary school curriculum, at least as represented in these novels, does not necessarily encourage the development of deep reading, however.[10] Rather, as we see especially in novels like *King Dork* or *Speak*, curricular engagement with texts is often at the level of an informational literacy transaction, designed to elicit vocabulary words for a test or "correct" interpretations for practice AP essays.[11] It is only by deliberately misreading, appropriating assigned texts for other purposes, developing communal reading strategies, and otherwise renegotiating the curriculum, that the teen protagonists of these novels model a more engaged reading practice for their own readers. So on the one hand the novels suggest that school is not a place to learn to read deeply—that school-promoted reading strategies are limited, shallow, and the opposite of engaging. Yet on the other hand the texts that the protagonists are assigned to read are themselves open to more engaged reading practices, practices that the novels do in fact model. The novels suggest that these practices may help teens develop power and agency. When they do so by learning the strategies that the schools actually promote, however, it may be a compromised power, a limited agency—as Trites suggests, these reading practices, however engaged, may "ultimately serve to sustain

[10] Patrick Sullivan concurs with this analysis, suggesting that the "readicide" of focusing on test-taking works against "'deep reading' [which] requires reflection, curiosity, humility, sustained attention, a commitment to rereading, consideration of multiple possibilities, and what the education scholar Sheridan Blau has called 'intellectual generosity'" (Sullivan 2016). (The term "readicide" is taken from Kelly Gallagher, whose book of the same title informs my own analysis of high school reading as well.)

[11] This is of course a deliberately reductive view of a secondary school curriculum. It is reflective of the depiction of English classes in most YA novels, however—which may reflect their authors' recollection of secondary school rather than current trends.

the status quo" (Trites 2000, 36; see also Carrington 2001). That limited power, however, provides a model for what could be greater power in less restricted circumstances. That is, adolescent power in schools is by definition limited, but these teens push the limits in intriguing and meaningful ways. Both the content of the curricular reading and the reading methods the teens develop contribute to their ability to develop their agency.

WHAT: CURRICULAR READING

For Frankie, it's Foucault; for Melinda, *The Scarlet Letter*; and for Tom Henderson, the central text is *The Catcher in the Rye*. While there is no single text associated with Miles's development as a reader in *Looking for Alaska*, his favorite class, Mr. Hyde's World Religions, becomes the touchstone for his development as a reader.[12] Each reader develops differently, however, demonstrating the many ways that canonical and curricular reading can be appropriated by teen readers.

Every literacy transaction is also a social transaction, as texts are "conver[ted] … from their apparent intended use to another"—in this case, by the institution of the school (Resnick and Resnick 1989, 186). For Tom's English teacher in *King Dork*, for example, *The Catcher in the Rye* seems merely to be a sourcebook for vocabulary words, while for Melinda's English teacher ("Hairwoman"), *The Scarlet Letter* becomes a hunting ground for symbols. These informational literacy transactions do not preclude pleasure, but they do make it beside the point. Tom derives pleasure, in fact, primarily from imitating his English teacher's mispronunciations of the vocabulary words, while Melinda's account of her English class focuses primarily on her former friend Rachel's resistance to Hairwoman's methods, methods that are particularly focused on uncovering "correct" interpretations.

One could derive a fairly conservative, canonical literature syllabus from the texts mentioned in YA novels set in school. In addition to those listed above, I could add: *Le Petit Prince*, *Moby-Dick*, *Ethan Frome*, *The Sound and the Fury*, *Things Fall Apart*, and *A Farewell to Arms* (*Looking for Alaska*), *I Know Why the Caged Bird Sings*, *Alice's Adventures in*

---

[12]Two decontextualized lines—"I go to seek a great beyond," reportedly François Rabelais's last words, and "How will I ever get out of this labyrinth of suffering?" from *The General in His Labyrinth*—become touchstones for Miles.

Wonderland, and *Dracula (Speak), A Separate Peace, Siddhartha, Le Peste (King Dork),* and perhaps the most obvious list of all, *To Kill a Mockingbird, This Side of Paradise, The Great Gatsby, Hamlet, Peter Pan, A Separate Peace* (again), *The Catcher in the Rye* (again), *On the Road, The Stranger, The Fountainhead, Walden,* and *Naked Lunch,* all in *The Perks of Being a Wallflower,* by Stephen Chbosky. Chbosky's novel is, in fact, so directly about the healing power of literature that it hardly bears discussion in this chapter, though it will come up from time to time. While some of the texts listed here are not clearly canonical, and in fact often come up on banned or challenged book lists, most are still reasonably familiar titles. Perhaps most strikingly, none is newer than Maya Angelou's memoir; these are more likely the recollected reading of the authors than the contemporary reading of today's teens. Chosen—as in fact many of today's assigned readings for teens are—for their assumed "timelessness" rather than contemporary relevance, many of the books mentioned are likely to strike a chord with most teen readers.[13] If they haven't read them, they've heard of them; they or someone they know has been assigned them in school. These form a significant part of the literary canon for young adults, even into the early twenty-first century.[14]

How: Misreading and Appropriation

Mining *The Scarlet Letter* for information in the middle of *Speak* has a twofold purpose. Melinda becomes a code-breaker of sorts, briefly enjoying Hairwoman's doomed efforts to engage the students in a hunt for

[13] Carrington speaks to the tendency of canonical literature to become weirdly ahistorical: "The objectification of official language codes in official texts acts to create what appears to be an ahistorical edifice. It gives these codes the appearance of naturalness, permanence, and an isolation from the ongoing struggles for social power, when in fact they are the site of these very struggles and represent the prize for the triumphant, that is, power to legitimize particular possible worlds via officialization" (Carrington 2001, 278).

[14] These novels do not really take up contemporary standards-based education following No Child Left Behind, again probably reflecting their grounding in the authors' own experiences rather than contemporary high schools. Nonetheless, most of the texts mentioned—or at least the authors—turn up on the sample reading lists in *Ready or Not,* the document that launched the Common Core, as well as on the Common Core exemplars for English Language Arts (American Diploma Project 2004, 101–130). While the sample reading lists from *Ready or Not,* like the novels I discuss here, contain few texts more recent than Maya Angelou's memoir, the Common Core exemplars skew much more contemporary. They also, somewhat puzzlingly, list *I Know Why the Caged Bird Sings* among informational texts.

symbols. Her gloss on the instructor's methods, while satirical, also suggests how readers might engage with the novel they are currently reading: "If he kept repeating 'She felt guilty, she felt guilty, she felt guilty,' it would be a boring book and no one would buy it. So he planted SYMBOLS, like the weather, and the whole light and dark thing, to show us how poor Hester feels" (Anderson 1999, 100).[15] Anderson's novel thus becomes self-explicating: Hairwoman next asks for symbolic associations with color, and in the following chapter Melinda paints with purple finger paints and her art teacher covers his own painting with black. Astute readers will work out the relationships.

At the same time, Melinda herself makes specific connections with the text she is reading, taking it beyond the informational transaction Hairwoman is requesting (one she never fulfills, in fact). Instead of searching for symbols, she connects empathetically with the protagonist: "I wonder if Hester tried to say no. She's kind of quiet. We would get along. I can see us, living in the woods, her wearing her A, me with an S maybe, S for silent, for stupid, for scared. S for silly. For shame" (Anderson 1999, 101).

We might call Melinda's musings a productive misreading. Hester is not in fact like Melinda, or not like the Melinda of this point in the text, who suffers silently and has little agency. This central passage, and the engagement through curricular reading with a canonical text, however, does appear to be a turning point in the novel. Wondering if "Hester tried to say no" is the most direct clue so far as to what has happened to Melinda. The novel develops further intertextual relationships (most directly with Maya Angelou's *I Know Why the Caged Bird Sings*) as it continues to unwind Melinda's trauma, but it is this scene in English class that most thoroughly explicates the reading practice that the novel implicitly endorses—an empathetic connection rather than (or in addition to) a hunt for symbols.[16]

While Melinda gains agency through a type of limited identification with the heroines of the texts she reads, *King Dork*'s Tom Henderson resists the notion that he might identify with Holden Caulfield, the protagonist of *The Catcher in the Rye*. In fact, his initial assessment of *The Catcher in the Rye* is dismissive at best: he's read it "like three hundred

---

[15] Barbara Tannert-Smith makes a similar point, noting that "breaking into [her] head and finding the key to [her] secrets" is "precisely the process Melinda demands of her own reader" (Tannert-Smith 2010, 407).

[16] See Chapter 3 for a more extended discussion of empathy in this novel.

times" and thinks "it sucks," and he characterizes Holden as "a kind of misfit kid superhero" who is "the ultimate guy" for teachers, "a real dream-boat" (Portman 2006, 12). It goes without saying that Tom does not put himself in that category. Tom recognizes that *The Catcher in the Rye* is often used, as Trites suggests much YA literature is, to "instill…a sense of tame rebelliousness in the above-average student" (Portman 2006, 34). The informational literacy transaction his own teacher engages the class in, however, is to "copy out chapter one, highlight the words with three or more syllables, define them, and use them in sentences" (Portman 2006, 34). It is hard to imagine a less pleasurable use of the novel, at least for a "Holden-y kid" (Portman 2006, 13).

Despite this unpromising beginning, however, Tom does derive both pleasure and a sense of identification from his engagement with not only *The Catcher in the Rye* but other novels he reads through the course of his own story. Tom's identification is especially with his father, through the medium of the book as an object: reading the particular copy of *The Catcher in the Rye* that his father owned, as well as his other books, begins to "put my dad in a picture made up of things that weren't entirely imaginary or theoretical. It allowed me to imagine myself in his place in the past" (Portman 2006, 318–319). This kind of imagining, which is a kind of empathy or theory of mind,[17] ends up extending to the fictional character he has heretofore rejected. His ongoing engagement with the book as an object outside of class actually does increase his engagement with the text itself.

Tom's engagement with *The Catcher in the Rye* comes about, as I've noted, primarily as an object, one of a box of books of his father's that he finds in the basement. This cache of his father's books becomes, he believes, the key to a mystery—about his father's death, perhaps, or about his own identity. The materiality of the books themselves is central, then, to his reading of them—he is interested in the markings his father made in them, the bookmarks he left, the stains and other physical reminders of his father's now lost presence. His engagement with *Catcher* extends further for two reasons—first, because it is assigned in his English class, which is why he retrieved it from the basement in the first place, and second, because he discovers in it what appears to be the key to a cipher, a cipher that he comes to believe may hold the key to

---

[17]See, e.g. Zunshine, Keen, Wolf, Oatley, as referenced in the introduction. I take up empathy as a reading strategy more fully in Chapter 3.

the mystery of his father's death. In this, the novel brilliantly parodies the tendency—also satirized in the *Scarlet Letter* passage in *Speak*—of beginning literary critics to try to "crack the code" of an author's intentions. This parody of literary criticism both animates the novel and strips the texts of any association with adult authority, since Tom becomes the arbiter of their meaning for his own life.

In his search for meaning, Tom reads the novel deeply, even in his rejection, analyzing the title reference in an extended passage:

> The title of *The Catcher in the Rye* comes from a misquoted poem by Robert Burns, which Holden Caulfield elaborates into a mystical fantasy about saving children from falling off a cliff. There are all these kids playing in a field of rye, and he stands guard ready to catch them if they stray from the field. A lot of people have found this to be a very moving metaphor for the experience of growing up, or anxiety about the loss of innocence, or the Mysterious Dance of Life. Or any random thing, really.
>
> To use HC's own terminology, it has always seemed pretty goddam phony and all to me ....
>
> The brilliance of it, though, is that the people in the *Catcher* cult manage to see themselves as everybody in the scenario all at once. They're the cute, virtuous kids playing in the rye, and they're also the troubled misfit adolescent who dreams of preserving the kids' innocence by force and who turns out to have been right all along. And they're *also* the grown-up moralistic busybody with the kid-sized butterfly net who is charged with keeping all the kids on the premises, no matter what. Somehow, they don't realize that you can't root for them all. (Portman 2006, 245–246)

Tom's recognition, here—that "you can't root for them all"—suggests a more subtle reading of the text than the one he believes has been foisted on him by teachers and parents, members of "the *Catcher* cult," as he terms it. He identifies here with the kids, who he sees as

> try[ing] to find a quiet place where you can be by yourself ... or to write a song about a sad girl, or to read a book once owned by your deceased father. But pretty soon someone comes along and starts throwing gum in your hair ... and publicly charting your sexual unattractiveness ... and forcing you to read and copy out pages from the same three books over and over and over. So you think, who needs it? You get up and start walking. And just when you think you've found the edge of the field and are about to emerge from Rye Hell, this AP teacher or baby-boomer parent dressed as a beloved literary character scoops you up and throws you back into the

> pit of vipers. I mean, the field of rye. … I'm sorry, but I'm rooting for the
> kids and hoping they get out while they can. (Portman 2006, 246–247)

It cannot be lost on most readers that Tom has just reinvented himself as Holden Caulfield here. Both want to save the children, but the terms of that salvation have changed. Where Holden sees a physical danger—the cliff edge—Tom sees an escape from conformity, from being forced into the same "field" as all the other "psycho normals" in school.

It is ironic that *The Catcher in the Rye* of all novels becomes so associated with adult authority. Books in general, however (and, we might add, books incorporated into the high school curriculum in particular), often become de facto representations of adult authority in children's and young adult literature, no matter what their content (Doughty 2013, 1; see also Carrington 2001). The double bind is clear: the novel may try to urge rebellion or resistance to authority, but it is also the representation of authority (a problem Tribunella also notes with *The Outsiders*). The escape from the double bind, if there is one, comes in appropriating the novel, refusing to read it in the manner prescribed, and using it, as Tom does here, both to achieve empathy with others and to undermine authority—in Tom's case, Mr. Teone's authority, a metonym for the authority of the school in general. In the end, what Tom achieves sounds surprisingly like what has been called the goal of "aesthetic reading": Tom is able, through the exploration of the book as object, to "enter the inner lives of others, and identify with" those who are quite unlike him—his father and even his stepfather (Barrs 2000, 292). This achievement of empathy may in the end be more important to him than the challenge to authority that the book also authorizes. Like Melinda, then, Tom becomes a figure of identification as well as resistance; their ability to empathize with characters who are ostensibly quite unlike them serves as a model for their own implied readers, and a reading method that extends far beyond their own texts.

How: Interpretation and Communal Reading

In *Speak* and *King Dork*, most of the reading that the novels represent is solitary.[18] While Melinda's and Tom's *reading* is generally solitary, however, for both, the most productive and rewarding acts of *interpretation*

---

[18] See Elizabeth Long on the tradition of representing reading, even classroom reading, as solitary.

are shared: Tom's somewhat abortive efforts to decipher his father's code with Sam Hellerman and, more importantly, Melinda's communal writing wall (discussed below).

In *Looking for Alaska*, reading also begins as a solitary act but ends up a communal one. Shared between Miles and Chip at first, it ultimately extends among a group of friends who "read" the events around Alaska's death in order to make sense of it for themselves. Their curricular reading becomes secondary to this extracurricular communal reading, but also melds with it in Miles's case, as he uses his interpretation of the events surrounding Alaska's death as material for his final exam in World Religions.

Like Tom Henderson, Miles is introduced to us as a reader, though of a very particular kind of literature: Miles reads biographies, including biographies of creative writers, but not the poems, plays, or novels that they have written. This kind of reading marks Miles throughout—he is amassing facts, trying to develop patterns. And he does it alone, like most readers. Indeed, his status as both reader and loner is part of what marks him from the beginning of the novel, when his mother throws him an almost-unattended going-away party, and he explains his decision to leave for boarding school to his parents by quoting the biography of Francois Rabelais: "I go to seek a Great Perhaps" (Green 2005, 5). Miles's reading of biographies is, it turns out, almost purely informational: he gleans them for last words.

Chip has his own informational literacy preferences—he reads almanacs, memorizing names of countries and their capitals. Seeing Miles's world map on the wall, he immediately starts reciting country names. We later learn a little bit more about Chip's reading practices when he tells Miles about his application essay to Culver Creek: "[He] wrote in his application essay about how he wanted to go to a school where he could read long books. The problem, he said in the essay, was that his dad would always hit him with the books in his house, so Chip kept his books short and paperback for his own safety" (Green 2005, 11). As they are for Tom Henderson, books are a sort of paternal talisman to both Miles and Chip—Miles marks up his father's books despite being warned against it, and Chip must dodge the books his father throws—but both also shift the focus away from the book as an object into the content of the book in their own explorations through reading.

When Miles first meets Alaska Young, he is transfixed almost as much by her library as by her beauty. "Her library filled her bookshelves and then overflowed into waist-high stacks of books everywhere, piled haphazardly against the walls. If just one of them moved, I thought, the domino effect could engulf the three of us in an asphyxiating mass of literature" (Green 2005, 15).[19] Again, as in *King* Dork, at first the focus is on the books themselves. When Miles asks Alaska if she's read all the books in her room, she replies, "Oh God no. I've read maybe a third of 'em. But I'm *going to* read them all. I call it my Life's Library. Every summer since I was little, I've gone to garage sales and bought all the books that looked interesting. So I always have something to read" (Green 2005, 20). For Alaska too, then, books are objects to be acquired, to display, and perhaps—eventually—to read.

If books initially seem to unite the three friends who are at the center of the novel, however, their curricular reading is less central. Like most boarding school novels, *Looking for Alaska* focuses primarily on social life: friendships, romance, rules and rule-breaking, and pranks. Miles, however, reminds us of his academic work even when his friends are focused on smoking and sex. He reads (or at least mentions) *Ethan Frome*, a textbook for World Religions, and the Gospel of Mark; he also notes not quite managing to read *Le Petit Prince*, *Things Fall Apart*, and *A Farewell to Arms*. While few of these texts play a significant role in the novel, the World Religions class threads through it from beginning to end as Miles attempts to make meaning first out of his experiences at Culver Creek—his bullying by the Weekday Warriors his first night there, for example—and most especially of Alaska's death. Dr. Hyde, whose lectures inspire Miles but seem to bore other members of the class, uses Alaska's first semester exam question (adapted from *The General in His Labyrinth*, one of her favorite books) as the class's final exam: "How will we ever get out of this labyrinth of suffering?" (Green 2005, 158, 215). He thus suggests both that their curriculum is may help them through their grief and that their reading should help them make meaning of their life (and, perhaps, vice versa).

In combining curricular and extracurricular reading, *Looking for Alaska* models the kind of reading most teachers would like to inspire their students to: a kind of connective, collective reading that almost organically moves between classroom and dorm room, from

---

[19]We may recall here that Frankie Landau-Banks appreciates her first boyfriend for the "piles of paperbacks" that adorn his "messy dorm room" (Lockhart 2008, 30). The sexuality-textuality connections here are barely hidden.

informational to pleasure-giving transaction. And yet pleasure might not be the right term for the kind of reading Miles and his friends engage in throughout the second half of the novel. While he and Chip and Alaska all derive pleasure from their various independent reading (of biographies and almanacs and novels), when Miles and Chip read more strategically in the second half of the novel they are doing so with a purpose: not the extrinsic motivation of the grade, but the intrinsic, meaning-making motivation of interpreting the clues that Alaska has left behind. They start with the book as object, with Alaska's book, in which she has written, next to the question: "How will I ever get out of this labyrinth?" "*Straight & Fast*" (Green 2005, 155, italics in original). Alaska's annotation becomes the first clue in the series of clues that the friends interpret as they try to come to terms with her death.

There is also an interesting connection between the friends' execution of their prank for Speaker Day, their attempt to solve the mystery of Alaska's death, and the questions raised in Dr. Hyde's World Religions class. In all three instances, the friends must piece together fragments from a variety of sources, "read" them critically, and construct a new narrative. This is deep reading, and it is a shared or communal effort—a kind of "public thinking."[20] Readers become writers as they construct new narratives out of old ones. Green's novel, written in the Internet age but set before it, models what readers have actually always done: read together.[21] Miles and Chip, along with others, pool their resources, working together to solve the mystery, or at least to lay it to rest.

Crucially, they need to broaden their circle before they can come to terms with Alaska's death. They make peace with the "Weekday Warriors" in order to pull off their final prank, for example. Their textual circle expands as well, with Takumi's note and Alaska's marginalia serving as the last two pieces of evidence in the puzzle. Significantly, like the other adolescents discussed here, the teen protagonists of *Looking for Alaska* are both readers and writers, scripting the prank and, of course, Miles's final exam essay for World Religions, included as the end of the novel (in

---

[20] I take the term from Clive Thompson, who uses it in *Smarter Than You Think*, especially Chapter 3.

[21] Although we usually think of reading as solitary, as Elizabeth Long notes, there is also a long tradition of communal reading, from family read-alouds to today's online fan communities, wikis, and fan fiction (phenomena far beyond the scope of this project).

another echo of *The Outsiders*). The interpenetration of reading and writing is another hallmark of the deep literacy we see in these novels.

The new narrative of the Alaska Young Memorial Prank (a stripper in the guise of a lecturer on adolescent sexuality) is an acceptance of Alaska's death and a celebration of their own vitality, the life force that Alaska herself embodied and that all adolescents (as the supposed lecturer notes) must explore. YA literature is marked by its engagement with both sex and death (see, e.g., Trites 2000); here, the discourses of sex and death intertwine and the friends use one to rewrite the other. Only after the prank is Miles able to write his final essay for World Religions, "How will I ever get out of this labyrinth of suffering?" Dr. Hyde and Miles both pay tribute to Alaska by using her favorite novel as a prompt for the final exam, and Miles in this essay draws on his reading to reflect on his own life, Alaska's death, and the meaning of friendship as he creates a new narrative out of the fragments he reassembles.

While Miles and his friends do pull together for collaborative reading, the novel does not ultimately depict a successful resistance to the school's attempts to mold them: again quoting Trites, they ultimately rebel only to conform. We see a similar model at work in *The Disreputable History*, but it is even less successful, as Frankie is not able to recruit others into her interpretive circle. We are first introduced to Frankie Landau-Banks, like Miles Halter, as someone who reads. Reading Dorothy Parker at the beach not only associates her with extracurricular reading but with wit, sharpness, and humor, all associations that hold true throughout the novel (though we never encounter Dorothy Parker again). *The Disreputable History of Frankie Landau-Banks*, like *Looking for Alaska*, centers in part on the intersection between prep school pranking and the hidden curriculum. While planning the Alaska Young Memorial Prank allows Chip and Miles to move from reading to "writing," however, Frankie's pranks are intended to teach others how to read. She plans increasingly elaborate pranks for the Loyal Order of the Basset Hounds to execute, hoping that they will both realize that she is the mastermind and that the pranks have a political agenda. As she discovers, however, prep school pranking is simply an expression of power, not a way of overthrowing it or calling it into question. So, for example, after the first prank, in which the Bassets hang brassieres on all the portraits in the school, some girls try to analyze the prank, wondering if it is making fun of them or of the male power structure represented by the portraits (Lockhart 2008, 241–243). But the boys who are members of the Bassets consider the prank to be just that: a prank. While she is delighted by the attention her pranks receive, "exhilarated … [while] listening to fifty-four students and three faculty members argue, speculate and wonder … about something she had done," the group speculating and wondering never seems to include the Bassets (Lockhart 2008, 262).

The pranks in *Alaska* and in *The Disreputable History* do become a kind of text, demanding interpretation—or reading—by those who witness them.[22] But in the case of *Alaska*, interpretation is both easy—adolescent sexuality involves the potential for both display and humiliation, perhaps in equal parts—and communal, in that the entire school witnesses the prank at once. Further, as there is no real question of authorship raised by the prank—all involved attribute it to its actual author, Alaska herself—interpretation is really secondary to appreciation. The really significant acts of reading and interpretation have already happened—and for the most part failed—by this time. The friends have read all the clues but failed to make sense of Alaska's death. The prank itself, then, unlike in *Disreputable History*, is not an interpretive act. The students plan, execute, and witness the prank; its meaning is transparent and its authorship known; and it is over. As with the Bassets' pranks, it involves no real challenge to the school's authority, inasmuch as Miles's father—a loyal alumnus—is a co-author, no school rules are explicitly violated, and there is no real lasting effect other than the celebration of Alaska's life that, implicitly, allows her friends to move on with their own lives. While the protagonists do develop (at least briefly) a collaborative reading/writing practice, then, it's not clear that it has any lasting effect, other than the entirely institutionally appropriate one of forcing the four main characters to study together in order to pass their finals. And the headmaster even approves—at least tacitly—their final prank: "But, Lord, 'subverting the patriarchal paradigm'—it's like she wrote the speech," he says, without sanctioning them for hiring a stripper to perform for Speaker's Day—or, indeed, realizing that Alaska actually did write the speech (Green 2005, 210).

In the case of the Bassets' pranks, however, interpretation is central. Alpha needs to "read" the pranks—and the messages—to determine who is directing the pranks, and both students and faculty wonder

[22]Both also involve actual written texts: in *Looking for Alaska*, the speech that Alaska has written and that the stripper delivers, and in *The Disreputable History*, the book of Basset history that Frankie deploys in her ever more elaborate pranks.

increasingly at the scope of the pranks, and therefore at their authorship as well. It is clear that at least one of Frankie's motives in directing them is to force Matthew and the other Bassets (but especially Matthew) into some close reading—into paying closer attention to the meaning of the pranks so they, and he, can better understand her. But Matthew is a very different kind of reader than Frankie. Matthew is a copy editor, concerned primarily with accuracy, with correctness—and this concern is at odds with Frankie's concern with meaning. Frankie plays with meaning, inventing words (the "inpea" or "imaginary neglected positive," for example, which she derives from her reading of P.G. Wodehouse), while Matthew seems incapable of such playfulness, looking up "gruntled" in the dictionary, for example, in order to prove her playful use of the word wrong. Reading for information rather than pleasure, Matthew is incapable of enjoying Frankie's wordplay or analyzing her pranks. Frankie's reading thus remains essentially isolated. While Alpha and she read each other, their reading never comes together in a productive way—in the way that she actually wants and intends it to. While Frankie's reading of Foucault directs her initial pranking (as well as a paper—Frankie, even more than Miles, is able to bring her extracurricular activities into her classwork), and her reading of the Basset Hounds' book suggests more pranks, she is unable to involve other readers in her projects. The institution remains unchanged by her efforts, despite her attempt to subvert it from within, and Frankie is unable to engage other readers in her projects. Gender clearly plays a role in the difference between the social reading undertaken by the friends in *Looking for Alaska* (note that Lara and Alaska herself are not really part of the core group of readers) and the solitary reading and writing of *The Disreputable History*. In the next chapter, I will explore the operations of gender and reading further, but here I will simply note that the types of reading the characters engage in are fairly stereotypical for their genders, and constitute yet another aspect of the way the novels fail to challenge the status quo in any serious way.

How: Power and Agency

Despite the gendered failure of communal reading and interpretation in *The Disreputable History*, however, perhaps the most successful acts of communal reading in this group of texts come in the least likely place, in *Speak*. While Melinda is resolutely isolated and alone through most of the novel, when she moves from reader to writer she gains power, agency, and community, finally refusing the victim status that has defined her through most of the novel.

As *Speak* begins, Melinda seems to be writing in a journal, perhaps one of the journals she suspects "the school must have gotten a good price on" (Anderson 1999, 6). Her English teacher "wants us to write in our class journals every day, but promises not to read them" (Anderson 1999, 6). This act of unshared writing, while it seems to respect the students' privacy, seems meaningless to Melinda, who writes "about how weird she [the teacher] is" (Anderson 1999, 6). The text we read—which may or may not be, like the text of *The Outsiders*, a class assignment—is, like three out of the four texts analyzed here, and like so many YA novels, a first-person narration, providing access to a voice that we otherwise never hear.[23] This seemingly transparent narration, however, hides, obfuscates, and shapes the experience the teen (or any) reader has of Melinda's story; fragments of other texts help shape not only Melinda's but the implied reader's awareness of the trauma that lies behind Melinda's silence. It is in English class, for example, that Melinda encounters Hester Prynne and imagines that they would get along. While she finally disdains her teacher's attempts to teach them "code-breaking," her question about Hawthorne ("Why couldn't he just say what he meant?") resonates in the context of a girl who is silent for the better part of a school year, unable herself to say what she means but able nonetheless to express herself (Anderson 1999, 100, 101).

In one of the novel's most interesting sequences, Melinda even turns her inability to speak into a kind of interpretive move. Faced with the requirement that she deliver an oral report, she instead hands out a typed copy of the paper, displaying a poster that reads:

THE SUFFRAGETTES FOUGHT FOR THE RIGHT TO SPEAK. THEY WERE ATTACKED, ARRESTED, AND THROWN IN JAIL FOR DARING TO DO WHAT THEY WANTED. LIKE THEY WERE, I AM WILLING TO STAND UP FOR WHAT I BELIEVE. NO ONE

[23] Jonathan Stephens, among others, notes the frequent use of first-person narration in young adult fiction (Stephens 2007, 44; see also O'Quinn 2001, 55). Chris McGee elaborates on the irony of the first-person narrator in *Speak*—like most young adult novels, an adult-authored novel which inevitably mimics a teen voice "speaking to other teenagers about what adults would most want to hear" (McGee 2009, 173). This irony is one of many that pervades first-person texts for teens but does not, I believe, undercut the implication of agency that Melinda derives from reading and writing.

SHOULD BE FORCED TO GIVE SPEECHES. I CHOOSE TO STAY
SILENT. (Anderson 1999, 156)

Her reading of the suffragettes, though, is limited. Although her lab
partner, David Petrakis, supports her in her presentation, he later points
out that "The suffragettes were all about speaking up, screaming for
their rights. You can't speak up for your right to be silent. That's letting the bad guys win" (Anderson 1999, 159). Although the issue is left
unresolved in the moment, it does represent the only time in the novel
when two characters work through an analysis together, even briefly, of
material they have both read. Sharing that analysis moves Melinda forward toward an agency that comes out of communal reading.

It is finally in acts of shared reading and writing that Melinda "tells"
her story: first to Rachel, in a notebook passed back and forth across a
table in the library, then in shared graffiti in a bathroom stall. The second experience is the most liberating. Melinda has written "GUYS TO
STAY AWAY FROM" and added the name "Andy Evans," the name
of her rapist. The idea comes to her after she has noticed what she calls
"a community chat room, a metal newspaper" on the bathroom wall
(Anderson 1999, 175). Days later, she returns to find her own entry
annotated:

> He's a creep.
> He's a bastard.
> Stay away!!!!!!!!!!!!!!!!!!!!!
> He should be locked up.
> He thinks he's all that.
> Call the cops.

(Anderson 1999, 185)

And so on. The "conversation" continues, validating Melinda's experience and letting her know that despite her fears, she is not alone. This
kind of communal sharing of reading and writing is now common-
place, of course—Facebook walls and Twitter feeds mimic the effect,
in the case of Facebook even down to the name. What Thompson calls
"public thinking" and attributes to the Internet clearly has its roots in
earlier practices. And in *Speak* the graffiti wall is powerfully liberatory,
even subversive, precisely because it is unexpected. The "sharing" is not
done with the click of a mouse or a smartphone app (not yet available,

less than 20 years ago); the wall is a physical object where other young women read Melinda's words and share their own anonymously but, like Melinda, with little expectation of action.[24] That physical text gives Melinda the knowledge that she has a community, and it is that community—a community that includes both fictional characters such as Hester Prynne as well as the writers on the wall—that gives her the ability to stand up to her attacker when they next meet. Text has a physicality in *King Dork* as well, a later novel that shares with its predecessor an earlier, pre-Internet (indeed, pre-personal computer) setting.

Reading and writing form the foundation of Melinda's ability to heal—between the emotional connections to canonical characters and writers (Hester Prynne, Maya Angelou) and the anonymous writers in the bathroom stall, Melinda discovers through reading and writing that she does indeed have a community and can tell her story as she chooses. As the novel ends, she is speaking—"Let me tell you about it," she says to Mr. Freeman in the novel's final words (Anderson 1999, 198). Finally, it seems, reading must be shared, must move off the page and into a larger community to have meaning that matters.

It must also, at least in these texts, become writing. Novels set in school engage in limited ways with the curricula of contemporary (or almost-contemporary) high schools, but they all share one important trait: They recognize the interrelationship of reading and writing. It is, of course, not surprising in the least that novelists would find ways to demonstrate the value of their craft. The characters read for information and escape; they write to make meaning of the reading; they even read and write together to make meaning of their own lives. In other YA novels, reading becomes even more crucial to the lives of young adults as it inspires or enables political resistance, or offers alternative models for development, or even becomes a metafictional player in the creation of

[24]Chris McGee resists the "empowerment narrative" in most readings of *Speak*, noting both that Melinda's "awareness of power … is sophisticated and profound" and that the wit and energy of her narration belie the victim narrative so many readers find in the text. He is thus disappointed by an ending that, as he sees it, requires "finally turning to an adult," suggesting that "everything is right once the teen comes to voice" (McGee 2009, 182, 184). By focusing on reading rather than speaking, I suggest instead that Anderson gives Melinda the authority in this passage as elsewhere in the novel: she reads and writes her story with her peers first, dictating the terms by which she will speak to her teacher—and to her reader. I think it is thus significant that she does *not* tell Mr. Freeman about it in the body of the novel.

the story. Beginning here, in school, provides the template for the kinds of agential development—partial, compromised, and yet still valuable—in which reading plays a part.

WORKS CITED

The American Diploma Project. 2004. *Ready or Not: Creating a High School Diploma That Counts.* Achieve, Inc. https://www.achieve.org/files/ReadyorNot.pdf.

Anderson, Laurie Halse. 1999, 2001. *Speak.* New York: Penguin.

Barrs, Myra. 2000. Gendered Literacy. *Language Arts* 77 (4): 287–293.

Brenner, Devon. 2012. They Read and Write, but Do They Critique? The Four Resources of Literacy Practice in Printz-Award-Winning Literature. *The ALAN Review* 39 (2): 39–48.

Carrington, Vicki. 2001. Literacy Instruction: A Bourdieuian Perspective. In *Difference, Silence, and Textual Practice: Studies in Critical Literacy*, ed. Peter Freebody, Sandy Muspratt, and Bronwyn Dwyer, 265–285. Cresskill, NJ: Hampton Press.

Doughty, Amie A. 2013. *"Throw the Book Away": Reading Versus Experience in Children's Fantasy.* Jefferson, NC: McFarland.

Gallagher, Kelly. 2009. *Readicide: How Schools Are Killing Reading and What You Can Do About It.* Portsmouth, NH: Stenhouse.

Green, John. 2005. *Looking for Alaska.* New York: Penguin.

Hinton, S.E. 1967, 1997. *The Outsiders.* New York: Puffin Books.

Ippolito, Jacy, Jennifer L. Steele, and Jennifer F. Samson. 2008. Introduction: Why Adolescent Literacy Matters Now. *Harvard Educational Review* 78 (1): 1–6.

Jacobs, Vicki A. 2008. Adolescent Literacy: Putting the Crisis in Context. *Harvard Educational Review* 78 (1): 7–39.

Latrobe, Kathy, and Judy Drury. 2009. *Critical Approaches to Young Adult Literature.* New York: Neal-Schuman.

Lockhart, E. 2008. *The Disreputable History of Frankie Landau-Banks.* New York: Hyperion.

Long, Elizabeth. 1993. Textual Interpretation as Collective Action. In *The Ethnography of Reading*, ed. Jonathan Boyarin, 180–211. Berkeley: University of California Press.

McGee, Chris. 2009. 'Why Won't Melinda Just Talk About What Happened?' *Speak* and the Confessional Voice. *Children's Literature Association Quarterly* 34 (2): 172–187.

O'Quinn, Elaine J. 2001. Between Voice and Voicelessness: Transacting Silence in Laurie Halse Anderson's *Speak*. *The ALAN Review* 29 (1): 54–58.

Portman, Frank. 2006. *King Dork*. New York: Delacorte.

Pratchett, Terry. 2003. *Wee Free Men*. New York: Harper Trophy.

Reimer, Mavis. 2009. Traditions of the School Story. In *The Cambridge Companion to Children's Literature*, ed. M.O. Grenby and Andrea Immel, 209–225. Cambridge: Cambridge University Press.

Resnick, Daniel P., and Lauren B. Resnick. 1989. Varieties of Literacy. In *Social History and Issues in Human Consciousness: Some Interdisciplinary Connections*, ed. Andrew E. Barnes and Peter N. Stearns, 171–196. New York: New York University Press.

Rollin, Lucy. 2001. Among School Children: The Harry Potter Books and the School Story Tradition. *The South Carolina Review* 34 (1): 198–208.

Salinger, J.D. 1951, 1989. *The Catcher in the Rye*. Boston: Little, Brown.

Stephens, Jonathan. 2007. Young Adult: A Book by Any Other Name ...: Defining the Genre. *The ALAN Review* 35 (1): 34–42.

Sullivan, Patrick. 2016. An Open Letter to High School Students About Reading. *Academe* 103 (3). https://www.aaup.org/article/open-letter-high-school-students-about-reading#.XBvYzPZKjOQ.

Tannert-Smith, Barbara. 2010. 'Like Falling Up into a Storybook': Trauma and Intertextual Repetition in Laurie Halse Anderson's *Speak*. *Children's Literature Association Quarterly* 35 (4): 395–414.

Thompson, Clive. 2013. *Smarter Than You Think: How Technology Is Changing Our Minds for the Better*. New York: Penguin.

Tribunella, Eric L. 2007. Institutionalizing *The Outsiders*: YA Literature, Social Class, and the American Faith in Education. *Children's Literature in Education* 38: 87–101.

Trites, Roberta Seelinger. 2000. *Disturbing the Universe: Power and Repression in Adolescent Literature*. Iowa City: University of Iowa Press.

CHAPTER 3

Misreading the Classics: Gender, Genre, and Agency in YA Romance

When I was a child, one of my favorite books was an old copy of Grimms' Fairy-Tales, illustrated by Wanda Gág, and later colorized by my mother's colored pencils. I was drawn to some of the less well-known fairy-tales in the book, like "Snow White and Rose Red," "The Musicians of Bremen," and "Spindle, Shuttle, and Needle." I found myself puzzled by them and therefore interested. The tales in the book were strange and other-worldly—animals and even domestic implements spoke and sang, while evil was punished and good, for the most part, prevailed. But what I liked best was knowing that they had been my mother's tales—that she, too, had been a little girl reading in bed, or lying on the floor, pencil in hand.

On the other hand, I can't remember when I first read *Jane Eyre*. It was never assigned to me in school—my high school teachers preferred Dickens and Austen to the Brontës. I enjoyed them as well, but what I really loved was my mother's collection of Georgette Heyer's Regency romances, whose debt to *Jane Eyre* (or, for that matter, to fairy-tales like "Cinderella" or "Beauty and the Beast") I couldn't yet recognize.[1]

---

[1] Tania Modleski, in *Loving with a Vengeance*, outlines the similarities thus:
A young, inexperienced, moderately well-to-do woman encounters and becomes involved with a handsome, strong, experienced, wealthy man, older than herself by ten to fifteen years. The heroine is confused by the hero's behavior since, though he is obviously interested in her, he is mocking, cynical, contemptuous, often hostile, and even somewhat brutal. By the end, however, all misunderstandings are cleared away, and the hero reveals his love for the heroine. (Modleski 2008, 28)

© The Author(s) 2019   51
E. R. Gruner, *Constructing the Adolescent Reader in Contemporary Young Adult Fiction*, Critical Approaches to Children's Literature,
https://doi.org/10.1057/978-1-137-53924-3_3

"We think back through our mothers if we are women" writes Virginia Woolf, and those mothers turn out in part to be linguistic structures, texts shared or written by other women.[2] In contemporary YA for girls, as in my own experience, those "mothers" are fairy-tales and romance novels, a feminized canon of literary foremothers that for the most part has escaped critical recognition until quite recently. I detail my own reading experience here because it is so similar to, and yet at the same time different from, the experience represented in the novels I am about to discuss. In the 1960s and 1970s, when I was a child, the combination of growing feminist critiques of fairy-tales and the last gasp of an all-male "literary"[3] canon (Jane Austen being the sole exception, in my high school education) combined to keep both commercialized fairy-tales (the Grimms' book was a notable, and notably non-standard, exception) and women authors off my official reading lists.[4] I read voraciously and widely on my own, but my choices were eclectic, coming from my parents' shelves, the library, and school assignments, and including far more genre novels (a smattering of early YA, but mostly mystery and romance) than any other kind.

In tenth grade, however, when I was about the age of the protagonists of the novels I treat in this chapter, we read "coming of age" novels in my prep school English class. The syllabus included *Great Expectations*, *A Separate Peace*, *The Catcher in the Rye*, and James Kirkwood's *Good Times, Bad Times* (1968), a boarding school novel that appears not to have stood the test of time.[5] My (male) English teacher announced to his (all girl) class that we could "identify" with the protagonists of these novels, as we, too, were "coming of age."

It was almost twenty years before I fully realized the implications of his comment. Not one of the novels I read in his class was by or about a woman; only the genre novels my mother shared with me offered me that experience. This is a history that has changed drastically in the last

---

[2] *A Room of One's Own*, Chapter 4.

[3] As opposed to "genre" fiction or children's literature, which has always been feminized, and in which I read widely.

[4] In those pre-video days, Disney movies were only available in the theater, and I can't remember seeing any of the fairy-tale movies until my own children watched them.

[5] Kirkwood is better known as the co-author of *A Chorus Line* and the author of *P.S. Your Cat Is Dead*.

forty years. In a variety of contemporary YA novels for girls, the protagonists have a wealth of literature to draw upon—and yet it still seems limited, if in different ways from my own experience. While the school stories I discussed in the previous chapter, unlike their older predecessors, feature coeducational schools and implicitly appeal to both male and female readers, in this chapter I focus on an explicitly feminized genre and audience. YA novels written for and about girls have several features in common: an emphasis on romance plots, on relationships, and on domestic life.[6] Many, moreover, are either structured by or make reference to fairy-tales and romance novels—especially the godmother of many contemporary romance novels, *Jane Eyre*.[7] These novels are therefore deeply intertextual and often metafictional: they reference, and can be structured by, earlier works of fiction. They may even call attention to the associations between themselves and their foremothers, highlighting their fictionality while still creating empathy for their teen protagonists.[8]

But referencing the earlier works and/or using them for structure has several effects, not all of them entirely positive. In some novels, a fairy-tale structure receives a feminist retelling—though such retellings often retain fairly traditional gender roles—and reading, though usually not reading of the tale itself, is part of the heroine's empowerment. *Sisters Red* (Pearce 2010), *Beastly*, and *Lindy's Diary* (Flinn 2007, 2012), for example, are explicitly revisions of traditional fairy-tales. In them, characters must become readers in order to escape or revise the fates of the original fairy-tale characters. Meg Cabot's *Princess Diaries* series and Stephenie Meyer's *Twilight* saga suggest correlations between their heroines' stories and those of earlier romance heroines, reshaping the

---

[6] Sara K. Day, in *Reading Like a Girl*, suggests that "adolescent women as a market and audience have been understood as particularly receptive to literature in emotional (rather than intellectual or analytical) terms" (Day 2013, 23). Her definition reminds us that the category of "girl books" is tautological: because certain books emphasize relationships, they are marketed to girls (with, for example, pink covers), which then creates a larger female audience for those books. Furthermore, of course, many YA novels neither construct nor imply gendered audiences.

[7] See Modleski (2008), Miller (2001), and Stoneman (1996), for more on the influence of *Jane Eyre* in varieties of popular culture, including romance novels.

[8] Sara Day suggests that these texts emphasize their readers' affective or empathetic responses to the protagonists (see, e.g., Day 2013, 23).

earlier texts into new stories for new generations even as the protagonists remain entranced by the originals. The readers in these novels seem
not fully aware of their enmeshment in the kinds of plots they read; the
greater their awareness, the better they are able to resist the demands
of plot. In such texts as *A Breath of Eyre* (Mont 2012), *Cloudwish*
(Wood 2015), and *We Are Okay* (LaCour 2017), the heroines recognize
correlations between their own stories and *Jane Eyre*, and seem to have
the greatest agency in shaping their own stories.

That a metafictional use of fairy-tales and romance novels[9] promotes
female agency might come as a surprise—after all, the romance tradition is often seen as detrimental or, at best, only ambiguously empowering to both heroines and female readers.[10] And, indeed, the surface
ideology of empowerment/agency is often undercut in these novels by
a passive allegiance to traditional gender norms—represented as much
by the construction of their audience as by the content of the novels.[11]
In Chapter 2, we saw YA literature both didactically present reading as
a means to developing agency and at the same time resist the straightforward association of textbook or assigned reading and educational
achievement. Young adult literature teaches its readers not only how to
read it, but why reading it is important. It is perhaps unsurprising, in
retrospect, to see reading play this role in educational fictions, however.
Widespread anxieties about adolescent reading virtually guarantee that
it would be figured as educationally empowering within adolescent fiction. Yet the late twentieth and early twenty-first centuries also saw an
explosion of fairy-tale and "classic" romance retellings, far removed from
the school stories dealt with in the previous chapter. These novels seem
on the face of them escapist, clearly disconnected from everyday reality,

[9] I treat fairy-tales and "classic" romance novels together in this chapter in recognition
of the romance tradition's development from the fairy-tale. My specific example of a frequently retold romance—*Jane Eyre*—is not only clearly indebted to fairy-tales, it is often
retold for adolescent women, making it a useful stand-in for other similar retellings and
reimaginings. See Stoneman (1996) and Miller (2001) for more on these retellings.

[10] See, for example, Karen Rowe's groundbreaking "Feminism and Fairy-Tales," as well
as Modleski (2008). More recent work in this field, such as Jones & Schacker's *Marvelous
Transformations*, has been more nuanced.

[11] Day notes that this construction is "white, middle-class, and heterosexual ... a norm
about which and to whom much popular culture is presented" (Day 2013, 10).

perhaps even politically conservative in their reclaiming of traditional fictions—yet it is in these that we can see how reading becomes specifically associated with developing female agency in adolescence. The fairy-tale and romance retellings I discuss in this chapter—texts not traditionally associated with reading at all—become the means through which a gendered reading leads to female empowerment. Yet that empowerment relies on some deeply conservative notions about empathy and humanization—notions that may in the end undercut the ostensive empowerment achieved by their teen girl characters.

Romances and their retellings are among our oldest forms of fiction, and we can find versions of these tales in many eras.[12] In this chapter, I focus on late twentieth- and early twenty-first-century retellings of fairy-tales and romances with updated settings intended for a young adult audience. Many retellings retain a fairy-tale like setting for their tales, such as most of those by Robin McKinley, Shannon Hale, Donna Jo Napoli, and Gail Carson Levine. My focus here on retellings with contemporary or realistic historical settings allows for a continuity of many concerns from the school stories previously discussed; contemporary settings also make a focus on reading more salient, as contemporary teens must, unlike those in traditional fairy-tales, interact with the education system, contemporary concerns about literacy, and even new technologies of reading.[13] Finally, then, the novels discussed in this chapter represent a certain kind of feminized reading—both within and outside of the novels themselves—as a means to developing agency, even if such agency is simultaneously compromised or even completely undercut.

---

[12] Here I draw on Northrop Frye's theory of modes, which classifies the romance along with folk tales and märchen as texts in which the protagonist is human though "the ordinary laws of nature are slightly suspended" (Frye 1957, 33). While the term is today used mostly reductively, as in discussions of fictions of romantic or sexual attraction (see, e.g., Trites 2000, 84–85) or in combination with other terms (as in "romantic comedy"), the fairy-tale romance and other romance texts (such as Philip Sydney's *Arcadia* or Cervantes' *Don Quijote*) form an important building block in the European literary tradition. As I'll explore further in this chapter, and as Tania Modleski and others have noted, many "girls' books" have their origins in the romance, drawing on such nineteenth-century classics as *Jane Eyre, Wuthering Heights,* or *Dracula.*

[13] I do, however, discuss a few fairy-tale-inspired fantasies in Chapter 6. In novels by Kristin Cashore, Shannon Hale, and Frances Hardinge, settings inspired by high fantasy can indeed include reading heroines.

REIMAGINING THE FAIRY-TALE

Both fairy-tales and YA literature are peculiarly susceptible to didacticism, to the operations of power and control.[14] In one of the inaugural articles in feminist literary criticism, "Feminism and Fairy Tales," Karen Rowe wrote that fairy-tales "which glorify passivity, dependency, and self-sacrifice as a heroine's cardinal virtues suggest that the culture's very survival depends upon a woman's acceptance of roles which relegate her to motherhood and domesticity" (Rowe 1979, 239). As Donald Haase has noted, "In Rowe's view, the fairy-tale–perhaps precisely because of its 'awesome imaginative power'–had a role to play in cultivating equality among men and women, but it would have to be a rejuvenated fairy-tale fully divested of its idealized romantic fantasies" (Haase 2004, 5). In the years since Rowe's essay first appeared, however, it has not been clear whether the structuring power of the fairy-tale could indeed be reworked for more egalitarian uses, or whether in fact the "replication of an old content and mode of representation [would only] result in the further replication of, for example, old masculinist and antifeminist metanarratives" (Stephens and MacCallum 1998, 22).

Christine A. Jones and Jennifer Schacker propose an alternative possibility, however, a tradition that focuses less on the happily-ever-after of the passive heroines in the classic romance fairy-tales and more on the ambivalently active linguistic facility of, especially, Little Red Cap and her sisters in romance.[15] We may trace the tradition they analyze in "Beauty and the Beast," one of the most frequently retold of the classic

---

[14] Cristina Bacchilega writes that "fairy-tales offer symbolically powerful scenarios and options, in which seemingly unpromising heroes succeed in solving some problems for modern children. These narratives set the socially acceptable boundaries for such scenarios and options, thus serving, more often than not, the civilizing aspirations of adults" (Bacchilega 1997, 5). As Trites comments about YA literature, "In a literature often about growth, it is the rare author who can resist the impulse to moralize about how people grow" (Trites 2000, 73).

[15] Jones and Schacker focus on reading itself in the Grimm's "Little Red Cap." While few fairy-tales actually incorporate scenes of reading, Jones and Schacker argue persuasively for the way that the text of this particular tale actually invites readers to participate in an interpretive game—a game which Little Red Cap loses, but which the huntsman, more skilled than she at both interpretation and speech, wins on her behalf. While their definition of reading includes many kinds of non-textual interpretation, their analysis neatly frames what I argue regarding the use of fairy-tales in YA literature: the mostly female readers depicted in a number of YA adaptations of fairy-tales develop agency through reading.

fairy-tales, and perhaps the most metafictional of them; we may find it as well, in another form, in Perrault's Cinderella, who teases her stepsisters for their misrecognition when she meets them at the ball. And we see the abject failure of reading in the many retellings of "Snow White," in which the eponymous heroine repeatedly fails to recognize her stepmother in the vendor who offers her poisoned combs, laces, and an apple. In YA adaptations and retellings of these tales—some so distant from their source material as to be only vaguely intertextually related, hardly fairy-tales at all—heroines who become readers and even writers avoid Little Red Cap's fate, taking on their own agency, rewriting their endings, and metafictionally engaging both fairy-tale and romance.[16] In most cases (though not all), these contemporary heroines must become literary, textual readers rather than the interpreters we find in their predecessors' texts. As we read these heroines' reading, we will also see the ways in which the YA novels about them make assumptions about reading and gender, often excluding boys entirely from the narrative, casting them as villains or beasts, or simply ignoring their readerly potential.

When YA authors retell fairy-tales in modern dress, these metafictional novels make reading far more salient than it was in the earlier tales. It is almost impossible to retell a fairy-tale after postmodernism without a knowing wink to the reader; the retellings I am concerned with here, however, go beyond a simply ironic, or postmodern, play with the reader's awareness of the retelling, to call attention to the status of the text itself as an artefact, blurring the lines between fiction and reality, and levels of fictionality.[17] Metafiction, in these YA retellings and reworkings of romantic fairy-tales, suggests that characters and readers alike are all caught in a web of story; only an awareness of the conventions of genre can provide the agency necessary to escape them.

---

[16] See Gruner (2011) for a consideration of three YA novels that are loose fairy-tale retellings in which the protagonists do develop their agency through the metafictional use of the tales. Some of the argument of this chapter draws on and extends the claims I first began working out in that essay.

[17] I am drawing here especially on Patricia Waugh's definition of metafiction in her book of the same name: "fictional writing which self-consciously and systematically draws attention to its status as an artefact in order to pose questions about the relationship between fiction and reality" (Waugh 1984, 2). As we have already seen, this definition underpins the usages of the term in such later critics as Joe Sutliff Sanders and Claudia Nelson.

This tendency is most obvious in Jackson Pearce's *Sisters Red* (2010), a reworking of "Little Red Riding Hood" in which the wolves are were-wolves and the eponymous sisters wear red to tempt and destroy the wolves. Like many Little Red remixes,[18] this one emphasizes the sexual danger posed by the werewolf predators; unlike them, it gives us her-oines who both seek out and research their antagonists. While reading plays a small part in the novel, it is significant—the girls and Silas pore over newspapers on microfilm, Internet postings, and "books on wild wolves, monsters, myths" in their effort to uncover the next poten-tial werewolf (Pearce 2010, 166). Their reading is purely strategic and informational,[19] and while the text initially depicts the fictional reading as ineffectual and frivolous, Rosie (the younger sister) ultimately pieces together the initial clues with the help of one of the library books: *Myths! Legends! Monsters!* by Dorothea Silverclaw (Pearce 2010, 224). The novel thus suggests that it and books like it may have a protective or predictive value; fairy-tales are not merely entertainment but versions of the truth, couched in fictional narrative. If, as Scarlett says of her grand-mother, "It was always difficult to tell when Oma March was imparting wisdom and when she was merely storytelling," this is because the posi-tion of the text is that the two are in fact one (Pearce 2010, 37).

But while *Sisters Red* makes a relatively straightforward, if unimagina-tive, didactic case for reading, other YA fairy-tales offer a more complex view. Meg Cabot's *Princess Diaries* series, for example, blends references to fairy-tales with explicit connections to *Jane Eyre*. In the long-running *Princess Diaries* series, knowing you are living out a Cinderella story is no protection against it, and reading *Jane Eyre* and other romances inspired by fairy-tales may simply incline one to believe in them rather than to acquire the necessary critical distance on them that we might expect in such a metafictional text. Cabot's heroine, Mia Thermopolis, is fully aware of her status as "Cinderella," though she fulfills the makeo-ver story more thoroughly than the fairy-tale romance. In 17 volumes of diary novels, Mia tells her own story. While, as I've argued elsewhere,[20]

---

[18] See Francesca Lia Block, "Wolf," and others as cited in Zipes (1983).

[19] It's worth noting that, as in the previous chapter, any kind of text can be used for an informational literacy transaction. In this case, the sisters are motivated to do the reading and find the information valuable—unlike the work Melinda (in *Speak*) and Tom (in *King Dork*) are assigned.

[20] Gruner (2011).

her ability to narrate gives her agency, allowing her to reshape the Cinderella story and providing her with the means, for example, to collapse the figures of fairy godmother and wicked stepmother into a single character (her grandmother, the Dowager Princess of Genovia), her reading is somewhat more ambivalent. In volume IV of the series, *Princess in Waiting*, we have the most detailed exploration of Mia's relationship with a single text: Charlotte Brontë's *Jane Eyre*. The novel, first recommended to her by her grandmother, becomes both touchstone and guidebook, a parodic source of dating advice that Mia takes all too seriously.

The references to fairy-tales pile up in *Princess in Waiting*, as Mia announces that her favorite movie is *Beauty and the Beast* (Cabot 2003, 42), attends a production of the ballet, *Sleeping Beauty* (Cabot 2003, 23), and fields a message from her boyfriend who asks, "Am I going to have to come to Genovia and climb up your hair to get you out or something?" (Cabot 2003, 14–15). If we hadn't already understood that Mia was living a fairy-tale life, references like these would remind us. (The novel also includes metafictional references to the film version of *The Princess Diaries*, which came out in 2001.)

Jane Eyre, however, is a different story. Both "Cinderella" and "Beauty and the Beast," it becomes a touchstone for Mia after her grandmother suggests that she read it to learn "a thing or two about how men and women relate to one another" (Cabot 2003, 64). The initial lesson Mia seems to glean from the novel is "don't chase boys"—a version of the "play hard to get" message her grandmother has been trying to send. It is in this vein that she recommends the book as well to her friend Tina Hakim Baba, who is having troubles with her own boyfriend, Dave. And although Lilly, Mia's best friend (and her boyfriend's sister), rejects the game-playing that both Mia and Tina are engaged in, she nonetheless endorses their reading of *Jane Eyre*: "According to Tina...Lilly says that *Jane Eyre* was one of the first feminist manifestos, and she heartily approves of us using it as a model for our romantic relationships" (Cabot 2003, 71).

Of course, neither Tina nor Mia "uses" *Jane Eyre* in this way. Both read the novel exactly as if it were one of its less feminist heirs, one of the romance novels Tina Hakim Baba also avidly consumes. That is, rather than focusing on Jane's autonomy, her independence, her fierce refusal to subordinate herself to her beloved, Mia and Tina learn from her only the most banal of lessons. For example, they develop a list of

"ROMANCE HEROINES AND THE VALUABLE LESSONS EACH TAUGHT US" (Cabot 2003, 173, emphasis in original). From *Jane Eyre,* they learn "Stick to your convictions and you will prevail." While this is unobjectionable, if limited, later "lessons" devolve into beauty tips and other sarcastic readings, such as these: "6. Jo March from *Little Women:* Always keep a second copy of your manuscript handy in case your vindictive little sister throws your first draft on the fire. 7. Anne Shirley from *Anne of Green Gables:* One word: Clairol" (173).

Reductive and snarky, the lessons parody the kind of "morals" that students frequently believe they are asked to uncover in the literature they read for class. In *Princess in Waiting,* Mia rarely comments on her English class (much of the novel takes place in between semesters, and what discussion of classwork there is usually focuses on Algebra, her bête noir). Her reading, then, is largely self-directed in this novel, and it ranges freely among the classics such as those listed here, fairy-tales, take-out menus, news items, and other ephemera. She is for the most part an immersive reader, one who takes pleasure in her reading and identifies with the heroines of the novels she reads—just as, one assumes, Cabot hopes her own readers will. The list, then, which includes such little-read classics as *Lorna Doone* and *The Scarlet Pimpernel* in addition to more canonical texts such as *Tess of the D'Urbervilles* and *Wuthering Heights,* figures as a kind of shadow syllabus for Cabot's readers, a suggested reading list that will direct them to novels beyond the standard syllabus and immerse them in both pleasure and canonical value. While reading *Jane Eyre* itself figures only parodically in the plot, then, the presence of these so-called romance novels functions more didactically, both authorizing Cabot's own novel within a tradition and providing its readers with suggestions for further reading.[21] The lessons, in other words, are a joke—the point of the list is the list itself.

The final metafictional moment of the text, of course, involves writing rather than reading—although the novel's readers are, ultimately, asked to validate it. Threaded throughout *Princess in Waiting* are the twin questions that also could be said to animate *Jane Eyre*: both "who am I?" and "am I loved?" Although Mia of course knows she is Mia Thermopolis, heir to the throne of Genovia, she does not—unlike

---

[21] See a similar tendency in more traditional school stories such as *King Dork* and *The Perks of Being a Wallflower,* both of which include reading lists generated either by the protagonist or by a teacher—reading lists which are now available for purchase through such service as Amazon.com's "listmania." See Chapter 2.

most of her friends—have a secure sense of a talent, and this is the "who am I" question that twines with the question of Michael's love for her throughout the text. As the implicit readers of the series are purportedly reading her journals, they are expected to be more aware of her talent than she is; it takes Michael to spell it out for her on the penultimate page of the novel: "I think it's pretty obvious, Mia, that you're a writer" (224). Mia's ability to shape her own story has been her hallmark, of course, throughout the series (and remains so for several more volumes[22]); here, the metafictional moment calls the reader's attention to herself as reader, just at the novel's close. To be like Mia, then, is to be—like *Speak's* Melinda or *Alaska's* Miles, perhaps—both reader and writer, but she is also list-maker and schoolgirl and fairy-tale princess all in one. Yet her gendered reading—books she never mentions to Michael, nor expects him to have any knowledge of—does not in and of itself provide her with the agency to make herself or shape her story. Unlike her role model Jane Eyre, in fact, Mia still requires the external authorization of her boyfriend, the approval of conventional romance, even to recognize herself as a writer. So while the lists she provides and the books she reads may indeed provide new outlets for her readers, her own agency remains limited, constrained by the genre she inhabits and revises.

Although Pearce and Cabot provide tales of empowerment through literacy, not all intertextual uses of fairy-tales provide such positive outcomes for their heroines. Two recent novels by Alex Flinn, *Beastly* (2007) and *Lindy's Diary* (2012), for example, explore the darkest possibilities of "Beauty and the Beast," though they ultimately offer an unearned happy ending. In retelling the familiar fairy-tale, "Beauty and the Beast," Flinn's novels rely most heavily, not surprisingly, on the 1991 Disney film as a source text, but nod to the eighteenth-century French version by Mme. Le Prince de Beaumont and to many other fairy-tales as well. Even more than the other texts I've analyzed in this chapter, Flinn's are overt fairy-tale rewrites—*Beastly* announces its connection to its source text in its title, tagline ("Love is a beast"), and cover image of a rose,[23] so associated with the fairy-tale.

[22] See Gruner (2011).

[23] The cover also recalls the popular *Twilight* series by using only black, white, and red. YA romances following *Twilight* have frequently employed these look-alike covers; there have even been repackaged Brontë and Austen novels that visually reference the popular *Twilight* look.

The reader of *Beastly*, we can then assume, is familiar with the "Beauty and the Beast" story. And because the implied reader is also a young adult in the early twenty-first century, the version of the tale she knows is the Disney story, which features—unlike almost any other fairy-tale—a reading heroine. Disney's Belle famously dances her way through the village, singing about her favorite book; later, the Beast woos her with his immense library. In a scene cut from the final theatrical version, but restored for DVD release, we also see her teaching the Beast to read. The celebration of reading in Disney's version is not, in fact, new with Disney, though it is heightened in the film version beyond what we might have seen in earlier iterations of the tale. Indeed, "Beauty and the Beast" may be at the same time the most didactic and the most metafictional of fairy-tales. From its earliest French versions, it operates both as a fairy-tale itself and, at the same time, as an implicit argument for reading fairy-tales.

Mme. Le Prince de Beaumont's "Beauty and the Beast" is an interpolated tale, one of many within her two-volume *Young Misses Magazine*, the conceit of which is to present a governess and her charges and their friends through their days. The text, presented most often in dialogue format, depicts the governess—Mrs. Affable—and her allegorically named charges and their friends learning their lessons and listening to stories. Although it is based on the much longer romance by Gabrielle Susanne Barbot de Gallon de Villenueve, it seems odd that Beaumont's interpolated tale would be the version to survive, surrounded as it is by, as Betsy Hearne notes, "tedious, didactic conversations among figures such as Mrs. Affable and Lady Witty" (Hearne 1989, 2). Yet the didactic context may be the key to its longevity after all—like all other versions of the tale, Beaumont's stresses the importance of learning to read, and to read well.

While the morals of such tales as "Cinderella," "Little Red Riding Hood," or "Rapunzel," say, are ambiguous at best—and sometimes contradictory—"Beauty and the Beast" appears always to have the same didactic aim: to quote the Disney version, it is "not to be deceived by appearances, /For beauty is found within" (*Beauty and the Beast* 1991). It is, in other words, an argument for deeper reading. Throughout Beaumont's tale and its larger frame, learning to read, reading well, and reading the right way (though not too much) are all emphasized, a point underscored by the usual didactic reading of the fairy-tale. It is probably worth mentioning from the outset that girls' reading is

Beaumont's focus, a focus that appears to be retained in other versions of the tale—but not necessarily in *Beastly*.

Beastly opens not with the Beauty figure, as in Beaumont's version, nor with the Beast's backstory, as in the Disney version. Instead, we begin in an Internet chat room—the Unexpected Changes chat group, facilitated by Mr. Chris Anderson. First to "speak" in the chat room is BeastNYC, followed by SilentMaid—who introduces herself as "A mermaid. Just a little one," Froggie—who notes that it is "Lnly being a frg when ur not rlly 1"—and Grizzlyguy, who is interested in two girls, Rose Red and Snow White—but "Not 'that' Snow White. A different one" (Flinn 2007, n.p.).[24]

The chat room—which never reappears in the novel—serves to signal to the reader that the novel is taking its place among those other works, and that BeastNYC is, indeed, a version of the fairy-tale Beast we all already know. This knowingness—signaled especially by Grizzlyguy's reference to "'that' Snow White"—does not, however, translate into knowledge that the characters themselves can use: the Little Mermaid still chooses to undergo transformation into a human being, for example, despite the warnings that the other characters give her. Instead, this metafictional play does little beyond reaffirming the reader's choice of reading material.[25]

But the novel is metafictional in at least two ways—in addition to the intertextual awareness signaled by the chat room, it is also the kind of metafiction Joe Sutliff Sanders discusses in his article on the critical reader: the "metafiction that documents the relationship between books and their readers" (Sanders 2009, 351). Unlike in any other version of the fairy-tale, this Beast's transformation requires him to become a

---

[24] The characters in the chat room come from several different fairy-tale sources. While it seems likely that BeastNYC and SilentMaid are from the two big Disney hits of the early 1990s, *Beauty and the Beast* and *The Little Mermaid* (based, of course, on earlier texts, but best known to contemporary readers from those sources), Froggie and Grizzlyguy derive from the Grimms' "Frog Prince (or Iron Hans)" and "Snow White and Rose Red." All, of course, are tales of lovers under mysterious enchantments.

[25] See Claudia Nelson on children's metafiction: in many metafictional texts for children, "we may see authors either in a mimetic light, as reporting on their own emotional experiences of reading, or in a didactic one, as seeking to establish for their audience the benefits that reading may have to bestow" (Nelson 2006, 227).

reader.[26] *Beastly* therefore picks up the thread about learning to read that was dropped in the Disney movie and uses it to stitch together its tale of transformation.

While the Beast character, Kyle, narrates *Beastly*, Lindy—the Beauty figure—is the first-person narrator of her own diary novel, and her tale, while it dovetails with Kyle's, diverges from it in significant ways. Perhaps most interesting is the fact that she reads her experience through literature throughout—really, from the very opening lines. In the second paragraph of the novella, for example, she announces that she reads Gabriel García Marquez and Ayn Rand for pleasure (in ninth grade). She compares her journal to Samuel Pepys', she agrees to the bargain that sends her to live with the Beast by comparing herself to Jane Eyre, and when she moves in with him, among the possibilities she imagines are "my captor in a hood or one of those medieval masks, invisible servants or clocks and candlesticks like in the Beauty and the Beast cartoon" (Flinn 2012, June 13, July 13, July 20). That is, Lindy is literate in the way her teachers might wish: she has wide-ranging reading interests and she uses them to interpret her experience. That her references also serve as clues to the knowing reader is a metafictional bonus—but, as with the chat room references in *Beastly*, a meaningless one, as it's unlikely that any reader will pick up *Lindy's Diary* who has not already read *Beastly*. Thus, these "clues" simply reinforce what has already been established.

In *Beastly*, Kyle does none of this kind of reading, at least at the beginning. The chat room introduction takes us to a flashback which gives us a non-reader, a handsome teenager who is, like Disney's Beast (and unlike Le Prince de Beaumont's), transformed as a punishment for bad behavior.[27] He comes to reading only after he is transformed into a Beast, and at first only out of boredom and necessity. He researches his plight, "googling words like *beast, transformation, spell, curse*—you know, just to see if this type of thing had happened to anyone else

---

[26] It's interesting to note that the 2017 live-action version with Emma Watson—metafictionally recognizable as Hermione to most of her fans—and Dan Stevens expands the library scene from the animated version, making the Beast a highly literate wooer of his Belle. The two exchange poetry over a snowy bridge and otherwise share texts, but the film makes clear that he is already a reader, more like Edward Cullen (see below) than Kyle.

[27] Like Disney's Beast, he cannot recognize "true beauty" when it is in front of him, focusing instead on superficial, external beauty. After rejecting a witch (again, much as Disney's Beast does), he is turned into a Beast and given two years to find a transformative love.

outside of Grimms' fairy-tales or *Shrek*" (Flinn 2007, 108). He finds the Internet chat room. He spends time on MySpace and Google Earth and, later, reads gardening books. He also, eventually, starts reading literature. First, *The Hunchback of Notre Dame*, then *The Phantom of the Opera*, *Frankenstein*, and *The Picture of Dorian Gray*. Reading about "people who live in darkness," as he says, begins to give him some distance on his own plight, and even some insight into his own past self: as he puts it, "Guys like Phoebus in *The Hunchback*, or Dorian, or the old Kyle Kingsbury—they can be scumbags to women and still get away with it because they're good-looking" (Flinn 2007, 126). This insight—that he has been "a scumbag to women"—is the beginning of his second, and final, transformation, back into a human.

While Kyle's initial reading in the novel is either self-directed or, occasionally, assigned by his tutor, his real education through literature comes after he encounters his Beauty, Linda. Furnished with the magic mirror that appears in most versions of the tale, he watches her, someone he had previously known only as one among the mostly undifferentiated masses of less-than-beautiful people at his school. At first, he watches her out of boredom and then out of curiosity: "usually, I watched Linda read. I couldn't believe she'd read so much in summer! Sometimes she laughed, reading her book, and once she even cried. I didn't know how anyone could make such a big deal about books" (Flinn 2007, 79). Here again the novel references the Disney film, this time with the Gaston motif: Kyle is not only the Beast but also the beastly male who can't see the value of literature.

The first book Kyle sees Linda read is *Jane Eyre*, and he thinks at the time that he might even be bored enough one day to read it himself. Later, when he does, it becomes another touchstone for him, another text in which he begins to see a potential version of himself. Once Linda comes to live in Kyle's "castle"—a Brooklyn brownstone where his father, appalled by his transformation, has sequestered him—they begin to read together, and the tale begins to turn into the story we know: they develop feelings, she leaves to care for her father (a drug dealer and addict who has traded her freedom for his own), she misses him, and she returns, almost too late, but in fact just in time for the final transformation.

Thus, *Beastly* not only turns the tale into the Beast's story, but makes it a story of transformative education, not only in the common way we use that term, but in the magical way of fairy-tale transformations.

It makes a claim for reading that goes beyond what we've seen in the earlier versions of the tale. But this claim ignores the playful metafictional qualities of the text, transforming them into mere touchstones of (a typically feminine) literacy. The novel becomes an almost painfully earnest celebration of the classics, challenging nothing in its reinscription of the unqualified "good" of reading. Thus, postmodern play collapses into post-ironic earnestness and into a traditionalist celebration of texts as talismans.[28]

What is also striking about Kyle's education in books is that it takes place at all. Bored by school and bored by books, Kyle Kingsbury is, in fact, the kind of boy addressed by programs such as Jon Scieszka's "Guys Read" program, BoysRead.org, and former First Lady Laura Bush's campaign to get more boys reading. He exemplifies the research of scholars like Michael W. Smith and Jeffrey D. Wilhelm who, in their book *Reading Don't Fix No Chevys*, summarize many years' worth of findings about reading and boys. Among them, we may see some of Kyle's tendencies, including an impatience with fiction (especially fiction about girls), a preference for instructional texts, and a desire to respond actively to reading (Smith and Wilhelm 2002, 10–11).

The kind of reading Kyle does is at first neither narrative nor expository; rather, he joins the chat room, tries to find a soul mate on MySpace, and orders an atlas and a travel guide to help him explore the places he views online. Pushed by his tutor into experimenting with gardening, Kyle begins to read more seriously, saying, "reading had become my perfect solution" to the problems he encounters growing roses (Flinn 2007, 142). Once Lindy enters the house, though, Kyle really begins to read. Like Disney's Beast, Kyle provides his captive with a library; this one, however, is custom-made: "I'd noticed her homework and tried to buy things she'd like, not only novels, but books about physics, religion, philosophy, and duplicate volumes for myself so I could read anything that caught her attention" (Flinn 2007, 165). It is, of course, the novels that Lindy reads and, therefore, that Kyle reads as well.

Jane Eyre, the most-referenced novel in the text, provides both a talisman for Lindy and a model for Kyle. When she finds an illustrated

[28] Here again I must reference Joe Sutliff Sanders's indispensable article on the critical reader in children's metafiction—what we see here is "any discomfort inspired by metafiction ... blunted by the solace and empowerment that come from relationships with books" (Sanders 2009, 351).

edition of the novel in the top floor of the brownstone, Lindy calls it "the most wonderful book in the world" (Flinn 2007, 210) and encourages Kyle to read it. When Kyle finally discusses the novel with his tutor, Will—after he has released Lindy to care for her father—he acknowledges his surprise at having enjoyed it. But, of course, he is now living it out, beginning to see himself and Lindy as versions of Rochester and Jane, a Beast who loves an unconventional Beauty. In *Lindy's Diary*, Flinn reinforces this intertextual connection by having Lindy wish for "a new servitude" just before she goes to Kyle's brownstone to live—the same wish Jane expresses before she first moves to Thornfield Hall to work for Mr. Rochester. This use of *Jane Eyre*, however, has none of the metafictional play we saw in Cabot's uses of the same novel in the earlier *Princess Diary* appropriation. While there the reader is in on the joke—that Mia and Tina are misreading the novel, which could provide them with a feminist grounding if they would only recognize it—here the use is far more conventional, more in line with the romance novel use to which they, too, put the text. Content is far less important in these novels than the simple fact that Kyle is actually reading, and reading what are typically termed "girl books." Rather than interrogating the term, the novel simply reverses its valuation, turning it to Kyle's and Lindy's advantage. This does, however, suggest that the self is malleable, reconstructable, refashionable—as we can see below (and as the even more conventional *Twilight* books do not suggest).

Of course, it is not fiction alone that transforms the beastly Kyle into the lovable beast and, ultimately, back into a newly realized Kyle again. We could point to his attention to the roses' growth, his enforced intimacy with those very different from himself, his magic mirror that allows him to see that his beautiful peers are, in fact, neither happy nor good, even the support he receives in the Internet chat room. But all of these involve reading: reading for information, initially, reading—as the traditional character of Beauty does—beyond the initial signs of class and culture, reading the chat room stories that suggest to him, more vividly than traditional fairy-tales, his own fate. The novel thus suggests, directly in line with the scholars of boys' reading, a multivariate approach to literacy, a literacy that builds on initial strengths and inclinations and then develops from there. This reading transforms Kyle more thoroughly than the witch's spell; as he notes well before the end of the novel, "I didn't even know who 'the real me' was anymore. I had been transformed—not just my body, but all of me" (Flinn 2007, 216). Potentially a postmodern subject, Kyle (re)constructs a "real me" out of language, out of reading.

Kyle's transformation through reading, then, is not a magic spell at all, but the result of hard work and creative thought. As the research on boys' reading suggests, he needs to turn his reading into action, even (perhaps) into a product, such as his roses. His transformation is also marked by the shift in his language—he notices, for example, that "since I'd been with her, I noticed that I'd started to talk differently … like the characters in the books she loved" (Flinn 2007, 243).[29] Only once he has begun to turn his reading into action is he ready to read and internalize the "moral" of *Jane Eyre*/"Beauty and the Beast"—ready to see himself as worthy of empathy and love rather than just pity and disgust. Not only is he worthy of empathy, of course, he is also able to feel it for the first time—as the research on reading (cited in the introduction) suggests, he has learned to recognize the humanity of others in part through reading novels that depict the inner workings of characters' minds.

And yet if this is the message of the novel, it is also a message that may not reach its intended readers, if—as the scholarship indicates—boys are less interested than girls in novels, in fantasy, in exposition. Kyle, after all, is still not fully convinced of the value of fiction until after he has let Lindy go, and only encounters it in the first place because of his monstrous transformation. The reading that has marked Lindy as "other," that has been part of her exclusion from the in-crowd and a fulfilling social life, is the same reading that ultimately transforms Kyle into someone worthy of his good looks (which are fully restored by the end of the novel). So the metafictional celebration of reading is multi-edged: developing multiple literacies can indeed help make a reader, even an empathetic reader. But those who perhaps most need to become readers—those "insider," adolescent males, the Gastons and Kyles of contemporary high schools—are the least likely to encounter the stories that will convince them of their need.

While reading transforms the Beast of *Beastly*, Lindy's case is different. Like *The Princess Diaries*, *Lindy's Diary* gives us a female protagonist who is an outsider, a reader, and a writer. And, again like Cabot's novels, it marks its protagonist as a fairy-tale heroine early on: "Sometimes,

---

[29] Kyle has begun to master what Maryanne Wolf calls "the language of books" (Wolf 2007, 87).

you wonder when your handsome prince is going to show up and rescue you" (Flinn 2012, May 10). Lindy's desire for a prince to rescue her is understandable—she's the motherless daughter of a drug addict. But the novel reiterates her wish, marking her as the fairy-tale princess in exile. To strike the point home, she is repeatedly linked with *Jane Eyre*—most obviously, of course, in order to weave her tale in with that of *Beastly*, but also to deepen the intertextual fairy-tale connections. Jane Eyre has frequently been read as either a Cinderella figure (especially during her time with her Reed cousins, who treat her as Cinderella's stepsisters do) or as Belle from "Beauty and the Beast," imprisoned with a beastly male whom she must tame; Lindy associates herself with Jane frequently throughout the novel, especially in moments of decision.[30]

But Lindy's version of *Jane Eyre* is more like Bella's, in *Twilight*, than like Brontë's (see below). Purged of its feminism, the *Jane Eyre* that Lindy and Kyle read is pure fairy-tale, a tale of true love and heroic rescue rather than one of self-determination and independence. While Kyle uses the novel and others like it to remake himself into a kinder, gentler teenage boy, Lindy's development is passively structured by the men around her—she moves almost without volition from her father to Adrian and back again. Despite her seemingly independent choices—she pays rent, she gets a scholarship—still her choices are constrained by the father/boyfriend binary.

In this, *Lindy's Diary* suggests another version of the *Twilight* series, which it otherwise resembles only in its assumed readership. But like that most popular of YA series from the early 2000s, *Lindy's Diary* gives us a reading heroine whose literacy suggests an agency that is, ultimately, false: her options are limited by the narrative she inhabits and the narrow interpretation of the ones she chooses. The metafictional play in Flinn's and Meyer's texts is self-limiting and conservative, reflecting the false-choice feminism of their Bush-era context. While the more anarchic play of *The Princess Diaries* suggests that critical literacy can be a path to agency, these more conventional texts provide only the comfort of recognition and the didactic insistence that reading is good for boys because it

---

[30] Campbell (2016) reads *Jane Eyre* through "Beauty and the Beast" and "Bluebeard." Readings associating *Jane Eyre* with "Cinderella" include Sullivan (1978) and Clarke (2000). The two most important Jane Eyre links in *Lindy's Diary* are her July 13 call for a new servitude and, on May 24, calling Kyle's name and thinking of the mystic call in *Jane Eyre*.

teaches them empathy. Their reading heroines serve only to reinforce the values of their implied readers and to reify gender stereotypes that ultimately provide few real options for girls.

FAILURES OF EMPATHY: *TWILIGHT*'S BORING BRONTËS

While, as I've noted, Kyle's transformation begins with multivariate literacy, it ends with a rather conventional celebration of literary reading of the most canonical sort. Thomas Newkirk quotes Judith Langer's claim that "Literature makes us better thinkers…and it moves us to consider our interconnectedness with others and the intrinsic pluralness of meaning; it helps us become more human" (Newkirk 2002, 75, quoting Langer 145). While this celebration of reading precisely describes what happens to Kyle, as Newkirk notes, the language suggests that such readers will become "more human *than those who don't read in this way*" (Newkirk 2002, 75, emphasis in original). This problematic claim ignores the obvious humanity of non-readers and the humanizing function of, for example, encounters with actual humans (Newkirk 2002, 76). It also elides what *Beastly* makes clear: the implicit equation of humanization with feminization.[31] The *Twilight* novels offer an interesting test case for the connection of reading, empathy, and feminization.

As I noted earlier, Peter Brooks, in his introduction to *The Humanities and Public Life*, writes that "In claiming a place for the humanities in public life, we [the contributors to the volume] are arguing that fictions are not distractions from reality but a central means to an understanding of where and how we live in reality" (Brooks 2014, 14). Leaving aside the linguistic sleight of hand that turns "the humanities" into "fictions," Brooks's argument is carried out in crude but effective fashion in the YA novels I've just been discussing. The fictions the protagonists read provide them precisely "an understanding of where and how [to] live." The very didacticism of this claim as it plays out in the novels, however, seems to work against it, especially, as we have seen, as it is gendered in the romances featuring boys but marketed toward girls, such as *Beastly* and

---

[31] This feminization is rarely valued in either contemporary popular culture or a political culture that seeks to defund, for example, both humanities programs and a variety of social and medical programs that disproportionately affect women.

Sisters Red. In the *Twilight* saga, the publishing phenomenon of 2005–2008, reading romance is again implicitly a guide to how to live for the novels' protagonists; it is less clear, however, that the practice has anything to offer its implied readers.

On her first day at Forks High School, newcomer Bella Swan's first class is English. Her teacher, Mr. Mason,[32] hands her a reading list: "It was fairly basic [she notes]: Brontë, Shakespeare, Chaucer, Faulkner. I'd already read everything. That was comforting ... and boring" (Meyer 2005, 15, ellipses in original). Like other literary newcomers she in some ways resembles—say, the Brontëan Lockwood and Jane Eyre, for example—Bella initially misreads her situation in Forks, expecting that past experience can guide her in the present. Perhaps because she is, unlike her predecessors, a reader of texts as well as situations, Bella quickly corrects, becoming a better interpreter than her predecessors in romance, both of whom repeatedly miss the cues that something is awry in their new settings. Although Bella can't yet name it, she intuits a problem shortly after her assessment of the English class, when Edward Cullen looks at her with hostility and fury. Though she misidentifies his reasons, she's right about the reaction—as she is about a number of other details. She notices, for example, that Edward gets her nickname right and that his eyes change color. Despite a slow Internet connection, she quickly puts together the clues Jacob gives her with her own observations and ferrets out Edward's identity without revealing it to anyone else. In *Wuthering Heights*, Lockwood needs Nellie to reveal Heathcliff's story to him—and misreads Catherine throughout the tale. Similarly, Jane denies the evidence about Bertha even when she sees Mason's wounds and Rochester's reactions. Unlike them, Bella is a quick study. Or, to put it differently, the *Twilight* series is less interested in the mysteries of identity than its literary predecessors. While *Wuthering Heights* and *Jane Eyre*, like so many Victorian novels, are essentially concerned with identity, its formation, revelation, and transformation, in the *Twilight* series identity comes fixed, already known; rather than unveiling new revelations, then, or exploring the ways in which identity shifts and transforms over time and in relationship,[33] Meyer's plots focus on

---

[32] There must be a reference to *Jane Eyre* in his name, though, as with many of the intertextual references in the novels I've been discussing, nothing comes of it.

[33] Even *Beastly*, as we have seen, at least gestures toward literature's transformative value.

the implications of bringing already-fixed identities together. Reading reveals, in other words—it does not transform. Focusing on instrumental uses of reading is one of the many standard defenses of the humanities,[34] of course, but as Brooks's anthology and others suggest, it is a limited one and may fail because it lacks both self-criticism and self-awareness—as we may see in the *Twilight* novels as well.

What the novel signals by evoking the literary canon (or a particular version of it) in that early scene, then, is not so much *Twilight*'s likeness to its intertextual predecessors as a particular way of thinking about reading. The paradoxical power of the canon is that it reifies texts that were themselves revolutionary in their time and that are thematically concerned with transformation rather than stasis. The "comforting…and boring" familiarity of canonical novels, in other words, may rob them of their revolutionary power.

I start with Bella as reader because it's one of the ways the text signals its intertextual affinities. Bella seeks solace in Austen (and doesn't find it when the first two heroes she encounters are named Edward and Edmund) (Meyer 2005, 148), argues with Edward about *Wuthering Heights* (Meyer 2007, 28–29), and tries to imagine a future for Juliet (Meyer 2006, 370–371). And Meyer prefaces each of the novels with an epigraph—from Genesis, *Romeo and Juliet*, Robert Frost, and Edna St. Vincent Millay—to further indicate the centrality of reading and texts to the *Twilight* experience. Commentary on the *Twilight* series—like that on its predecessor in popularity, J.K. Rowling's Harry Potter series—repeatedly references the length of the books and the significance that these are, first and foremost, reading experiences. Review essays and articles repeatedly reference other texts, too: Caitlin Flanagan in *The Atlantic Monthly*, for example, (I think wrongly) claims that "Edward treats Bella not as Count Dracula treated the objects of his desire, but as Mr. Rochester treated Jane Eyre. He evinces the most profound disdain and distaste for this girl" as well as placing Edward's revelation of his love for Bella in a telling context: "Not since Maxim de Winter's shocking revelation—'You thought I loved Rebecca? … I hated her'—has a sweet young heroine received such startling and

---

[34]The Web site for my own department promises that "deep engagement with literary study [is] a pursuit that develops writing and critical reading abilities along with strengthening communication skills and critical thinking" (english.richmond.edu, accessed Jan 15, 2018).

enrapturing news" (Flanagan 2008). The constellation of modern gothics that Flanagan cites is telling: *Rebecca* is itself, of course, a text of imitation, a reworking of *Jane Eyre*. Flanagan is onto something else with her evocation of *Jane Eyre* as well. As we've seen before, the novel is central to the romance tradition. Modleski's bare-bones summary of the novel, cited earlier, fits *Twilight*—especially its first volume—quite nicely.

And yet, of course, Bella is not Jane. In key moments, Jane supports Rochester: from their first meeting when he falls off his horse, to the revelation that Mason is in the house ("I have got a blow"), to their marriage, it is Jane who is stronger than her Edward despite her small stature and her insignificant social status. Bella, on the other hand, requires Edward Cullen's intervention more than once (in the parking lot, in the streets of Port Angeles, etc.) to save her life. Her clumsiness structures the relationship between the lovers, in fact; Edward repeatedly begs Bella to be careful and repeatedly incurs her gratitude (though sometimes also her wrath) by saving her life. While Brontë works hard to establish an equality between her patently unequal lovers, Meyer revels, it seems, in the inequality of hers. And where Jane discovers a vampirish secret in Rochester's past—the first time she sees Bertha, she tells Rochester she was reminded of "the foul German spectre—the Vampyre" (C. Brontë 1847, 317)—and then helps him displace it, Bella must become a vampire in order to establish equality with her older, stronger lover.

Nor, of course, is Edward really Rochester, despite the age gap and the shared first name. As Flanagan further notes, "*Twilight* centers on a boy who loves a girl so much that he refuses to defile her, and on a girl who loves him so dearly that she is desperate for him to do just that, even if the wages of the act are expulsion from her family and from everything she has ever known" (Flanagan 2008). *Jane Eyre*, however, centers on a man who loves a girl so much he proposes precisely to "defile" her (Flanagan's terms are strangely Victorian here), and a girl who loves him so dearly that she won't allow him to. That is, again, the *Twilight* novels utterly restructure the power relationships evident in *Jane Eyre*. Jane, both narrative and moral center, is able to speak for herself, and act for herself, in ways that Bella, despite her own narrative control, is remarkably unable to do.

Patsy Stoneman notes that one of the effects of the first-person narration in *Jane Eyre* is that it "'teaches' her readers how to 'read' the enigmatic Rochester" (Stoneman 1996, 200).[35] Strikingly, this is at first one of the things Bella is least able to do. While she figures out *what* Edward is in relatively short order, the first three novels are consumed with her inability to "get" him, at least in relationship to her. Again, this reverses the pattern of *Jane Eyre*, in which Jane *knows* Rochester deeply despite her ignorance of his past. Edward, for his part, is also remarkably unable to "read" Bella—she alone in all the world is immune to his vampirish mind-reading ability. Thus, he again falls short of Rochester's status as, in Judith Furman's words, "the great Recogniser" (Stoneman 1996, 201, quoting Furman 1989, 122). Of course, it is their failure to read each other that generates most of the narrative interest in the first three novels—the play of misunderstanding that is the meat of the romance novel, from *Evelina* and *Pride and Prejudice* on, continues long after the lovers have mutually confessed their love, at least in part because of their repeated inability to "read" each other. This inability serves as well, at least in places, to undermine one of the central functions of intertextuality—the sense of "fatedness" that John Hannay notes. As he says, in a novel with a generic plot, "we know what comes next because we recall analogous stories and so discern the proleptic logic of the one we are reading" (Stoneman 1996, 148, quoting Hannay 1986, 1–2). This aspect of intertextuality fails Bella—and her implied readers—repeatedly. While we may predict the *Jane Eyre*-ish "happy ending" of the first novel—and indeed of the series—the way Meyer takes us there repeatedly frustrates a proleptic reading. That is, familiarity with *Twilight*'s predecessors will not help the reader "discern the logic" of Meyer's saga, because she repeatedly refuses Brontëan logic.

Another reason for this frustration—beyond the play of mutual misrecognition—is, perhaps ironically, the series' overly intertextual nature. We are not just dealing with the generic romance drawn from *Jane Eyre*, in other words. Indeed, when Bella mentions a Brontë novel in *Twilight*, it's always *Wuthering Heights*, not *Jane Eyre*. While the two novels are, as Stoneman elucidates, frequently lumped together as generic "romance" or "women's" novels, they deal with very different kinds of romance,

---

[35] Although Day does not cite Stoneman, it seems to me that both are making similar arguments here about the function of reading, especially of reading first-person romances, for female readers. Again, here we have the focus on reading as interpretation of almost any situation—a focus that again shifts in the YA reworking into a narrower emphasis on textual reading.

and their intertextual significance is quite different. *Wuthering Heights* first comes up in *Eclipse* as a negative example. As Edward points out: "The characters are ghastly people who ruin each others' lives.... It isn't a love story, it's a hate story" (Meyer 2007, 28). While Bella defends the novel's appeal—"it's something about the inevitability. How nothing can keep them apart—not her selfishness, or his evil, or even death, in the end ..."—Edward remains, at least initially, unconvinced (Meyer 2007, 29). (A similar pattern emerges in *New Moon*, in which Edward tries and fails to convince Bella that Romeo is not a worthy romantic hero.) Edward is here the more attentive reader; one of the mysteries of the *Twilight* saga is that Bella's more romantic readings repeatedly prevail.[36]

In some ways, of course, *Eclipse* does rewrite the tragic triangle of *Wuthering Heights*, casting Jacob as Heathcliff and Edward as Edgar— or, perhaps, as the reverse. At first, the hairy, dark, outcast Jacob appears in the Heathcliff role while the wealthy, attractive, Edward appears as Edgar. Reading the pairings this way would suggest, perhaps, that Meyer is rewriting Brontë to provide not only a happy but an oddly conventional ending, in which the "right" suitor actually does prevail. Yet the roles shift later in the novel, when Edward identifies with Heathcliff, telling Bella "I'm discovering I can sympathize with [him] in ways I didn't think possible before" (Meyer 2007, 265). Later Bella opens the book to this passage, in which Heathcliff tells Nelly:

> And there you see the distinction between our feelings: had he [Edgar Linton] been in my place and I in his, though I hated him with a hatred that turned my life to gall, I never would have raised a hand against him. You may look incredulous, if you please! I never would have banished him from her [Catherine's] society as long as she desired his. The moment her regard ceased, I would have torn his heart out, and drank his blood! But, till then—if you don't believe me, you don't know me—till then, I would have died by inches before I touched a single hair of his head! (Meyer 2007, 266, quoting E. Brontë 1847)

As Bella recognizes immediately, Edward has now cast himself as Heathcliff, willing to sacrifice his own happiness for his lover's—and,

---

[36] Edward's superior reading skills may seem to give the lie to my earlier argument that boys are infrequently associated with reading in romance retellings; Edward's "otherness" here seems to trump his masculinity.

of course, threatening to drink his rival's blood if he fails her. Casting Edward as Heathcliff this way does several things. For most of *Twilight*'s implied readers, who may not have encountered Brontë's novel yet, it may direct their reading: the *Twilight*-inspired reader of *Wuthering Heights* may, given Edward's earlier disdain, be less likely than the average reader to seek out and find a "love story" in Brontë's disturbing novel. Second, it sets up the not unreasonable possibility that they will encounter another vampire in that earlier text. Third, for the reader who does have some familiarity with *Wuthering Heights*, it may increase the tension in *Eclipse*, setting up the possibility of a tragic ending rather than the comic one predicted by the *Jane Eyre* paradigm. (A similar thing happens with *Romeo and Juliet* as the intertext of *New Moon*.) This doubled intertext, then, may have the effect of misleading the proleptic reader.

Meyer, after all, rewards her heroine's choice. Where Brontë reveals Isabella's foolishness in succumbing to romantic convention, Meyer celebrates her heroine's naïve reading.[37] *Wuthering Heights* reveals Heathcliff to be cruel, pitiless, and unchanging: his connection to Catherine, so celebrated by Bella, brings about her death. Nor is his famous promise—"I cannot live without my life! I cannot live without my soul!" (E. Brontë 1847, 169)—borne out by the text; in fact, he lives another eighteen years after Catherine's death, drearily amassing the wealth that will, eventually, enrich Catherine's daughter. In *Wuthering Heights*, the identity that Catherine and Heathcliff seem to share is part of the problem. Unable to change, both ultimately die rather than facing the possibility of transformation.[38] The *Twilight* saga, however, celebrates stasis. Even *Breaking Dawn*, the novel that might seem to focus on Bella's transformation—into both vampire and parent—is more a novel of revelation than of transformation. As a vampire, Bella comes into her own, discovering that, as the ancient Volturi vampire Aro says, she may have been "designed for this life" of immortality

---

[37] Cabot's humorous reworkings in *The Princess Diaries* are here more aligned with Brontë's satire of Isabella.

[38] While readings of *Wuthering Heights* are notoriously divided on the promise of its second half, I am inclined to read it as a positive revision of the first story. The fact that the second Catherine instructs her cousin Hareton Earnshaw in reading—a scene that forms part of what Gilbert and Gubar denigrate as a diminishing domesticization—to me suggests a positive restructuring of the relationships of the first half (see, e.g., Gilbert and Gubar 1979, 299). But the novel's bifurcated structure does also gesture to an openness that is strikingly lacking in the *Twilight* series.

(Meyer 2008, 696). Even her nearly instant adaptation to life as a vampire is not as swift as her discovery of maternity, however.

> From that first little touch, the whole world had shifted. Where before there was just one thing I could not live without, now there were two. There was no division—my love was not split between them now; it wasn't like that. It was more like my heart had grown, swollen up to twice its size in that moment. All that extra space, already filled. The increase was almost dizzying.... I wanted [the baby] like I wanted air to breathe. Not a choice—a necessity. (Meyer 2008, 132)

Bella discovers her latent vampire qualities and her latent maternity, nearly simultaneously. There's no work involved, no drama—she simply becomes the new thing that she in some sense always already was. (We've seen her mother her own mother and father for three volumes by this point.) Unlike the first Catherine in *Wuthering Heights*, who dies rather than face the transformation that maternity requires, or the second, who does change and mature through her experiences, Bella is nearly as static as the vampire characters who surround her, and revels in that stasis.[39] Reading has neither revealed character nor even served to signal surprises of the plot, then: Bella's reading, and her readers', function largely to reinforce cultural norms and provide escapist comfort. When Bella or her reader empathizes with a fictional character, then, this connection forestalls rather than engendering deep reading.

In her article "Brontë for Kids," Kelly Hager identifies a genre of children's and young adult novels that take Brontë novels and biographies—specifically, *Jane Eyre*, *Wuthering Heights*, and the Brontë biographical myth—as both intertextual referent and model. She argues convincingly that:

> The stories of Jane Eyre, of Catherine and Heathcliff, and of the Brontës growing up at Haworth provide both writers and their protagonists with strategies for narrating the experience of adolescence. Whether we think of the story of the Brontës themselves ... or of their novels—the story of

[39] Lydia Kokkola, in "Virtuous Vamps," argues that "despite her transformation into adult and vampire, Bella seems remarkably *untransformed* by her transition into motherhood ... In undermining the transformational power of motherhood, Meyer draws on another well-established convention in children's literature: the fear of growing up" (Kokkola 2011, 176).

> Jane Eyre, making her way alone in the world and trying to make sense of and justify her attraction to Rochester; of Catherine, growing up with Heathcliff as her best friend and the object of her embryonic erotic desire—we realize that these are all stories about children going through adolescence, trying to reconcile their desire for independence with the complications presented by their emerging sexuality. (Hager 2005, 328)

She goes on to note that this use of the Brontës works precisely because the characters in the contemporary novels are always aware they are not *really* Brontë characters; unlike quixotic readers who lose themselves in novels, they preserve a distance between themselves and their texts. In the *Twilight* saga, *Wuthering Heights* is implicitly deployed for a similar function: both implied reader and fictional character will understand Bella's adolescence better, the novel suggests, when they read it through the lens of *Wuthering Heights*. Yet unlike the novels Hager discusses, the *Twilight* saga fails to provide the distance that creates what Mary Poovey calls "a buffer against overidentification" (Hager 2005, 328, quoting Poovey 88). That is, when Edward begins to suggest that he, too, might claim "I am Heathcliff"—when Bella repeatedly casts herself as, like Catherine, the point of a triangle between two incompatible lovers (here even their species, not just their class status, must divide them)—all distance collapses. Bella's reading, in other words, provides almost none of the benefits of reading that defenders of the humanities like Peter Brooks suggested it could. Rather than providing her necessary skills or, especially, critical distance on any contemporary values, for example, her empathetic reading simply directs her to replicate its most conventional plots.

Defending the Humanities?

More recent novels influenced by the Brontës return their focus to *Jane Eyre*, using it—as Mia Thermopolis does—as a guide to life. Unlike *Princess in Waiting*, however, these novels provide their heroines an earnest identification with Jane. In Fiona Wood's *Cloudwish*, for example, the protagonist, Vân Ước Phan, asks herself "What would Jane [Eyre] do?" whenever she is in doubt as to her course of action. Often, her version of Jane would "have some more muscle in the way she dealt with the world" than Vân Ước herself actually does (Wood 2015, 79). Her Jane, in other words, is outspoken, feminist, and confident. Sometimes she is represented by quotations from the text, other times by Vân Ước's imaginary conversations with her. Always, however, she is more confident, more sure of herself, than Vân Uớc—she is, indeed, a feminist role model. In Nina LaCour's *We Are Okay*, however, protagonist Marin identifies with Jane's orphan status, her fear, her loneliness. And in Eve Marie Mont's *A Breath of Eyre*, Emma Townsend literally enters the text of *Jane Eyre*, building on her earlier identification with Jane and then moves beyond that identification to recognize the necessary interrelationship of Jane and Bertha, both in the novel and in her own identity.[40]

Both *We Are Okay* and *Cloudwish*, despite their clear reliance on *Jane Eyre* as a role model, provide a more nuanced use of the text—a deeper reading—than the novels of the *Twilight* saga or even *Princess in Waiting*. Vân Uớc, the protagonist of *Cloudwish*, is the daughter of Vietnamese immigrants, while Marin, of *We Are Okay*, is queer—both, then, provide more radical versions of otherness in their identification with Jane than do the earlier novels. Even Mont's Emma, a scholarship student whose best friend, also a scholarship student, is the child of West Indian immigrants, shares a class identity with Jane: living within, but not a part of, a more elevated class status than her own.

All three novels are both structured by and make frequent reference to *Jane Eyre*; the characters' reading of the novel provides them with comfort and direction, and their plots frequently intersect with or echo scenes in the earlier text. For example, in *A Breath of Eyre*, Emma Townsend goes to a boarding school named Lockwood Prep and has a roommate (Michelle Dominguez) who is, like her, a scholarship student (though Michelle's anger is far from Helen Burns's preternatural calm). There's lightning (she is hit by it), a fire (stables burn down; Michelle is blamed), a Blanche Ingram figure in Elise Fairchild, and family secrets, including one that haunts her love interest, Gray Newman. *Cloudwish* involves, among other things, a love interest for Vân Uớc who both teases her and possesses a level of wealth and privilege (and, unlike Rochester, good looks) that initially lead her to mistrust him despite her attraction.

---

[40]Emma's paper on *Jane Eyre* makes an argument clearly influenced by Gilbert and Gubar's *The Madwoman in the Attic*, though the text is never referenced and her own paper is received as "too risky," and characterized by "bold and controversial statements" (Mont 2012, 302). In 2012, the year of the novel's publication, her reading would be far from controversial, even in most high schools.

But it is *We Are Okay* that is perhaps the most interesting of these three Brontë-inspired novels. While, like the other two, it is (in Hager's words) a "stor[y] about children going through adolescence, trying to reconcile their desire for independence with the complications presented by their emerging sexuality," it also quite clearly places *Jane Eyre* within a tradition rather than taking it as a singular model (Hager 2005, 328). Like *Princess in Waiting* or the school stories of Chapter Two, *We Are Okay* provides its readers with a shadow syllabus. Unlike them, the "syllabus" exists to be read critically rather than used as a model text.

The novel's protagonist, Marin, meets her (now ex-) girlfriend Mabel in English class, because (in Mabel's words) "Brother John had us analyze some stupid poem, and you raised your hand and said something so smart about it that suddenly the poem didn't seem stupid anymore. And I knew you were the kind of person I wanted to know" (LaCour 2017, 49). Their connection through literature continues throughout the novel, as Mabel writes a paper on orphans in the literature (*Jane Eyre* and *The Turn of the Screw* figure prominently) and Marin one on ghosts and hauntings (which includes both of the former novels as well as *One Hundred Years of Solitude*). Poetry by Plath and Sexton also figure briefly in the text. More important than the syllabus, however, is the attitude toward literature that Marin articulates: "It's better if it's complicated," she says in English class, arguing that the teacher's two possible interpretations of *The Turn of the Screw* ("the governess is hallucinating" or "the ghosts are real") are not enough (LaCour 2017, 24). She follows with the claim that complexity is itself the "point of the novel":

> We can search for the truth, we can convince ourselves of whatever we want to believe, but we'll never actually know. I *guarantee* that we can find evidence to argue that the staff is playing a trick on the governess. (LaCour 2017, 24)

The novel and its characters ultimately suggest that deep reading can ensue from empathy. They connect with each other and with their textual forebears, building an affective association that allows Marin to recognize herself as, by turns, both Bertha and Jane, both monster and orphan. Unlike the more didactic "reading" of *Jane Eyre* that we see in *A Breath of Eyre*, *We Are Okay* plays with its predecessor, suggesting, at least implicitly, that its own implied readers might also want to the way Marin does—deeply, affectively, and with empathy.

Like the children Hager refers to in "Brontë for Kids," or the immersive readers analyzed in Sara Day's *Reading Like a Girl*, Marin identifies with her favorite novel's protagonist. Recounting her time in a motel before she started college, Marin tells Mabel about a woman, wailing in the room next door.

> I felt like Jane when she sees [Bertha] in the mirror. I was afraid. I'd listen to her at night and sometimes I felt like I understood what she was trying to say. I was afraid I'd turn into her.
>
> The fact of her was scary enough, but the fact of me, in an identical room, just as alone as she was, that was the worst part. There was only a wall between us, and it was so thin it was almost nothing. Jane, too, was once locked up in a room with a ghost. It was terrifying, the idea that we could fall asleep girls, minty breathed and nightgowned, and wake to find ourselves wolves. (LaCour 2017, 131–132)

Like Emma in *A Breath of Eyre*, Marin is alert to the connection between Jane and Bertha. And, like Emma again, she connects with both of them, collapsing the distance between reader and character. But *A Breath of Eyre*, like *Cloudwish*, seems to undercut its suggestion that empathic reading is also deep reading: for Emma and Vân Ước, identity trumps critique as the protagonists simply reinscribe the heteronormative conclusion of *Jane Eyre*. While Elaine Scarry argues that "empathetic narrative require[s] one to think counterfactually, to think the notion that one does not oneself hold to be the case," these novels comfortingly suggest that such reading is unusual, unlikely, or even, ultimately, wrong (Scarry 2014, 45). Reading the classics reinforces and reifies rather than reinvigorating or reinterpreting a tradition, in these texts: no change is really, they suggest, necessary. Thus, while these reimagined romances do indeed suggest that reading is important—indeed, critical—to the development of young adults, it is so only for the most conservative of reasons: the reinscription and reinstatement of the romance centered on the heteronormative couple, with the teenage girl doing all the affective work of both reading and relationship maintenance.

Only in the conclusion to *We Are Okay* do we get an inkling of what a more deeply affective reading might mean. As Marin and Mabel watch the movie adaptation of *Jane Eyre* near the novel's end, Marin thinks, "For a few minutes, Jane believes that she'll be happy, and I try to believe it, too" (LaCour 2017, 230). The novel's conclusion does not provide the heteronormative ending of the courtship novel that all the other novels discussed here do; rather, it reinscribes the ending of *Jane Eyre* with a difference by offering reunions: Marin with Mabel's family, with the memory of her grandfather, and—perhaps most importantly— with her mother's past. Like Jane "an independent woman" who is her "own mistress," Marin concludes her story in the bosom of family, both present (like the Riverses) and absent (like her mother and St. John) (C. Brontë 1847, 501).

Girls who read, these reimagined romances suggest, are indeed empowered by their reading. Their ability to imagine themselves into the lives of their fictional predecessors—their development of empathy— allows them to take (a limited) control of their romantic lives. As Scarry, Brooks, and others suggest, then, the empathy that reading engenders can indeed provide "a central means to an understanding of where and how we live in reality" (Brooks 2014, 14). In the chapter that follows, I explore texts that suggest reading's centrality not only to understanding but in fact to (re)shaping that reality, as I explore the way reading is central to how racialized minorities "dream [themselves] into existence" (Elliott 2010).

WORKS CITED

Bacchilega, Cristina. 1997. *Postmodern Fairy Tales: Gender and Narrative Strategies*. Philadelphia: University of Pennsylvania Press.

Beauty and the Beast. 1991. Dir. Gary Trousdale and Kirk Wise. Walt Disney Studios. Film.

Beauty and the Beast. 2017. Dir. Bill Condon. Walt Disney Pictures. Film.

Brontë, Charlotte. 1847, 2006. *Jane Eyre*. London: Penguin.

Brontë, Emily. 1847, 2003. *Wuthering Heights*. London: Penguin.

Brooks, Peter. 2014. Introduction. In *The Humanities in Public Life*, ed. Peter Brooks with Hilary Jewett, 1–14. New York: Fordham University Press.

Cabot, Meg. 2003. *The Princess Diaries, Volume IV: Princess in Waiting*. New York: HarperCollins.

Campbell, Jessica. 2016. Bluebeard and the Beast: The Mysterious Realism of *Jane Eyre*. *Marvels and Tales* 30 (2): 234–250.

Clarke, Micael M. 2000. Brontë's "Jane Eyre" and the Grimms' Cinderella. *Studies in English Literature, 1500–1900* 40 (4): 695–710.

Day, Sara K. 2013. *Reading Like a Girl: Narrative Intimacy in Contemporary American Young Adult Literature*. Jackson: University Press of Mississippi.

Elliott, Zetta. 2010. The Writer's Page: Decolonizing the Imagination. *The Horn Book*, March/April. https://www.hbook.com/2010/03/decolonizing-imagination/.

Flanagan, Caitlin. 2008. What Girls Want. *Atlantic*, December. https://www.theatlantic.com/magazine/archive/2008/12/what-girls-want/307161/.

Flinn, Alex. 2007. *Beastly*. New York: Harper Teen.

———. 2012. *Beastly: Lindy's Diary*. New York: Harper Teen, Epub edition.

Frye, Northrop. 1957, 2000. *The Anatomy of Criticism: Four Essays*. Princeton: Princeton University Press.

Gilbert, Sandra M., and Susan Gubar. 1979. *The Madwoman in the Attic: The Woman Writer and the Nineteenth-Century Literary Imagination*. New Haven: Yale University Press.

Gruner, Elisabeth. 2011. Telling Old Tales Newly: Intertextuality in Young Adult Fiction for Girls. In *Telling Children's Stories: Narrative Theory and Children's Literature*, ed. Michael Cadden, 3–21. Lincoln, NE: University of Nebraska Press.

Haase, Donald (ed.). 2004. *Fairy Tales and Feminism: New Approaches*. Detroit: Wayne State University Press.

Hager, Kelly. 2005. Brontë for Kids. *Children's Literature Association Quarterly* 30 (3): 314–332.

Hearne, Betsy Gould. 1989. *Beauty and the Beast: Visions and Revisions of an Old Tale*. Chicago: University of Chicago Press.

Jones, Christine A., and Jennifer Schacker (eds.). 2012. *Marvelous Transformations: An Anthology of Fairy Tales and Contemporary Critical Perspectives*. Peterborough, ON: Broadview.

Kokkola, Lydia. 2011. Virtuous Vampires and Voluptuous Vamps: Romance Conventions Reconsidered in Stephenie Meyer's "Twilight" Series. *Children's Literature in Education* 42 (2): 165–179.

LaCour, Nina. 2017. *We Are Okay*. New York: Dutton.

Meyer, Stephenie. 2005. *Twilight*. New York: Little, Brown.

———. 2006. *New Moon*. New York: Little, Brown.

———. 2007. *Eclipse*. New York: Little, Brown.

———. 2008. *Breaking Dawn*. New York: Little, Brown.

Miller, Lucasta. 2001, 2004. *The Brontë Myth*. New York: Knopf.

Modleski, Tania. 2008. *Loving with a Vengeance: Mass-Produced Fantasies for Women*. New York: Routledge.

Mont, Eva Marie. 2012. *A Breath of Eyre*. New York: K-Teen.

Nelson, Claudia. 2006. Writing the Reader: The Literary Child in and Beyond the Book. *Children's Literature Association Quarterly* 31 (3): 222–236.

Newkirk, Thomas. 2002. *Misreading Masculinity: Boys, Literacy, and Popular Culture*. Portsmouth, NH: Heinemann.

Pearce, Jackson. 2010. *Sisters Red*. New York: Little, Brown.

Rowe, Karen. 1979. Feminism and Fairy Tales. *Women's Studies: An Interdisciplinary Journal* 6: 237–257. Rpt. 2009. *Folk and Fairy Tales*, 4th ed., ed. Martin Hallett and Barbara Karasek. Peterborough, ON: Broadview.

Sanders, Joe Sutliff. 2009. The Critical Reader in Children's Metafiction. *The Lion and the Unicorn* 33 (3): 349–361.

Scarry, Elaine. 2014. Poetry, Injury, and the Ethics of Reading. In *The Humanities and Public Life*, ed. Peter Brooks with Hilary Jewett. New York: Fordham University Press.

Smith, Michael W., and Jeffrey D. Wilhelm. 2002. *Reading Don't Fix No Chevys: Literacy in the Lives of Young Men*. Portsmouth, NH: Heinemann.

Stephens, John, and Robyn MacCallum. 1998. *Retelling Stories, Framing Culture: Traditional Story and Metanarratives in Children's Literature*. New York: Routledge.

Stoneman, Patsy. 1996. *Brontë Transformations: The Cultural Disseminations of Jane Eyre and Wuthering Heights*. New York: Prentice Hall.

Sullivan, Paula. 1978. Fairy Tale Elements in *Jane Eyre*. *Journal of Popular Culture* 12 (1): 61–74.

Trites, Roberta Seelinger. 2000. *Disturbing the Universe: Power and Repression in Adolescent Literature*. Iowa City: University of Iowa Press.

Waugh, Patricia. 1984. *Metafiction: The Theory and Practice of Self-Conscious Fiction*. London: Methuen.

Wolf, Maryanne. 2007. *Proust and the Squid: The Story and Science of the Reading Brain*. New York: Harper Perennial.

Wood, Fiona. 2015. *Cloudwish*. New York: Poppy/Little, Brown.

Woolf, Virginia. 1929, 1981. *A Room of One's Own*. New York: Harcourt Brace Jovanovich.

Zipes, Jack. 1983. *The Trials and Tribulations of Little Red Riding Hood: Versions of the Tale in Sociocultural Perspective*. South Hadley: Bergin & Garvey.

CHAPTER 4

"Dreaming Themselves into Existence": Reading and Race

When I was a child, I lived in a house with a magic door. The closet in the front hall led, through a secret door in the back, directly into a church. Not, of course, just any church—my father's church. My father was a man who wore robes and said solemn things and made magic happen. And our house was the portal into the place where he did his magic.

Of course, my father is not a magician and our house was not a portal. But the experience of living in a house that was not, always, just a house, made books like *The Lion, the Witch, and the Wardrobe* or *Alice's Adventures in Wonderland* seem, well, potentially true. Why shouldn't there be a wardrobe that led into a wood, a well that was a portal to a fantasy world? My parents say that when we were young my brother and I sometimes sat near the closet door and listened to the choir singing on the other side of it. Mystery, magic—it seemed they could be anywhere.

Passages through portals, exciting though they were, didn't particularly surprise me, especially because the children who passed through those portals—though I didn't think about it at the time—looked much like me: the four Pevensie children of the Chronicles of Narnia, Alice, and their kindred were all, like me, White children living in all-White worlds.

In her essay, "Decolonizing the Imagination," writer Zetta Elliott describes herself as a child much like me, or like some of the characters we've already discussed. "I grew up," she writes, "dreaming of magical wardrobes and secret gardens." She goes on:

© The Author(s) 2019
E. R. Gruner, *Constructing the Adolescent Reader in Contemporary Young Adult Fiction*, Critical Approaches to Children's Literature,
https://doi.org/10.1057/978-1-137-53924-3_4

Doors figured rather prominently in my imagination, and books were indeed windows into other worlds. They were not, however, much of a mirror for my young black female self. I learned early on that only white children had wonderful adventures in distant lands; only white children were magically transported through time and space; only white children found the buried key that unlocked their own private Eden.

Perhaps the one benefit of being so completely excluded from the literary realm was that I had to develop the capacity *to dream myself into existence.* (Elliott 2010, emphasis in original)

What might it take for minority children and teens to dream themselves into existence? What kinds of books might suffice? Elliott's autobiographical essay follows, and draws on, earlier work by Nancy Larrick ("The All-White World of Children's Books," 1965) and Rudine Sims Bishop ("Mirrors, Windows, and Sliding Glass Doors," 1990). Their essays were among the first to articulate to a wide audience what minority readers already knew: that most books for children and teens represent whiteness as universal, including people of color most often as "background" or supporting characters if they appear at all. Similarly, works by ethnic minority writers are significantly underrepresented in children's and young adult literature (and, indeed, throughout the publishing world).[1] As Walter Dean Myers and Christopher Myers have pointed out, the lack of minority characters deprives minority children of both "mirrors" and "maps" (C. Myers 2014; W.D. Myers 2014). Like Elliott, they note that children of color do not see themselves or their experiences mirrored, as White children do, in the books they read, and books that represent whiteness as normative deprive both children of color and White children of "maps" that might direct them to a more inclusive future. The We Need Diverse Books (#WNDB) movement, founded in the same year (2014) as the Myerses wrote their essays, attempts to address both problems. Drawing on the ground-breaking work of Larrick and Bishop, and lamenting that their work is not yet complete, #WNDB has a mission of "Putting more books featuring diverse[2] characters into

---

[1] This underrepresentation, of course, also significantly affects school curricula—which, however, often even neglect the diverse options that are available, as the first two chapters suggest.

[2] The WNDB Web site defines diversity broadly: "We recognize all diverse experiences, including (but not limited to) LGBTQIA, Native, people of color, gender diversity, people with disabilities*, and ethnic, cultural, and religious minorities" (https://diversebooks.org/about-wndb/).

the hands of all children" and a vision of "A world in which all children can see themselves in the pages of a book" ("Mission Statement" 2019).

The young female characters of Chapter 3, of course, could "see themselves" in fairy-tale heroines or Jane Eyre. While the benefits of such identification are, as we've seen, somewhat ambiguous, they do not necessarily involve the kind of "cross-reading" that many minority readers face—though, of course, for characters such as Vân Ước and Marin, femininity trumps other identity categories such as nationality and sexuality in their empathic connections to Jane. Some such readers thus reject reading itself because they cannot see themselves in the literature they are given. For example, while Zetta Elliott remembers a childhood reading Anglophone children's classics such as *The Secret Garden*, *The Chronicles of Narnia*, and the like, Kiese Laymon comments that he was more drawn to African-American musical traditions than to books, because "most American literary classics were not courageous, imaginative, or honest enough to imagine our people or our experience as parts of its audience" (Laymon 2013a, loc. 58).[3] Many writers of color—as well as some White writers representing characters of color—thus incorporate literary and artistic traditions beyond the White canon as literary forebears, creating a more inclusive literary tradition. As these characters "dream [themselves] into existence," however, they run the risk of reinscribing the marginalized status of the works they include. The readers they represent draw on different traditions, both inclusive and exclusive. Yet, as Zetta Elliott writes, it is difficult to "decolonize the imagination," and not all YA novels depicting minority readers can do so.

In some YA novels, literacy is multivalent, both socializing the protagonists into the world of institutional power and, eventually perhaps, giving them the tools to interrogate and even subvert it. As with the school stories analyzed in Chapter 2, however, the actual possibilities for subversion may be limited by the fact that the characters are simultaneously interpellated into institutional power structures even as they overtly resist them. Other texts, especially those featuring underrepresented

---

[3] I am indebted to Phil Nel for pointing out this quotation as well as the earlier-quoted comments about failures of representation by Zetta Elliott (Nel 2017, 7–8). Laymon goes on to note that "my most meaningful discoveries about the act of being human have come through the solitary act of … reading, and rereading," and he names specific African-American classics, including *Kindred* and *The Bluest Eye*, as part of his heritage (Laymon 2013a, 62).

youth, depict an even more complicated relationship between literacy and power. The world of institutional power appears far more subtly in these novels, but may be even more pervasive, as the characters are marked as racially "other" to that world. For example, Jackie of Jacqueline Woodson's *Brown Girl Dreaming* (2014) is grounded in her community and finds the support network of African-American storytellers to be central to her development. Although the world of institutional power creates the conditions of her geographical location, she herself is only tangentially aware of it. City Coldson, of Kiese Laymon's *Long Division* (2013b), is similarly removed from the norms of power, yet simultaneously able to manipulate them—his removal gives him the vision to see, at times, what those more enmeshed in power structures cannot. Other novels, including Fiona Wood's *Cloudwish* (2015), M.T. Anderson's *Octavian Nothing* novels (2006, 2008), Kwame Alexander's *Booked* (2016), and E.R. Frank's *Dime* (2016) take on both historical and present-day systems of power in more diverse environments, reading their way into new relationships with both their "home" environments and the structures of institutional power. We might say that they learn new "metaphors to read by," as Ebony Elizabeth Thomas has said (Thomas 2016, 116). Race, class, gender, and sexuality braid together in these novels in different ways, suggesting both the necessity and the limits of reading to develop agency. Not only the novels but the readings they demand are intersectional, requiring a consideration of the interactions among and between the many components of identity (see Crenshaw 1989 for a definition of intersectionality).

Many of these novels represent characters who read, learn from, and enjoy texts from the same White literary tradition that Zetta Elliott referenced above. Yet that tradition, however engrossing, remains inadequate to the characters' needs. Novels such as *The Astonishing Life of Octavian Nothing, Traitor to the Nation*, as well as *Cloudwish, Dime*, and *The Absolutely True Diary of a Part-Time Indian* are steeped in a White Euro-American literary canon. Despite the novels' implicit endorsements of the White literary tradition, however, characters in most of these texts must also seek out a broader literary tradition in order to develop the critical literacies, and the agency, we have already seen in other novels.[4]

---

[4] Ebony Elizabeth Thomas quotes Latrise Johnson: "Students don't just need diverse literature because it's diverse. They need literature that inspires and awakens their potential to be the narrators of their own existence and to imagine a more just world" (Thomas 2016, 117; quoting Johnson 2016).

Other novels draw instead on a specifically African-American storytelling and reading tradition, such as *Long Division* and *Brown Girl Dreaming*. The novels thus model two different ways of being a racially marked reader: assimilation (and, perhaps, subversion), or resistance. The novels themselves—complicated, multilayered, drawing on a variety of traditions—may thus become the literature their characters seek out. This matters not only, of course, for characters and readers from racial and ethnic minorities. Empathy and imagination gaps—gaps between those readers who have always seen themselves in the literature they read, and those who have not—can also, perhaps, be bridged by these novels—though we rarely see such bridges within them.

Engaging the White Literary Tradition

As we have already seen, Fiona Wood's *Cloudwish* engages almost exclusively with one novel, Charlotte Brontë's *Jane Eyre*. The novel opens with an epigraph from Alice Walker that calls attention to Vân Uớc's "cross-reading": "I recognized myself in *Jane Eyre*. It amazes me how many white people can't read themselves in black characters. I didn't feel any separation between me and Jane. We were tight. –Alice Walker, Sydney Writers' Festival, 2014" (Wood 2015, n.p.). Vân Uớc, of course, does "recognize [her]self in *Jane Eyre*": an artist who finds herself split between two social classes, a "poor, obscure" girl who "cannot bear to be solitary and hated," she reads events throughout the course of the novel in terms of Brontë's text (Wood 2015, 71 and 124). *Cloudwish* draws structural and thematic elements from *Jane Eyre* that encourage Vân Uớc to see her relationship with Billy through the lens of Jane's with Rochester and authorize her belief in magic. And while *Cloudwish* briefly references other canonical high school texts, including three Jane Austen novels, Sylvia Plath's *Ariel*, *The Great Gatsby*, *To Kill a Mockingbird*, *Dubliners*, and *The Catcher in the Rye*, *Jane Eyre* occupies a central place in Vân Uớc's imagination and therefore in the novel.

Perhaps the most significant connection between the two novels, however, is not in the romance plot, but in the uncovering of family secrets that propel the *denouement* of both. Early in the novel, Vân Uớc imagines herself "stern-eyed, tapping her polished boot impatiently," a modern Jane Eyre demanding to learn the secrets that her mother, in particular, keeps from her. It is not until late in the novel that Vân Uớc learns those stories, stories that are unique to her Vietnamese heritage and her parents' refugee status. It is only by incorporating them with her great love of *Jane Eyre* that she can reject the "magic" that she believes has attracted Billy, and start to create a more whole, open, and egalitarian relationship with him. As in *Jane Eyre*, this may be an ambivalent conclusion: Billy never fully rejects his "bad boy" image, and, while her mother's reconciliation with her aunt gives her more family members (much as the Moor House episode provides Jane with a family in *Jane Eyre*), the family's material status is not changed by this realization, and Vân Uớc remains "the only one in the family who was ever going to read books like *Jane Eyre*" (Wood 2015, 30).

Other novels with minority protagonists take even less from their oft-cited literary references. In books like *Aristotle and Dante Discover the Secrets of the Universe* or *Death, Dickinson, and the Demented Life of Frenchie Garcia*, we might expect reading to figure largely in the action of the plots, simply based on the titles. The action of the novels, however, engages only fleetingly with reading. And despite the fact that both novels have minority protagonists (although only *Aristotle and Dante* explicitly recognizes its characters' ethnicity), what little reading they do engage in represents an entirely White canon. Although Frenchie asserts a sympathy with Emily Dickinson's poetry, quoting it throughout the novel, her engagement with it is actually quite limited, serving only to reinforce character traits she is trying to shed. Similarly, although Dante gives Aristotle both poetry and novels to read, it's unclear how William Carlos Williams, Tolstoy, or Steinbeck actually affects him. While at times both novels suggest that literacy could serve as a kind of self-making, more often it seems escapist. Aristotle, for example, claims that "High school was just a prologue to the real novel. Everybody got to write you—but when you graduated, you got to write yourself" (Sáenz 2014, 335).[5] This claim is, however, almost immediately followed by an image of Ari's mother removing the book from her husband's hands to get him to join in a family meeting—implicitly, then, the book serves not as self-making but as an escape (Sáenz 2014, 347).

While these novels enact the fairly common trope of an underrepresented reader's relationship to a White-authored text, Laurie

---

[5] As with Melinda of *Speak*, Miles of *Alaska*, or even Mia of *The Princess Diaries*, Ari's reading implicitly leads to writing, though the language here is disconcertingly dismissive of reading as a lifelong pursuit.

Halse Anderson's *Speak* is the rare novel that represents the opposite. Melinda, the protagonist of the novel, as we've already seen in Chapter 2, draws on a variety of other texts: perhaps most notably, fairy-tales and *The Scarlet Letter*. However, her evocation of Maya Angelou's *I Know Why the Caged Bird Sings* is in many ways the most meaningful of these encounters. Covering the mirror in her closet with Angelou's image, Melinda metaphorically claims an identification with her, seeing Angelou's image instead of her own.[6] She chooses the image because, as she says, "the school board is afraid of her" (Anderson 1999, 50). Readers familiar with Angelou's work, however, will also note that, like Maya, Melinda retreats into silence after a sexual assault; Melinda may also, then, recover her voice at least in part through books, as Maya does. Untouched by the racism that permeates Angelou's experiences, Melinda nonetheless identifies with her at least as much as with Hester Prynne, the other literary heroine who inspires her.

These examples of cross-reading suggest, as with the examples in Chapter Three, that literary empathy may indeed contribute to the development of adolescent agency. But not all readers learn to empathize, nor do all readers even read.

READING/NOT READING: BOOK LISTS AS/AND SELF-MAKING

Sherman Alexie's *Absolutely True Diary of a Part-Time Indian* (2007) opens with an epigraph from Yeats: "There is another world, but it is in this one." The novel thus, like *Cloudwish*, marks itself as part of a White literary tradition even before its opening pages. But while Junior, the novel's protagonist, frequently mentions reading, and even provides a list of his favorite books (much like Charlie in *The Perks of Being a Wallflower*) we do not actually see him interact with the books on his list—or many others—within the text. The books on the list are telling, as most of them are either YA novels themselves (*Feed, Catalyst, Fat Kid Rules the World, Tangerine*) or books frequently assigned to high school students (*The Catcher in the Rye, The Grapes of Wrath*). And all of these are by White authors, concerning White characters. The outliers are three diverse books: two by Native American authors—the graphic novel *Jar of Fools*, by Jason Lutes, and James Welch's *Fools Crow*—and Ralph Ellison's

---

[6] Anderson here neatly reverses Sims Bishop's mirror/window metaphor: Melinda implicitly finds a mirror in Angelou's story.

Invisible Man. It is as if the author is here providing a reading list for his own implied readers. Junior makes no more mention of the books, nor does he say why they make his list, but they do provide his location in both time and space, as well as a literary heritage for the novel itself.

Adrienne Kertzer suggests that Junior's list can illuminate the novel by "allow[ing] the possibility of reading that makes dialogue [between White and Native readers] possible" (Kertzer 2012, 71). She notes, for example, that most of the YA novels on his list "characters are deeply affected by one, or at most two, deaths" (Kertzer 2012, 62). Since Junior documents at least five deaths in his circle during one year, his experience differs significantly from these characters'—and, as Kertzer notes, from Roberta Seelinger Trites's assertion that death in YA novels is "often depicted in terms of maturation when the protagonist accepts the permanence of mortality" (Trites 2000, 119). White readers may learn from this juxtaposition the limitations of their typical reading: the novel may suggest that there are more models of maturation than one premised on the acceptance of mortalitity.

Yet of course, as Kertzer also notes, "readers who do not know the books on Junior's list will be oblivious to the deliberately imperfect mimicry that [she argues] is characteristic of Alexie's work" (Kertzer 2012, 75). Her comments demonstrate both the expansive and, indeed, liberatory possibilities of intertextual reading and, at the same time, the impossibility of imagining a coherent implied reader for the novel. Further, unlike (for example) *Cloudwish* or *The Astonishing Life of Octavian Nothing*, *The Absolutely True Diary* never really depicts its protagonist reading. Junior does, however, credit Gordy with "teaching" him how to read:

'Listen,' he said one afternoon in the library. 'You have to read a book three times before you know it. The first time you read it for the story. The plot. The movement from scene to scene that gives the book its momentum, its rhythm.
…
The second time you read a book, you read it for its history. For its knowledge of history. You think about the meaning of each word, and where that word came from … If you don't treat each word that seriously then you're not treating the novel seriously.
…
[And] you should approach each book—you should approach life—with the real possibility that you might get a metaphorical boner at any point. (Alexie 2007, 94–97)

Thus, the first lesson Junior takes from Gordy is that literature—like Junior's cartoons—can be used "to understand the world" (Alexie 2007, 95). But Junior goes beyond thinking of literature as, in Bishop's words, a window on the world, to propose an equivalency between literature and life: "I suddenly understood that if every moment of a book should be taken seriously, then every moment of a life should be taken seriously as well" (Alexie 2007, 95).

This is, perhaps, the most didactic passage in the novel—one can imagine the author over the reader's shoulder here, encouraging a second and even a third look at the text. Yet, as I've already noted, we don't really see Junior enact Gordy's suggestions. While his lists may reflect the "three readings" model, the novel never depicts it. Thus the novel's invitation to the implied reader here may be an example of "do as I say, not as you see me do."

Reading lists like Junior's, of course, seem to be a common element of novels for children and young adults—I've already noted the one in *The Perks of Being a Wallflower* (discussed briefly in Chapter 2) for example, as well as those in *The Princess Diaries* and *Cloudwish* (both discussed in Chapter 3). One particularly interesting one can be found in Kwame Alexander's *Booked* (2016). Asked to choose a book for a middle school book discussion group, the main character provides a list of recently published popular and less well-known middle-grade books in the form of a sentence. The list, like the one we see in *Absolutely True Diary*, is both diverse and wide-ranging in style and subject matter, though all of the books are either middle-grade or Young Adult novels:

Dear Know it All **Percy Jackson**
If You're Reading This, It's TOO LATE!
Planet Middle School
May B.
CATCHING FIRE!
　　　BECAUSE OF WINN-DIXIE

SMILE,
　　　I Will Save You
　　　When You Reach Me
　　　Where the Sidewalk Ends

> *Until We Meet Again*
> **Peace,** *LOCOMOTION, Darius and Twig:*
> *The Outsiders*
>
> *P.S. Be Eleven* (Alexander 2016, 243)[7]

Although the sentence/poem is a clever trick, the books are otherwise completely undiscussed. The list then functions almost purely as a didactic encouragement to the implied readers of the novel, just like Junior's description of Gordy's reading method. Something similar, though even less explicit, occurs in Renee Watson's *This Side of Home*, in which the main characters are named Nikki and Maya, after two giants of African-American literature, but otherwise have little engagement with a literary heritage.

Absolutely True Diary only clearly indicates that Junior reads two works of literature in addition to the comic books he reads with Rowdy. The first is *Medea*. Junior finds a language for his own experience in *Medea*, beginning with the line, "What greater grief than the loss of one's native land?" (Alexie 2007, 173). Later, he also reads *Anna Karenina*—or, at least, the opening, to which he strenuously objects: "Well, I hate to argue with a Russian genius, but Tolstoy didn't know Indians. And he didn't know that all Indian families are unhappy for the same exact reasons: the fricking booze. Yep, so let me pour a drink for Tolstoy and let him think hard about the true definition of unhappy families" (Alexie 2007, 200). While *Medea* may be a mirror, then, *Anna Karenina* fails the test.[8] Junior's tricky reading strategy—both inclusive and limited, both suggestive and obscure—may, indeed, allow for dialogue across ethnicities, as Kertzer suggests, but only to an already-well-read audience. Indeed, all of these novels seem to suggest more about their implied readers than their characters with these book

---

[7]Emphasis in original. The authors of the books are, in order, Rachel Wise, Rick Riordan (the first two are series titles, both in the first line), Pseudonymous Bosch, Nikki Grimes, Caroline Starr Rose, Suzanne Collins, Kate DiCamillo, Raina Telgemeier, Matt de la Peña, Rebecca Stead, Shel Silverstein, Renee Collins, Jacqueline Woodson and Walter Dean Myers (on the same line), S.E. Hinton, and Rita Williams-Garcia.

[8]Kertzer also notes brief allusions to *A Tale of Two Cities* and Yeats's poem, "A Second Coming," both accessible only to those who have already read Dickens and Yeats, as the texts are not named.

lists: they congratulate the reader who recognizes the books on the lists, challenge the one who does not, and in either case underscore their didactic point that reading is an essential (if invisible) part of self-making.

MAKING A TRADITION

While the novels I've discussed so far in this chapter for the most part depict the common experience of a minority youth trying to "find" themselves in mostly White literary canon, E.R. Frank's *Dime* and M.T. Anderson's *The Astonishing Life of Octavian Nothing, Traitor to the Nation* complicate that pattern. And while the earlier novels also involve minority authors depicting minority youth "cross-reading," the two novels I treat in this section are written by White authors "cross-writing." Their protagonists, however, find value in a more expansive canon than we have yet seen.

Like *Absolutely True Diary*, E.R. Frank's *Dime* (2015) announces its intertextuality with an epigraph, this time from *To Kill a Mockingbird*: "*I ain't cynical ... Tellin' the truth's not cynical, is it?*" (Frank 2015, n.p.; attributed to Dill, *To Kill a Mockingbird*). The words signal the stance of the narrator, Dime, whose story never actually verges on cynicism but does insist on its foundation in experience.[9] Insisting on her story's truth, Dime as narrator nonetheless clearly shapes it throughout, announcing from the first that she must strike the right tone, find the right voice, in order to be heard. Dime finds comfort and escape in books throughout the novel, and books also spark emotions for the other "wifeys" in her "family" of unwilling sex workers—especially Lollipop, who remembers picture books only faintly from her childhood, and Brandy, who reacts violently to Lollipop's memories, suggesting that they hold a significant place in her memories of an earlier life. Lollipop remembers familiar, canonical picture books: *Goodnight, Moon, Where the Wild Things Are,* and *The Snowy Day.* Even these seemingly random references, however, provide a metafictional commentary on the action of the plot. Despite the language of family that surrounds them, the children in Daddy's apartment are not able either to go to bed or to play outside comfortably, as the children in *Goodnight, Moon* and *The Snowy Day* do.

---

[9] Frank, a psychotherapist who specializes in trauma, thanks the staff and clients of Polaris New Jersey, a program dedicated to eliminating human trafficking. She also provides resources on human trafficking and sex slavery at the end of the novel. While the novel is obviously a fiction, Frank is careful to suggest its origins in fact.

And the wild things in their world are not imaginary beasts conjured by a disobedient child, but abusive men who seek out children and teens for exploitation and/or their sexual satisfaction. The narrative refers briefly to other children's books (*Mandy*, by Julie Andrews Edwards; Walter Farley's *The Black Stallion*; Avi's *The True Confessions of Charlotte Doyle*; books from both the Harry Potter and Narnia series), creating a list for implied readers to connect with much as we saw in *Absolutely True Diary*.[10] Again, this is a list of works by White writers and, except for *The Snowy Day*, all depict the experiences of White children.[11]

Dime, unlike *Absolutely True Diary*, draws specifically on texts read by the protagonist. Thematically, the two most significant texts that Dime reads are Harper Lee's *To Kill a Mockingbird* and Alice Walker's *The Color Purple*. Both novels, of course, center on real or alleged sexual abuse, and inequities of race and class permeate them as they do Dime's own life. Despite these similarities, the novels also represent Dime's window to a world outside Daddy's apartment and "the track," where she and the other girls pick up their clients.

At times, *To Kill a Mockingbird* blurs with Dime's own story, as when she writes "Mrs. Dubose finally died, right as Daddy pulled off the highway by a rest area sign" (Frank 2015, 166). The drug-addicted Mrs. Dubose captures Dime's imagination, implicitly teaching her more about Brandy than Brandy herself has revealed. References to the novel also function, then, to increase interest in it, leaving out key plot elements while representing Dime's investment in the story. Like many other YA novels, *Dime* didactically encourages (further) reading in its young readers—or congratulates them for their knowledge of other novels.

Dime draws strength from *To Kill a Mockingbird*, quoting Atticus Finch to herself as she begins to formulate a plan to leave Daddy: "*Courage is not a man with a gun in his hand. It's knowing that you're licked before*

---

[10]The list here is not aspirational, as are the lists in *Cloudwish*, *The Princess Diaries*, or *The Perks of Being a Wallflower*—or even *Absolutely True Diary*, which lists at least a few novels some readers might not be familiar with. The novels listed in *Dime*—with the exceptions noted below—are all picture books and middle-grade novels, easily read by and familiar to most American children.

[11]Two other books get brief mentions in the novel. The first is *Flowers in the Attic*, not strictly for adolescents though frequently read by them, and, like *The Color Purple* and *To Kill a Mockingbird*, centered on the sexual, emotional, and physical abuse of children. The other, *Their Eyes Were Watching God*, is another novel depicting a legacy of rape and domestic violence, and the only Black-authored text mentioned besides *The Color Purple*.

you begin but you begin anyway and see it through no matter what" (Frank 2015, 191, emphasis Frank's). As the quotation indicates, however, Atticus's power is limited—not expecting to clear Tom Robinson, his courage is only in providing a competent defense, not in changing or even protesting the power structures that place Tom in the position of accused. Atticus is a confusing role model for Dime: a White man defending a Black man against rape charges brought by a White woman. Dime, exploited by Black and White men alike, and without access to the privileges of race that both Mayella Ewell and the children in the novel possess, can admire Atticus's courage or Dill's commitment to the truth, but cannot enter further into the novel's commitments. Indeed, despite the ways in which the novel touches her own situation, even obliquely, Dime reads it—as she reads most books—primarily for escape, not for insight into her own condition.[12] In Bishop's words, it offers her a window, not a mirror.

But despite the epigraph from *To Kill a Mockingbird* and her evocation of Atticus in a moment of need, Dime identifies most with the African-American characters in *The Color Purple*, noting for example that "Shug is the sort of person I wish I could be, even though Celie is the one I'm more like" (Frank 2015, 14). While the novel makes fewer references to *The Color Purple* than to *To Kill a Mockingbird*, the former novel seems considerably more important to Dime, offering her a vision of recovery from horrific abuse and an egalitarian, if utopic, mutually supportive Black community.[13] Dime sees herself in *The Color Purple* because it is the closest thing to a mirror she has. Tellingly, then, Brandy hides the phone number of the women's shelter under the mirror in her compact—only once she has seen herself reflected both literally and literarily can Dime escape the life she is trapped in.

M.T. Anderson's *Octavian Nothing* volumes, like the other novels discussed so far in this chapter, draw heavily on a White literary tradition. In this historical novel, set both before and during the American Revolution, Africans and African-Americans are most often denied literacy by their White captors. When it is acquired by Octavian, Pro Bono, and other enslaved people, it marks them as other, but simultaneously provides at least some of the conditions for resistance, perhaps even freedom.

---

[12] Dime refers to her books as an escape more than once. See, for example, 125–127 and 179–180.

[13] The abuse in *The Color Purple*, as in *Dime*, is intersectional, attributable to the interrelationship of race, class and gender.

In *Octavian Nothing*, literacy is complex, socializing Octavian into a White literary and educational tradition which will never fully accept him, but leaving him isolated within his community. While in the novels discussed so far literacy seems an unalloyed good, Octavian's literacy comes at great cost. Reading is often, as it is for so many YA protagonists, a refuge for Octavian. But his status on the one hand as an enslaved person and on the other hand as an educated African leaves him without his own tradition or roots. Found reading by his companions in Lord Dunmore's Ethiopian Regiment, for example, Octavian is embarrassed—"covered with blushes"—and recognizes his book as the "artifact of the conqueror" (Anderson 2008, 141). Not for the first time in the text, Octavian lapses into silence after a significant event. Earlier, however, it has been obvious physical or emotional trauma that has brought on his silence; here, it is simply the evidence of his literacy.

While literacy and literacy education are central to both volumes of Anderson's dense historical novel, my focus is on a line that threads through Volume II. It begins with Bono and Octavian. Both have been enslaved by the members of the Novanglian College of Lucidity, an experimental institute for studying the educability of people of African descent. Only Octavian, however, has undergone that education; Bono has been a servant. The shame Octavian experiences when his literacy is remarked begins with his awareness of his difference from Bono. Bono can read and write, but his creative and subversive use of literacy stands in counterpoint to Octavian's more conventional one throughout the text. For example, Bono has Octavian translate pornographic passages from Latin for him; he also creates a catalog of evidence of the mistreatment—torture—of slaves for himself, tearing pages out of gazettes and papers that are being discarded. Octavian's literacy is useful to Bono, but his own, unlike Octavian's, speaks directly to his experience. For much of the novel, he both uses and derides Octavian.

When he belatedly learns of Octavian's mother's death, however, Bono softens toward him. First, he introduces Octavian to Olakunde, another person of his mother's homeland, who may be able to shed some light on her origins. Octavian has lived his whole life with a story of his mother's royal parentage (and therefore his own): a story Olakunde casts doubt on. But Olakunde also tells Octavian the story of Oshun, the story, as Octavian says, "of the Venus of my mother's people, their Aphrodite" (Anderson 2008, 346). This story, of a beautiful woman misled by powerful men (or gods) and, like Octavian's mother, sickened by smallpox, prepares the way for Bono to tell Octavian the story of his conception. When Bono tells him that he was conceived when his mother was raped on board ship, Octavian records it in his journal in Latin. Over 700 pages into his story, he finds out the truth of his parentage, and he records it in such a way as to distance it from both himself and his future readers (including this one). A footnote provides the translation.[14]

While Octavian and Bono are both literate, then, it takes the combination of their two literacies—and others—to make either one whole, as well as to convey their disparate tales to readers. Many contemporary readers may of course be stymied by the text's historical context, use of Latin, and obscure vocabulary. But the assemblage of texts—including, always, the critical voice of Pro Bono, but also a variety of other voices, critical and complimentary, both surprised by Octavian and frustrated by him—gives the reader a point of contact, a place to land as well. Erica Hateley suggests that "By using texts that are *about* young people being or becoming critical readers, [English teachers] can immediately signal a desire to resist normative classificatory systems of a 'national literature' or a 'literary canon' and involve students in a conversation *about* canonicity" (Hateley 2012, 77). *Octavian Nothing*, like the other texts I've discussed in this chapter, calls attention to the tradition it calls on, both expanding Octavian's canon and itself becoming part of a newly expanded canon at the same time. Throughout *Octavian Nothing*, Octavian returns to canonical literature—because it has, effectively, been his bedtime reading. Although Bono mocks him for reading Virgil, it is almost literally all he has, and while it sets him apart from his companions, it is also comforting. When he learns more stories, however— the stories, especially, of his mother's people, and of the other enslaved Africans who have not eaten "beef every supper" or been "taught to play the fiddle," as Bono chides him—he is able to put the stories from Virgil and Ovid in a new context, and make them mean differently: both for him and for his implied readers (Anderson 2008, 253). Like the communal readers of Chapter 2, Bono and Octavian—and their companions— read together, but with the critical difference that they are reading and telling stories from across traditions.

---

[14] Jackie in *Brown Girl Dreaming* and City in *Long Division* also uncover difficult personal histories and include them at arm's length in their narratives, though not in Latin.

After Octavian starts sharing stories from Greek and Latin mythology with Olakunde, whose Oyo stories he craves, they begin to develop a shared literacy, a common ground. For example, Olakunde tells tales of "Ogun, the god of iron, beloved by smiths and warriors, which potent deity was despised by the other *orishas* for teaching man the mysteries of the forge and smithy; and [Octavian] in return told them of Prometheus, similarly condemned, and of the lame Hephæstus, blacksmith of the gods, toiling in his Ætnan gulph" (Anderson 2008, 374). These shared literacies suggest that readers, too, may bring their own stories to this one. For example, the reader of 2006, when *The Pox Party* first appeared, may have been inclined to connect Bono's catalog of slave tortures to the recently revealed horrors of Abu Ghraib prison, to which they bear a remarkable, and horrific, similarity. Reading the novel in the following decade of the twenty-first century, however, a reader may also find resonances with the musical *Hamilton*, which depicts another (possibly mixed-race) bastard outcast who reads and then writes his way into history, and who, like Octavian, finds Jeffersonian rhetoric about freedom somewhat hollow when it fails to extend to those of African descent. These resonances, unavailable to the author writing the novel, recall Octavian and Olakunde's connections between Oyo and classical mythology—connections similarly unavailable when the stories were first told, but meaningful to their inheritors. Readers always bring their own contexts to a text, that is—even the represented readers of the novel.[15]

Octavian's literacy narrative, then, suggests both the difficulty of becoming a reader (either canonical or functional), and the value: ambivalent about his education, Octavian nonetheless returns to the college at the end of the novel to confront its principal one more time, to show him that he has created his own narrative out of the assemblage of texts they left him. While their canon is oppressive, it has also—but only in combination with the other tales he has heard, read, told, and retold—helped to free him.

The kind of literacy that *Octavian Nothing* both depicts and demands goes far beyond basic reading skills into a multimodal literacy, in which "readers … sort through, analyze, and organize what they read to put together a coherent whole" (Koss and Teale 2009, 570). The complexity of the reading Octavian does is replicated in the text of the novel.

---

[15] See introduction for a brief discussion of reader-response theory.

And thus the novel models a literacy appropriate to its subject: truth is slippery, interpretation both imperative and impossible. While the specifically canonical education Octavian has received at the College of Lucidity is not, of itself, sufficient to prepare him for his new reality, it becomes part of a larger context of shared literacies that he develops—and that Anderson encourages his readers to develop as well—in order to face an uncertain future.

Anderson's text privileges the Western canon of literature as an expansive tool, available to readers like Octavian, Pro Bono, and even the illiterate Olakunde. While this canon may not be familiar to young readers of the twenty-first century, the final sentence of the novel echoes the end of one of the most canonical novels in the American literary tradition, Mark Twain's *The Adventures of Huckleberry Finn*: "And so I light out for the unknown regions"[16] (Anderson 2008, 561). Yet it is not until he encounters Olakunde's stories, stories from the African diaspora, from Octavian's buried heritage, that he is able to act rather than to react. A single tradition cannot provide the mirrors and windows that the diverse reader—or protagonist—requires.

READING AND WRITING AGAINST HISTORY

Novels such as Kiese Laymon's *Long Division* and Jacqueline Woodson's *Brown Girl Dreaming* are far less indebted to a White literary tradition than any of the other novels treated in this chapter. Both novels are attempts to write against at least 400 years of literary history, and to find a place where someone like City Coldson or Jackie Woodson, the narrators of their tales, can locate themselves in a text. They thus play with the idea of the reader in the text—locating their protagonists in time and space, and turning reading into an interactive network rather than an introspective, unidirectional activity. This network is an essential part of the arguments the We Need Diverse Books movement is making on behalf of young readers. If *Octavian Nothing* and *Dime* (both the novels and the characters) needed to combine a White canonical literary tradition with an African (American) one in order to develop a multimodal literacy that empowers the characters to action—indeed, to

---

[16]Compare: "But I reckon I got to light out for the Territory ahead of the rest, because Aunt Sally she's going to adopt me and sivilize me and I can't stand it. I been there before" (Twain 1884, 229).

freedom—other texts, such as those by Laymon and Woodson, work almost exclusively within an African-American tradition, but to much the same purpose.

Reading, in both novels, is both a marker of social and cultural success and deeply suspect; it is also, as in *Octavian Nothing*, both powerful and dangerous. Jackie and City, the protagonists of the novels, make the reverse circuit from Octavian. While he moves from reading to storytelling, they are not (at least at first) readers, but they are both storytellers, who come to reading through their own words, their own stories. Unlike the other novels discussed in this chapter (with the exception of *Booked*), these novels depict reluctant or hesitant readers, characters who need to find themselves in a book before they can develop into readers. Although they challenge the racist canard that minority youth cannot be good readers, these novels do not posit a simple one-to-one relationship between reading and either academic or financial success. Like the *Octavian Nothing* volumes, both *Brown Girl Dreaming* and *Long Division* are also formally challenging: one is in verse, telling its story fragmentarily, while the other involves a book within a book, and time-travel, telling its story circularly. They thus reject any transactional purpose for reading, developing more complex, even ambivalent, defenses of reading.

Novels like *Brown Girl Dreaming* and *Long Division* may reinforce the claims of studies like those cited in the introduction, studies that suggest, for example, that frequent reading correlates with reading pleasure and choice.[17] In these novels, we have reluctant readers, readers who have not (yet) found themselves in a book, readers who find reading either boring, difficult, and/or disconnected from their realities. The novels themselves, like others discussed in this chapter, might then function as that book in which readers can "find themselves." But they also, and importantly, offer a different model of reading. Reading becomes a

[17] See, for example, the "Kids and Family Reading Report" published by Scholastic in 2008: "Among kids age 9-17, 'having trouble finding books that I like' is among the top reasons for not reading more books for fun" (15). Scholastic does not provide disaggregated data by race or ethnicity, although the 2017 report is more attentive to diversity than previous reports. The 2009 NEA Report, "Reading on the Rise," while generally optimistic about the state of reading in the USA, noted significant gaps in the "literary reading rates" of Whites as compared to African-American and Hispanic American readers. While these gaps were narrowing in the period studied (2002–2008), they were still significant and indicated that fewer than 50% of minority youth were frequent pleasure readers.

network for these characters, a means of connecting with others. They may, indeed, depict a new purpose for (literary) reading. Steven Fischer traces two earlier purposes:

> As of the late seventeenth century Western European readers began prioritizing *extensive* over *intensive* reading. Hitherto, with little access to printed information, readers had read their few available publications (the Bible, a Book of Hours, pedlar's booklets and pamphlets) slowly, repeating each word over and over again in purposeful contemplation. That is, they read intensively. But by the late 1600s, when individual readers could purchase several books, their purpose shifted to the widest possible coverage of a given topic, or even to variety itself. They began reading extensively. Whereupon one's very concept of reading's primary function altered: from focus to access.
>
> It changed society profoundly. Ever since, reading has been viewed not as a place, but as a road. (Fischer 2003, 255)

If the reading in *Cloudwish* and *Dime* is intensive, limited to one or two novels, whether by inclination or necessity, we might call the reading in *Octavian Nothing* and the implied reading in *Absolutely True Diary* and *Booked* extensive, covering a breadth of interest and genre. In *Long Division* and *Brown Girl Dreaming*, however, while reading can be both place and road, it is also network—not carrying its reader to a new place so much as connecting the reader to others distant in time and/or place. Thus City Coldson in *Long Division* and Jackie in *Brown Girl Dreaming* connect to ancestors, precursors, places from which they are distant, but also others like them, others in their communities—and they model these connections for the implied readers of the novels themselves.

Of course, books have always been a kind of connection—a network before there were digital ones. Books that refer to other books and books that draw together multiple stories are already networks, or at least nodes in them. These recent novels, however, signal their (potential) function overtly. They teach their readers how to read them, in other words—how to use them not only for access but for connection. In an increasingly alienated society, that is a significant function, especially for marginalized characters and readers.

Long Division and *Brown Girl Dreaming* are, like many of the texts discussed earlier, metafictional texts. Laymon's novel is particularly interesting in this regard, as it is not overtly intertextual with specific canonical works, as most of the metafictional texts discussed earlier are.[18] The main character reads a book called *Long Division*, by a character much like him, who himself both reads and writes a book called *Long Division*. As we've already seen, the novel takes place in three distinct time periods, in each of which a character called City Coldson moves through essentially the same spaces with both similar and different concerns. *Brown Girl Dreaming* is more chronologically straightforward, but as a text that references its own creator's writing, it, too, operates as a metafictional text.

Long Division embeds a literacy narrative[19] within its larger story, depicting City's early rejection of reading and his growing awareness that reading and writing are central to his development. While school itself plays only a minor role in the novel, City's relationship with a particular book—and, with that, his growing interest in reading and his developing awareness of history—is central to his story. A similar arc characterizes *Brown Girl Dreaming*, in which the protagonist Jackie begins as an illiterate child, and struggles to become a reader as proficient as her older sister, Dell. It is only through story—specifically, her ability to tell and retell a variety of stories—that Jackie becomes a reader and, more importantly, a writer grounded in the stories of the past that come to her through her family as well as her reading for school. Like City, however, Jackie must also find herself in a text in order to incorporate reading into her storytelling. In both cases, moreover, the literacy that is required of its readers is modeled by the texts: the novels themselves educate their readers in the histories and stories, the critical reading, and the adaptation of literacy to personal ends that the characters also take up.

Unlike the other novels I've discussed in this chapter, *Long Division* makes no overt allusions to a White literary tradition, connecting instead throughout to larger African-American literary and artistic traditions. The novel's epigraph comes from a song, not a novel or a poem: "'Twice upon a time, there was a boy who died/and lived happily ever after/ but that's another chapter.' –André Benjamin, 'Aquemini'" (Laymon 2013b, 5). Citing André Benjamin—better known, perhaps, as André 3000 of Outkast—signals the novel's commitment to a wide variety of textual

---

[18] *The Book Thief* refers primarily to imaginary texts, though of course *Mein Kampf* exists in consensus reality.

[19] See Chapter 5 for a fuller discussion of literacy narratives. I take the term from Janet Carey Eldred and Peter Mortensen, who use it to describe the acquisition of a new social language (Eldred and Mortensen 1992, 512).

representations of African-American life. And in a novel where the main character is baptized in a revival service, the biblical and baptismal references in "Aquemini" are particularly relevant. Even the reader unfamiliar with Outkast's lyrics, however, will recognize that City lives at least "twice upon a time," metaphorically dying in the hole in the ground that leads him into his own past. Laymon's intertextuality here moves beyond canonical novels into a specifically African-American tradition—one that he also invokes in his book *How to Slowly Kill Yourself and Others in America*. In the Author's Note accompanying the essay collection, itself almost a companion to the novel, he writes that "I couldn't find literary models of what I wanted to do, but I had plenty of musical models.... For me, this was partially because most American literature, unlike lots of American blues, soul and hip-hop, did not create an echo" (Laymon 2013a, loc. 51). The African-American literary tradition that he does find— Toni Morrison, James Baldwin, Ralph Ellison, and Octavia Butler—permeates the novel, though in unacknowledged ways. For example, City as narrator writes after his explosion at the dynamic sentence contest, "Mama didn't even tell me what I did wrong. Quiet as it's kept, she barely said a word to me" (Laymon 2013b, 45). Only readers already familiar with *The Bluest Eye* will recognize the phrase "quiet as it's kept," which opens Claudia's narration in the novel. As with *Absolutely True Diary*, then, it may be difficult to imagine a coherent implied reader for *Long Division*. In this case, however, it seems that the novel itself models one.

The blank pages at the end of the different versions of *Long Division* that the kids read within the novel suggest, of course, that they must finish the story, must write their own endings. But it is the figure of the ellipses that is even more important—the tattoo on LaVander Peeler's wrist, the punctuation mark claimed by Baize Shephard as her favorite. Both the blank pages and the ellipses suggest that the story continues, but the ellipses also suggest a beginning earlier than we know, a reminder that readers simply dip into stories for a moment, and they are ongoing. As Baize says, "The ellipsis always knows something more came before it and something more is coming after it" (Laymon 2013b, 245).

Ellipses also, however, indicate a gap. In a meaning not explored overtly by the characters of the novel, but unavoidable in a novel so riven with loss, disappearance, and absence, the ellipses mark the losses that haunt each generation of the novel, both real and fictional: Lerthon Coldson, Baize Shephard, Trayvon Martin, Principal Reeves's husband, and the flood victims in New Orleans and Mississippi. The many alternate versions of *Long Division* write these "lost" characters back into the story, back into history, while the ellipses acknowledges the gaps that their stories still leave. The novel also, and perhaps just as importantly, writes characters like City Coldson—"black like me, stout like me … [and] written like you actually thought" into literary life. Just as Toni Morrison did almost 50 years ago with *The Bluest Eye*, Laymon writes for and about non-readers here. Rereading the novel, and rewriting it, as both versions of City do, allows the characters and the readers to "identify and clarify multiple points of view," construct knowledge and fill in gaps (Jacobs 2008, 14 and 15). Or, to put it differently, their reading and writing make them better readers and writers, encouraging them to continue to read themselves into history.

Brown Girl Dreaming is, of course, a very different novel than *Long Division*. A novel in verse, it engages with the author's own history to tell the story of her gradual coming into her writerly identity. Yet there are important similarities. As I've already noted, for example, both novels are semi-autobiographical and formally inventive. Both novels might also be said to invoke the Gothic tradition.[20] According to Gisele Liza Anatol, who reads *Brown Girl Dreaming* as a post-colonial Gothic, "Loosely described, Gothic writing for young people features fear or the pretense of fear; a deep sense of foreboding when it comes to confronting the forbidden (especially sexuality, [if this element is present]); a supernatural atmosphere; death and decay; and the motifs of old mansions or castles (typically haunted) and labyrinthine or subterranean passageways, alongside diabolical villains who threaten the innocence of the protagonist" (Anatol 2016, 407–408). This description is remarkably apt for *Long Division* as well as *Brown Girl Dreaming*. But their Gothicism is a specifically African-American one, haunted by the long history of slavery and discrimination. The "diabolical villains," in this case, are the agents of White supremacy.

Like *Long Division*, *Brown Girl Dreaming* begins with an evocation of a specifically African-American literary history: in the poem, "Second Daughter's Second Day on Earth," for example, the narrator tells us that "James Baldwin/is writing about injustice, each novel,/each essay,

---

[20]Of course *Jane Eyre*, the important pre-text to so many of the novels discussed in the previous chapter, is also a key Gothic text. However, in the reworkings its Gothicism is often masked or muted. The African-American Gothic treated here seems an even more salient tradition.

changing the world" (Woodson 2014, 4). Unlike City, however, Jackie lives within a family of readers, her sister Dell often "under the kitchen table, a book in her hand,/a glass of milk and a small bowl of peanuts beside her" (Woodson 2014, 60); her brother Hope with his "head bent/inside the superhero comic books my grandfather/brings home on Fridays" (64). Jackie listens to the stories her sister reads, and the text turns metafictional:

> In the books, there's always a happily ever after.
> The ugly duckling grows into a swan, Pinocchio
> becomes a boy.
> The witch gets chucked into the oven by Gretel,
> the Selfish Giant goes to heaven.
> Even Winnie the Pooh seems to always get his honey.
> Little Red Riding Hood's grandmother is freed
> from the belly of the wolf.
>
> When my sister reads to me, I wait for the moment
> when the story moves faster—toward the happy ending
> that I know is coming. (Woodson 2014, 206)[21]

This reading does not come as easily to Jackie as to her sister, however:

> Words from the books curl around each other
> make little sense
> until
> I read them again
> and again, the story
> settling into memory. (Woodson 2014, 206)

Reading "again and again," however—a recursive reading not unlike what we see in *Long Division*—makes Jackie not only a reader, but, like City, a writer. She can engage with the stories her sister speeds through, making them her own and remaking them into new stories. Before that

---

[21] Like *Dime*, *Brown Girl Dreaming* evokes a White tradition of children's literature here. Unlike most of the other novels treated in this chapter, however, *Brown Girl Dreaming* begins by citing an African-American tradition and only slowly incorporates the White fairy-tales cited here, reversing the movement seen in other texts. And unlike the novels treated in Chapter 2, *Brown Girl Dreaming* is neither structured nor inspired by the fairy-tales it references.

can happen, however, she—again like City—must find herself in a book. The poem "stevie and me" expresses this succinctly.

stevie and me
I stop in front of the small paperback
with a brown boy on the cover.
Stevie.
…
someone who looked like me
could be in the pages of the book
… someone who looked like me
had a story. (Woodson 2014, 226–228)

Like City, when Jackie finds "someone who looked like me" in the pages of a book, she starts to become a reader. As with City, the process is complex and multilayered: she does not become a reader or a writer all at once. Like Vân Uớc, Jackie must engage with her history, her family, and her past. When she does, she becomes not only a reader, but a writer and activist. Near the end of the novel, she includes these lines, in the poem "the revolution":

the revolution

Don't wait for your school to teach you, my uncle says,
about the revolution. It's happening in the streets.
…
I want to write this down, that the revolution is like
a merry-go-round, history always being made
somewhere. And maybe for a short time,
we're part of that history. And then the ride stops
and our turn is over.
…
And after I write it down, maybe I'll end it this way:

My name is Jacqueline Woodson
and I am ready for the ride. (Woodson 2014, 308–309)

Characters like City and Jackie, then, engage with multiple histories, multiple texts, in order to develop into literate people. They engage with systems of oppression and opportunity, with texts both near to and far from their own experiences. Jackie's and City's stories are complex, requiring them to engage with both an oppressive past and a specifically African-American literary tradition in order to move toward a more confident future. Their trajectory begins to rewrite our story of reading, as it indicates the significance of the #WeNeedDiverseBooks movement, and of our common engagement with a wide variety of texts and the histories that inform them. For reading to become, or continue to be, a network—these texts teach us—it must *both* speak directly to its readers and expand their field of vision, modeling the reading it also teaches.

Novels depicting underrepresented readers have a double burden: they are expected to reflect a diverse experience to diverse readers, but also to conform to familiar enough genres to engage both majority and minority readers. The characters in these novels suggest that they can "dream themselves into existence" through their reading, modeling a reading strategy for their audience. While their influences are diverse (some more than others), for the most they make little effort to read those influences critically. City Coldson's multiple readings of a text that changes each time he reads it offers a useful reminder that it is not just what we read, but when, where, and how, that makes reading deeply meaningful. In the two chapters that follow, we see readers who read both critically and deeply, and whose reading becomes profoundly liberatory. As they read sacred texts against the grain, and read critically for citizenship, we see adolescent readers becoming agents of their own futures.

WORKS CITED

Alexander, Kwame. 2016. *Booked.* New York: HMH Books for Young Readers.

Alexie, Sherman. 2007. *The Absolutely True Diary of a Part-Time Indian*, illus. Ellen Forney. New York: Hatchette-Little, Brown.

Anatol, Giselle Liza. 2016. Brown Girl Dreaming: A Ghost Story in the Postcolonial Gothic Tradition. *Children's Literature Association Quarterly* 41 (4): 403–419.

Anderson, Laurie Halse. 1999, 2001. *Speak.* New York: Penguin.

Anderson, M.T. 2006. *The Astonishing Life of Octavian Nothing, Traitor to the Nation, Volume One: The Pox Party.* Cambridge, MA: Candlewick.

———. 2008. *The Astonishing Life of Octavian Nothing, Traitor to the Nation, Volume Two: The Kingdom on the Waves.* Cambridge, MA: Candlewick.

Bishop, Rudine Sims. 1990. Mirrors, Windows, and Sliding Glass Doors. *Perspectives* 6 (3): ix–xi.

Crenshaw, Kimberlé. 1989. Demarginalizing the Intersection of Race and Sex: A Black Feminist Critique of Antidiscrimination Doctrine, Feminist Theory and Antiracist Politics. *University of Chicago Legal Forum* 1, article 8: 139–167.

Eldred, Janet Carey, and Peter Mortensen. 1992. Reading Literacy Narratives. *College English* 54 (5): 512–539.

Elliott, Zetta. 2010. The Writer's Page: Decolonizing the Imagination. *The Horn Book*, March/April. https://www.hbook.com/2010/03/decolonizing-imagination/.

Fischer, Steven Roger. 2003. *A History of Reading*. London: Reaktion Books.

Frank, E.R. 2015. *Dime*. New York: Atheneum.

Hateley, Erica. 2012. 'In the hands of the Receivers': The Politics of Literacy in *The Savage* by David Almond and Dave McKean. *Children's Literature in Education* 43: 170–180.

Jacobs, Vicki A. 2008. Adolescent Literacy: Putting the Crisis in Context. *Harvard Educational Review* 78 (1): 7–39.

Kertzer, Adrienne. 2012. Not Exactly: Intertextual Identities and Risky Laughter in Sherman Alexie's *The Absolutely True Diary of a Part-Time Indian*. *Children's Literature* 40: 49–77.

Koss, Melanie D., and William H. Teale. 2009. What's Happening in YA Literature? Trends in Books for Adolescents. *Journal of Adolescent & Adult Literacy* 52 (7): 563–572.

Larrick, Nancy. 1965. The All-White World of Children's Books. *Saturday Review* 48 (37): 63–65.

Laymon, Kiese. 2013a. *How to Slowly Kill Yourself and Others in America*. Chicago: Bolden (E-pub).

———. 2013b. *Long Division*. Chicago: Bolden Books.

"Mission Statement." 2019. We Need Diverse Books. https://diversebooks.org/about-wndb/.

Myers, Christopher. 2014. The Apartheid of Children's Literature. *The New York Times*, March 16. https://www.nytimes.com/2014/03/16/opinion/sunday/the-apartheid-of-childrens-literature.html.

Myers, Walter Dean. 2014. Where Are the People of Color in Children's Books? *The New York Times*, March 16. https://www.nytimes.com/2014/03/16/opinion/sunday/where-are-the-people-of-color-in-childrens-books.html.

Nel, Philip. 2017. *Was the Cat in the Hat Black? The Hidden Racism of Children's Literature, and the Need for Diverse Books*. New York: Oxford University Press.

"Reading on the Rise: A New Chapter in American Literacy." 2009. NEA Research Report, January. https://www.arts.gov/sites/default/files/ReadingonRise.pdf.

Sáenz, Benjamin Alire. 2014. *Aristotle and Dante Discover the Secrets of the Universe*. New York: Simon & Schuster.

Sanchez, Jenny Torres. 2013. *Death, Dickinson, and the Demented Life of Frenchie Garcia*. Philadelphia: Running Press.

Scholastic Kids and Family Reading Report. 2008. *Reading in the 21st Century: Turning the Page with Technology*.

————. 2017. http://www.scholastic.com/readingreport/files/Scholastic-KFRR-6ed-2017.pdf.

Thomas, Ebony Elizabeth. 2016. Stories *Still* Matter: Rethinking the Role of Diverse Children's Literature Today. *Language Arts* 94 (2): 112–119.

Trites, Roberta Seelinger. 2000. *Disturbing the Universe: Power and Repression in Adolescent Literature*. Iowa City: University of Iowa Press.

Twain, Mark. 1884, 1977. *The Adventures of Huckleberry Finn*. New York: Norton Critical Edition.

Watson, Renee. 2015. *This Side of Home*. New York: Bloomsbury.

Wood, Fiona. 2015. *Cloudwish*. New York: Poppy/Little, Brown.

Woodson, Jacqueline. 2014. *Brown Girl Dreaming*. New York: Penguin.

CHAPTER 5

Magic, Prophetic, and Sacred Books: Making Communities of Readers

As I noted at the beginning of Chapter 4, I grew up in rectories (though only one had a magic door). As the daughter of an Episcopal priest, I am part of a hermeneutic tradition that stresses critical thinking. The bumper stickers in our church parking lots said things like "Darwin was an Anglican," "Coexist," and "Question Authority." Where I live now, however, I sometimes see a bumper sticker that reads: "God said it, I believe it, that settles it." It is often paired with another one: "Bibles that are falling apart usually belong to people that aren't." The two combine to suggest an approach to reading and religion that suggest that religious reading is fundamentally anti-interpretive; that reading the Bible (or, possibly, other religious texts) provides direct access to truth—that religious texts are, in a word, magical.[1] This attitude reflects, of course, the rise of fundamentalism in the latter half of the twentieth century—a very different tradition from the hermeneutic tradition of my youth.[2]

---

[1] I use "magic" here to suggest that these are texts that *do* things for which we have no explanation in consensus reality, whether it is predicting the future, giving guidance for the present, or explaining the past. Sacred texts, divinely inspired, similarly exceed the bounds of consensus reality. English fantasy literature for children dating from at least George MacDonald has used magic as a metaphor for divine intervention. We may think, for example, of the Princess Irene's grandmother in *The Princess and the Goblin* or Aslan's "Deep Magic" in the Chronicles of Narnia. See, for example, Pat Pinsent, "Revisioning Religion" (2006).

[2] It's beyond the scope of this project to explore the history of fundamentalism in the West. Karen Armstrong, however, argues convincingly that the tendency to read sacred texts as

© The Author(s) 2019

E. R. Gruner, *Constructing the Adolescent Reader in Contemporary Young Adult Fiction*, Critical Approaches to Children's Literature, https://doi.org/10.1057/978-1-137-53924-3_5

I grew up a skeptical reader, and in the protagonists of the novels I treat in this chapter, I find idealized (far more adventurous and creative) versions of my younger self. At the same time, these novels acknowledge the magic of books. Texts can be sacred, they seem to say, but that quality inheres in the reading, not in the text itself. Open and skeptical, faithful and apostate, the young readers I treat in this chapter learn to read both extensively and in community and that reading empowers them to write new stories for themselves and for others.[3]

In the young adult novels I discuss in this chapter, texts (of many sorts) may provide access to truth, even spiritual and religious truth, but such access requires interpretation just as much as, if not more than, any other kind of reading. Sacred or magical texts appear to offer access to truth; they promise magical qualities such as prophecies or answers to eternal questions. The young readers I treat in this chapter, however, discover that they must interpret sacred and magical texts if they are to develop their own agency in the world—and that a too-credulous reliance on any book is not only limiting but dangerous.

While in Chapter 2 I focused on *where* young adults read—both in and out of school—and in Chapters 3 and 4 on *who* some of those readers are, in this chapter, I focus on a specific subset of *what* they reading: sacred, prophetic, or magical books. I treat a disparate group of both realistic and fantasy novels together for their commonalities: in each, readers encounter texts that promise (or that they believe provide) access to truth. In each, readers must learn to read these texts deeply, even skeptically, creating rather than accepting the truth they find in texts. Their deep reading, especially when done in community, begins to grant them an agency that they lack as more accepting or credulous readers,

---

expressions of historical truth is a product of, rather than a reaction to, the rise of empiricism (see, e.g., Armstrong 2000, xiii–xv).

[3] For a discussion of "extensive" reading, see Stephen Fischer: "As of the late seventeenth century Western European readers began prioritizing *extensive* over *intensive* reading. Hitherto, with little access to printed information, readers had read their few available publications (the Bible, a Book of Hours, pedlar's booklets and pamphlets) slowly, repeating each word over and over gain in purposeful contemplation. That is, they read intensively. But by the late 1600s, when individual readers could purchase several books, their purpose shifted to the widest possible coverage of a given topic, or even to variety itself. They began reading extensively" (Fischer 2003, 255).

or as non-readers. But sacred or magical texts can also endanger their readers, as we shall see.

Magical books have a long history in children's and young adult literature. A brief sampling from the twentieth century includes the Magician's Book in C.S. Lewis's *The Voyage of the Dawn Treader* (1952), the book of Gramarye, through which Will Stanton receives his magical education in *The Dark Is Rising* (1973), or Ogion's spellbook, which Ged steals a look at in *A Wizard of Earthsea* (1968). These books join a host of others, some nearly sentient, that populate contemporary young adult literature; and like them, many are dangerous. The seductive spells in the Magician's Book, like so many spells, have a way of delivering what they promise, but not what Lucy wants. When Ged reads a spell for summoning the spirits of the dead in Ogion's book, he inadvertently enacts it, unwittingly calling up a spirit of danger. Only the Book of Gramarye is safe for its reader, and even that book imposes a burden. In contemporary young adult fiction, something similar is true. In the Harry Potter series, books such as *The Monster Book of Monsters*, which threatens to bite its reader, or Tom Riddle's diary, which nearly engulfs Ginny Beasley, are both magical and dangerous. The talking Book in *Un Lun Dun* and the sacred texts in *Evolution, Me, and Other Freaks of Nature* and *Where Things Come Back* do not threaten physical danger, but nonetheless carry the potential for harm, as do the fairy-tales and sacred texts of the Tiffany Aching series and *His Dark Materials*. These threatening books require careful, often communal, critical reading in order to make them safe and productive for their readers. (Nothing can make *The Monster Book of Monsters* either safe or productive, however.)

But, of course, books have long been dangerous. Ideas spread by books from *The Communist Manifesto* to the *Little Red Book*, from Martin Luther's *95 Theses* to Tyndale's Bible, Darwin's *Origin of Species* to Parnell and Richardson's *And Tango Makes Three*[4] have threatened authorities and both inspired and endangered their readers. Some have built communities, others have threatened or even shattered them. Young adult novels that depict readers engaging with magical, prophetic, or sacred texts literalize the potential dangers that certain books have

---

[4] The picture book, *And Tango Makes Three* (2005), is about two male penguins who jointly hatch an egg and raise the chick in Central Park Zoo. It was first or second on the ALA's Banned and Challenged Books list from 2006 to 2010 (http://www.ala.org/advocacy/bbooks/frequentlychallengedbooks/top10).

always engendered. The novels I discuss in this chapter represent readings that may present various kinds of danger: they may cause either the creation or the destruction of community, or they may incite risky but ultimately beneficial action. They demonstrate both the promise and the threat of literacy.

In the previous chapters, I have discussed reading in a variety of settings and of various kinds of literature. But in those chapters, I discussed how fictional teens read fiction and poetry: works of art, for the most part, rather than works of faith, prophecy, or magic. While in the novels discussed in earlier chapters teen reading both represents and develops teen agency, the implied readers of sacred and prophetic texts are constrained by their reading: limited to the prescribed outcomes of the texts they read. As David P. Resnick and Lauren B. Resnick note: "The expected behavior of the sacred text user is to learn the texts themselves (perhaps by heart) and to acquire a body of standard interpretations of the text" (Resnick and Resnick 1989, 175–176). That is, the reader's interpretation is not encouraged; standard or authorized interpretations already exist—and may not even be acknowledged as interpretations even as they must be mastered.

Resnick and Resnick define a sacred literacy transaction as one in which "the reader ... gains access through reading and proper interpretation to participation in a particular marked community that accepts the text as sacred" (Resnick and Resnick 1989, 178). The boundaries on the interpretation of sacred texts, then, develop in community. A relatively new Web site, "Harry Potter and the Sacred Text," however, reverses the order of the text's sacral quality and reading in community. Rather than claiming that *a priori* sacred texts must be read in community, their Web site proclaims that "By reading the text slowly, repeatedly and with concentrated attention, our effort becomes a key part of what makes the book sacred. The text in and of itself is not sacred, but is made so through our rigorous engagement. Particularly by rigorously engaging in ritual reading, we believe we can glean wisdom from its pages."[5] For these readers, it is not the quality of the text itself that demands rigorous reading, but the quality and kind of reading that imbue a text with the sacred. We see both approaches to sacred texts in literature for young adults: some texts come marked as sacred and require a certain kind of

[5] http://www.harrypottersacredtext.com/methodology-1/.

reading, while others are sacralized by readers' attention to them. Either approach makes for a fundamentally different way for teens to interact with texts than we have seen in earlier chapters—and both can be either dangerous or empowering.

In novels as disparate as the fantasy series *His Dark Materials* (Pullman 1995–2000), and the Tiffany Aching subset of the Discworld fantasies (Pratchett 2003–2015); fantasy novels including Laini Taylor's *Strange the Dreamer* (2017) and China Miéville's *Un Lun Dun* (2007); and realistic novels such as *The Hired Girl* (Schlitz 2015), *Evolution, Me & Other Freaks of Nature* (Brande 2007), and *Where Things Come Back* (Whaley 2011), teen readers encounter sacred texts of various sorts. In some cases, reading can create community for the characters, as we see in *The Hired Girl* and *Strange the Dreamer*. Readers who approach texts alone, however, may operate completely outside of community norms. In *Where Things Come Back* and *Strange the Dreamer*, for example, solitary reading is dangerous both to the reader and to others.

Perhaps most interesting are the readers who refuse or fail to master the sacred texts they encounter within the boundaries of their communities, as in *Evolution, Me, and Other Freaks of Nature, Un Lun Dun,* and the Tiffany Aching novels. Their readings may expose the readers to danger, but may also grant them greater agency than more conventional readers exhibit. As reading characters engage with a variety of both sacred and prophetic texts, they learn to read and sometimes revise the stories that constitute their realities, pointing the way for their own implied readers to do the same. These novels suggest that not only do sacred and prophetic texts require interpretation, then, they require exactly the same kind of critical attention that literary texts do. Such attention, moreover, may either reinforce or shake faith. David Jasper argues that, "The task of interpretation, the reading and criticism of great literature, is ultimately the task of a new theodicy, recognizing the necessity of repeatedly deferred meanings, in justifying that which has ultimate meaning in time and in eternity" (Jasper 1989, 75). Those same endlessly deferred meanings, however, may not point to "ultimate meaning" at all—or may do so for some readers and not for others. In the chapter that follows, I examine YA novels in which skeptical and faithful readers pursue meaning in sacred and prophetic texts. In so doing, they may or may not change places, but they learn—both from texts and from each other—how to read.

READING THE WORD AND THE WORLD IN REALIST FICTION

In realistic novels such as Laura Amy Schlitz's *The Hired Girl*, Robin Brande's *Evolution, Me, and Other Freaks of Nature*, and John Corey Whaley's *Where Things Come Back*, the sacred texts come from recognizable religious traditions in the USA: the Christian (implicitly Protestant) Bible and the Catholic Missal. These novels emphasize critical reading and thinking rather than a purely literalist or fundamentalist approach to texts. While Whaley's characters engage with a book from the Apocrypha, the Book of Enoch, both Mena of *Evolution, Me...* and Joan of *The Hired Girl* struggle with their interpretations of more familiar Christian texts. All three find their interpretive communities inadequate to their needs and must develop both new ways of reading and new communities in order to come to terms with their texts and with their relationships to lived experience.

In *The Hired Girl*, the first books we see Joan Skraggs reading are nineteenth-century novels, and in many ways, the novel resembles those reworkings of *Jane Eyre* discussed in Chapter 3. Like those other rereaders, Joan reads herself as Jane, but in the course of the novel, she becomes a more critical reader of both Brontë's novel and the religious texts that she turns to for instruction. The novels she has received from her teacher, Miss Chandler—*Jane Eyre*, *Dombey and Son* and *Ivanhoe*—are initially her most cherished possessions. The novels represent both Miss Chandler's faith in Joan and Joan's conviction that her life has more meaning than to be a drudge on her father's farm. "During bad times," she writes, "I've turned to them the way a pious girl might turn to her Bible" (Schlitz 2015, 58). *Jane Eyre*, her favorite novel, inspires her to leave her abusive home: "When Jane Eyre was tired of teaching at Lowood, she prayed for a new servitude. I remember that, her saying, 'Grant me at least a new servitude!' She didn't think she could attain anything better like Liberty or Excitement or Enjoyment, but she thought she might stand a chance with a new job" (Schlitz 2015, 62).[6] Inspired by Jane, Joan flees her father's home and becomes the servant to a wealthy Jewish family in Baltimore, the Rosenbachs.

In moving into the Rosenbachs' home, Joan begins to see her reading come to life. As she says to Mrs. Rosenbach, she has not met any Jews before, "but I've read about them in the Bible. And in *Ivanhoe*,

[6]As we saw in Chapter 3, this seems to be a popular takeaway from *Jane Eyre*.

Rebecca was a Jewess, and she's my favorite character in the whole book" (Schlitz 2015, 93). (Mrs. Rosenbach later gives her *Daniel Deronda* as a more accurate depiction of Judaism.) As she becomes their "Sabbath goy," however, doing the work that the family and their housekeeper Malka cannot do on the Sabbath, Joan learns more of the family's religion, and her curiosity and incorporation into their community spark a more critical reading of her own religious texts. While her catechist, Father Horst, emphasizes "the IMPRIMATUR" in her missal, insisting that she memorize her catechism, Mr. Rosenbach encourages her questions and offers her a variety of texts—fiction, philosophy, and art (Schlitz 2015, 219). (He also reminds her to read her own Bible.) While Horst calls her "a disobedient and quarrelsome child" (Schlitz 2015, 237) for challenging his authority, Mr. Rosenbach is impressed by "the little girl who loves books so much that she stays up all night and sets the house on fire!" (Schlitz 2015, 148—it's really only her hair). Not only does he give her *carte blanche* in his library, but he specifically suggests Marcus Aurelius's *Confessions* and Plato's *Theaetetus* as aids to her religious and philosophical questions. While fourteen-year-old Joan actually prefers the sensational novels she finds in his shelves, his willingness to engage her in interpretive questioning stands in stark contrast to Father Horst's intransigence. Bakhtin's distinction between "authoritative discourse" and "interior persuasiveness" seems to characterize Horst in relation to Rosenbach. Ann Trousdale, citing Bakhtin, writes:

> Authoritative discourse is characterized by distance from oneself, a lack of dialogic possibilities, a lack of play, of 'spontaneously creative stylizing variants'; discourse that is static with its own single calcified meaning.
>
> A second type of discourse is one which Bakhtin describes as having interior persuasiveness. This type of discourse does not necessarily appeal to any external authority but is flexible, with malleable borders. It is contextualized and can be related to one's own life. (Trousdale 2004, 178–179, citing Bahktin, *The Dialogic Imagination* 342–343)

Mr. Rosenbach helps Joan develop a context for her reading that frees her from an authoritative interpretation of religious texts. This context, or community, is flexible, including at different times both of his sons, Malka, Mrs. Rosenbach, and even Father Holst. Holst's authoritative discourse gives way to the more flexible reading practices that Joan develops in the Rosenbachs' home. The novel ends with Joan entering a charity school Mr. Rosenbach has founded: here, in a school open to both Christians and Jews, she may find her best interpretive community.[7] We never see Joan stop trying to find a Mr. Rochester among the men she meets; she is a naïve reader of novels, but a questioning one, and she brings that same attitude to her religious reading.

Mena in Robin Brande's *Evolution, Me, and Other Freaks of Nature* goes in the opposite direction, focusing her Bible-trained eye on fiction when she first starts to read beyond her tradition. Like *The Hired Girl, Evolution, Me…* similarly focuses on the dangers of reading a sacred text too literally—especially when a community of readers constrains interpretation of its sacred texts. Members of the Paradise Christian Church read their Bibles literally, if selectively, condemning (among other things) homosexuality and a belief in evolution. When protagonist Mena Reece is shunned by her church community, she seeks a new community of friends.[8] While she begins the novel still committed to her fundamentalist reading of the Bible, if not to her church community, her lab partner Casey, his sister Kayla, and her teacher Ms. Shepherd provide her the security both to reread the texts her former community had reified and to read new ones they had condemned.

Brande's novel provides other insights into how to read through Mena as well. Before she begins to assemble her community, for example, she sees a glimpse of it in *A Tale of Two Cities*, which she reads for her English class. "What I wouldn't give to meet people like that," she writes in her notebook, "—noble, brave, self-sacrificing" (Brande 2007, 70). As she becomes closer to Casey and his family, she reads more: *A Tale of Two Cities, The Fellowship of the Ring,* the Harry Potter series, and Casey's father's novels. Thus as her community expands, she moves from intensive to extensive reading.

---

[7] It's worth noting here that the novel, which has many parallels to *Jane Eyre*, ends with Joan's placement in a boarding school where she anticipates a happy ending—a sly revision of the Lowood episode of the original.

[8] We learn fragmentarily that Mena's friends believed that their classmate Denny was gay, and therefore harassed him, acting on Pastor Wells's preaching on the sin of homosexuality. After Denny attempts suicide, Mena writes him a letter explaining who is responsible and why. This letter becomes the basis for a lawsuit against members of the church, and it is the lawsuit—and the fact that the insurance Mena's father sold to church members will not cover bullying—that occasions both Mena's and, later, her family's shunning.

Straddling two communities, two ways of interpreting the world, Mena is able to make connections between them, and especially between their "sacred" texts, that others might not. Because her sheltered upbringing has prevented her from reading *The Lord of the Rings*, or the Harry Potter series, for example, when she first hears of Gandalf's return after his seeming death, she thinks to herself, "kind of like Jesus" (Brande 2007, 142).[9] And when she begins to learn about evolution, she sees unexpected parallels between the biblical text and scientific thought, recognizing that the story of how Jacob increases his flock is an example of survival of the fittest, as well as "sexual selection and selective breeding for certain traits" (Brande 2007, 129, 132; Genesis 30, 25–41). As "BibleGrrrl," then, she finds congruence, not conflict, between Biblical texts and the theory of evolution.

Her former pastor, like *The Hired Girl*'s Father Horst, leaves no opening for critical or skeptical readings of the Bible, instead insisting on his own narrowly defined terms. Yet he later uses the language of critical thinking to attempt to shut down the biology teacher's discussion of evolution. As he leaves the classroom, "Ask questions," Pastor Wells boom[s] ... "Demand to hear both sides. God gave you brains. Don't be ashamed to use them" (Brande 2007, 120). Wells's injunction to the students would, of course, not be out of place in any class on critical thinking. But "both sides" are not opposed. As Ms. Shepherd points out, they are trying to answer different questions, and she is teaching science, not religion (see, e.g., Brande 2007, 244–250).[10] It is Ms. Shepherd, then, who provides a vivid lesson in critical thinking when she gives Casey a stuffed jackalope, claiming it is an authentic species. When the students return to class and question her further based on their research, the class moves into "a whole discussion about whether we should believe everything we read, and how it's destructive to society to trust someone else's observations over our own, and that it's the scientist's duty to always test other people's hypotheses and not fall into lazy thinking" (Brande 2007, 50). Ms. Shepherd, Casey, and Kayla thus provide Mena with the community of readers she needs in order to read her Bible more critically.

[9] Melody Briggs and Richard Briggs suggest that fantasy literature is uniquely suited to "fill the gap" between scientific and religious modes of interpreting the world, and Mena seems to serve as an example of their claim (Briggs and Briggs 2006, 31).

[10] Obviously, this is a contested issue; Ms. Shepherd gets the last word on it in the novel.

In fact, both sides read their Bibles selectively. Mena, as Bible Grrrl, cherry picks stories and parables that may demonstrate a basic understanding of genetics and, perhaps, the survival of the fittest. Pastor Wells uses the story of Judas to shame Mena's family, suggesting that Mena's action is akin to Judas's treachery. While Wells relies on (false) analogy whereas Mena relies on close reading for metaphor, both extrapolate from the text within their community contexts. While the implied audience for *Evolution, Me...* will applaud Mena's "conversion" to scientific thought (which, not incidentally, includes a really hot boyfriend), neither Mena nor the congregation of Paradise Christian really engages in critical reading. Mena's community desacralizes her reading of the Bible, but they do not read it together, while Pastor Wells pre-determines the "sacred" context for his congregation's reading, imposing a hierarchical community rather than inviting shared participation. Neither represents true communal reading, though both do provide some glimpses into it. The implied reader will hold out hope for Mena, restored to her parents' good graces and hoping to attend a new church that, like Ms. Shepherd, does not find evolution to be incompatible with Christian faith.

Where Things Come Back, like *Evolution, Me...*, features a contrast between fundamentalist and critical readers. The two types of reading, however, do not come together until the end of the novel—each conveyed and represented by a different narrator.[11] One section is narrated by Cullen Witter, the protagonist. The first-person narration implies a subjectivity about the story that is borne out by the events: Cullen must always recalibrate his reading of both text and circumstance. The omniscient narration that characterizes the other story—a story of failed literalist readings—implies an objectivity or truth value. In this second narrative, Benton Sage and, later, his college roommate Cabot Searcy are both searchers after the truth, and they believe they have found it in the apocryphal Book of Enoch. In this text, they find both explanations for evil and directions for life. Their readings, however, lead Benton to suicide and Cabot to madness—literalism or fundamentalism is thus ironically depicted as an untenable reading strategy in the "objective" section of the book.

---

[11] The reader knows before the characters do that the two plotlines are connected through Cabot Searcy's failed marriage: his wife Alma is from Cullen's home town of Lily, Arkansas.

While the third-person omniscient narrator of Benton and Cabot's story tells a particular, and peculiar, story, the first-person narration does not build the "narrative intimacy" that Sara Day finds in books directed mostly at girls and that we saw a version of in Chapter 3.[12] That is, the first-person narration, while it may encourage a certain amount of identification, also distances. Cullen frequently prefaces the most emotionally charged portions of his narration with a distancing impersonal construction, as well as a keen awareness of the restrictions of genre. For example, he writes:

> When one is watching the girl he thinks is his girlfriend whispering into the ear of her ex, he immediately imagines Russell Quitman [the ex] suddenly yanking out the tubes from his neck, breaking free of his wheelchair, and lifting Ada Taylor off the ground in one quick swoop. He sees the Quit Man slowly plant a long movie-star kiss on her lips and then put her down, laughing. His face goes from normal to zombie and back and forth. And behind them all the people cheer and clap and suddenly their faces too begin to shift and contort.... (Whaley 2011, 159)

The sudden shift into the impersonal "one" from the far more personal "I" signals not only Cullen's discomfort with emotion, but also his exploration of metafiction. Here, we see that Cullen understands how zombie stories work—he's been thinking about writing one since early in the novel—and his narrative complies with its form, demonstrating "zombification" at the seeming emotional climax of the story. While we see Cullen himself read only a few texts, he is clearly aware of narrative conventions. His narrative, then, reminds the reader of the need to question the text, to explore its implications, to imagine alternatives just as Cullen does.

Both a too-literal reading of scripture and the lack of an interpretive community hamper roommates Benton Sage and Cabot Searcy throughout the novel. Benton's mission to Ethiopia fails in part because he reads his experiences too literally through his understanding of scripture. As he says to Rameel, his missionary guide,

---

[12] Day's concept applies specifically to novels aimed at girl readers, with female first-person narrators. She helpfully reminds us, however, of Maria Nikolajeva's rejection of the "identification fallacy" that assumes an affinity between reader and narrator. Cullen's narration quite openly rejects that fallacy.

"It's in Hebrews. It says, 'Are they not all ministering spirits sent out to serve for the sake of those who are to inherit salvation?'"

"And?" Rameel sat up farther in his bed.

"I always thought this was God telling us to go out and save people."

"And you doubt that now?" Rameel asked.

"No, I doubt that I am helping God in any way other than providing food and water. I feel as if we are doing nothing more than reading a few scriptures and then moving on." (Whaley 2011, 38)

Rameel understands that the first (food and water) *could* potentially lead to the second (conversion)—and that *could* be what the text means—but Benton is wedded to his interpretation. Benton reads scripture both literally and personally, as if it were addressed directly to him. Like Pastor Wells, he interprets historically situated stories and letters as if they were transparently true for him as well. When he discovers the Book of Enoch, he finds himself unable to fulfill what he sees as its directions to him and commits suicide: the novel thus literalizes the dangers of a fundamentalist reading in his brief story.

Cabot Searcy, Benton's roommate, follows him in his obsession with Enoch, which he also reads as if it were a set of operating instructions. His obsession with the book deprives him of his job, his family, his marriage, and possibly his sanity. "He had," the narrator says, "taken Benton's notes and not blown them out of proportion so much as he had strapped an atom bomb to every letter of every word" (Whaley 2011, 166). The striking image reinforces the suggestion that a too-literal reading is dangerous, even deadly—not only to the reader, but to those in his circle as well. And so it is: he (accidentally) kidnaps Cullen Witter's younger brother Gabriel, because he has interpreted his experience through the lens of the prophetic book of Enoch, which has convinced him that he is in the presence of the archangel himself and is fulfilling God's wishes in keeping his human avatar.

Cullen and Gabriel are very different readers than Benton or Cabot— Gabriel particularly. Neither reads literally nor do they read within a sacred tradition. Gabriel, who seems to read more than his brother, carries a copy of *The Catcher in the Rye* in his back pocket and spends each morning reading on the porch (Whaley 2011, 102, 108).[13] Both,

---

[13]While Tom Henderson in *King Dork* ends up seeing a version of himself in Holden Caulfield, we see no evidence that Gabriel does so. The book is a touchstone, but not a prophecy.

however, reject the notion of a destiny guiding their actions, including their reading. While Cabot, following his roommate, sees only fate in his reading and limits himself to that one topic, Cullen, Gabriel, and their friends question and reject the idea of destiny, and expand both their reading and their communities rather than contracting them.

Cullen's narrative does include more than one destiny-driven character, however. John Barling, who comes to Lily, Arkansas to find the elusive Lazarus woodpecker, claims his search for it is his destiny. His quest, like Benton's, seems to destroy his life—or at least his marriage. Ada Taylor, on the other hand, tries to reject what she thinks is her destiny: her status as the "Black Widow," whose two previous boyfriends have died and whose ex, Russell Quitman, is paralyzed in an accident. While neither destiny is driven by a book (as we will see with texts discussed later in this chapter), both conform to the familiar narrative structures of the quest and the teen "sex = death" narrative.[14] The titles Cullen imagines for the books he never writes, however—*"You May Feel a Slight Sting," "This Popcorn Tastes Like People," "Five A.M. is for Lovers and Lawn Ornaments"* (Whaley 2011, 15, 55, 133)—offer an ironic commentary on the action, rather than signaling any particular genre or narrative arc. Indeed, the novel itself refuses narrative conventions by beginning with a death and ending with Gabriel's unexpected return. Just as *The Hired* Girl unsettles the narrative arc of *Jane Eyre* and *Evolution, Me...* moves from the closure of fundamentalism to the random direction of evolutionary development, *Where Things Come Back* similarly plays with narrative sequencing by starting with a death and ending with the anticlimax of Gabriel's non-kidnapping. As the novels subvert narrative expectations, they give their implied readers experiences that parallel the characters'. Unlike the teleological prophetic narratives, they revise, these novels privilege openness. And unlike the solitary readers who endanger themselves and others by their lonely intensive reading, the protagonists develop increasingly extensive canons and larger reading networks, leading them to greater agency.

---

[14] See Trites for the frequent association of sex with death in, especially, early YA literature. Judy Blume is said to have written *Forever* to counteract the connection (see Trites 2000, 91).

FANTASY, PROPHECY, AND NARRATIVE CAUSALITY

Where Things Come Back involves characters who seem to believe they are destined—that they are, we might say, in a fantasy novel—but they are not. They are, like the protagonists of *The Hired Girl* and *Evolution, Me, and Other Freaks of Nature*—and, indeed, all the novels I've discussed so far—bound by the constraints of realism. We find readers in realistic YA novels because reading is such a recognizable part of most teens' lives. But fantasy novels stress action: quests generally involve movement and adventure, not reflection. The fantasy tradition draws deeply on fairy-tale models which, as we saw in Chapter 3, rarely involve much reading. But what if the protagonist of the fantasy narrative is in fact a reader? Can a critical reader resist—or alter—a prophecy? In several recent fantasy novels or series, resistant readers reshape their stories, suggesting, as with other texts I've already discussed, that their critical reading develops agency, redirecting their stories. In Laini Taylor's *Strange the Dreamer* (2017), China Miéville's *Un Lun Dun* (2007), Philip Pullman's *His Dark Materials* trilogy (1995–2000), and Terry Pratchett's Tiffany Aching novels (2003–2015), reading protagonists resist and revise prophetic texts.[15]

Lazlo and Deeba, Tiffany and Lyra, are both bound by and resist a force Pratchett calls "narrative causality." Pratchett defines "narrative causality" as "the idea that there are 'story shapes' into which human history, both large scale and at the personal level, attempts to fit" (Pratchett 2000, 166). In *Witches Abroad*, he writes: "the theory of narrative causality … means that a story, once started, takes a shape. It picks up all the vibrations of all the other workings of that story that have ever been. … Stories don't care who takes part in them. All that matters is that the story gets told, that the story repeats" (Pratchett 1991, 2).[16] Protagonists of fantasy literature, in particular, are subject to narrative causality—they inhabit stories such as the hero's journey, biblical

---

[15]Lyra Belacqua, unlike the other protagonists, is not much of a reader, at least initially—and certainly not of books. Her reading of the alethiometer, however, similarly demonstrates the necessity of interpretation when seeking the truth.

[16]Pratchett's term seems to me to combine the concepts of genre and fate to convey the ways that characters are bound to certain futures, especially in fantasy literature.

narrative, fairy-tales. However, protagonists who have read or heard such stories can, while re-enacting the story, retell and rework it as well. In the fantasy novels I discuss in this chapter, the protagonists are the subjects of, or participants in, prophecy. As such, they seem to bear the peculiar burden of fulfilling a destiny for a larger community than themselves. They may thus also seem to be stand-ins for their implied readers, or even for all young adults, who bear the burden of fulfilling the future for a generation that is passing leadership on—a generation that may have passed on the stories to them. Of course, the story of critical reading is not without its dangers, and those who challenge or subvert prophecies are likely to face them. Critical readers in these novels face down those dangers most often by creating communities of readers. When their communities support, and even come into being through, their willingness to reinterpret and retell the stories they encounter, they offer a positive model of critical reading to their own implied readers.

Strange the Dreamer features a protagonist, Lazlo Strange, whose reading suggests truths that his community of librarians and scholars reject. The "children's stories" he explores, along with more mundane writings such as "old journals and bundled correspondences, spies' reports, maps and treaties, trade ledgers and the minutes of royal secretaries," give him access to another world, another community (Taylor 2017, 23). *Strange the Dreamer* endorses Lazlo's reading of fantasy and fairy-tale, just as the Tiffany Aching books do for Tiffany. Although Tiffany's initial encounters with fairy-tales are comic, the novels become increasingly serious about the truths embodied in the tales; like Lazlo, then, Tiffany must become familiar with the "children's stories" that her elders reject, so that she can use them rather than passively inhabiting them. While *Strange the Dreamer* and the Tiffany Aching books require their characters to recognize which texts are and are not sacred, in both *His Dark Materials* and *Un Lun Dun*, the sacred texts are given and the protagonists must learn to read them. The two heroines, Lyra and Deeba, become co-creators within their texts, storytellers who alter their own destinies by rereading, revising, and reworking familiar tales and by resisting the extremes of narrative causality. All four characters develop their agency *as readers*. Without reading, they remain children subject to the tales told about them; with it, they change the world.

Like Tiffany Aching, Lazlo Strange begins his tale as a solitary reader, in the dusty stacks of a forgotten corner of the Great Library. Reading in the sublevel of the library entices him, but it might also be dangerous: "Lazlo might have lived down there like a boy in a cave for who knows how long. He might have grown feral: the wild boy of the Great Library, versed in three dead languages and all the tales ever written in them, but ragged as a beggar in the alleys of the Grin" (Taylor 2017, 16).[17] Books and stories, Lazlo learns, transmit knowledge across national, cultural boundaries. He learns of Weep, the Unseen City, first from stories, but many other reading materials deliver their meaning to him as he reads them more and more carefully. Unlike Kyle in *Beastly,* however, his interest is neither fully transactional nor informational—Lazlo is creating stories out of ledgers, receipts, and children's tales, not a how-to manual. And when he learns the stories of Weep, he shares them.

Rather than becoming feral, then, Lazlo becomes part of a community: the cohort of travelers recruited to rescue the lost city of Weep. His only skill—or the one that he offers to Eril-Fane, the cohort's leader—is that he "knows a lot of stories" (Taylor 2017, 78). Those stories might be dismissed as fairy-tales, but Lazlo "understood that they were reflections of the people who had spun them, and were flecked with little truths—intrusions of reality into fantasy, like...toast crumbs on a wizard's beard" (Taylor 2017, 41, ellipses in original). The seemingly heroic Thyon Nero, on the other hand, reads only in solitude, taking Lazlo's gift of "*Miracles for Breakfast*" only after denigrating the gift, and never acknowledging it as the key to his alchemical success.[18] His theft of Lazlo's volumes of notes and speculations about Weep is also a solitary act: He never speaks of it nor reveals what he has learned from the books until the visitors from Weep arrive to recruit their cohort. Thyon's alienation from the community only increases as Lazlo becomes more and more a part of it. Lazlo is, indeed, so imbued with the power of stories that his "guess" about Weep's predicament is very nearly accurate; his faith in stories then connects him across boundaries to Sarai,

[17] There's also a physical danger to Lazlo's reading: his nose is broken by a "falling volume of fairy-tales his first day on the job" (Taylor 2017, 17).

[18] Thyon more closely resembles Kyle, as he reads for a singular purpose; like Kyle as well, he does eventually learn empathy—though in Thyon's case this comes less from his reading than from his experiences with others, including the reader Lazlo Strange.

the daughter of the Mesarthim, as well as to his hosts in the Unseen City. Crossing those boundaries will be the key to restoring the city and releasing the children.

Like the other readers discussed in this chapter, Lazlo reads to learn, reading extensively, rejecting the intensive focus on a single story for a broader, expansive view. While the books he has compiled out of his research have seemed magical to him, when Thyon requisitions them, he realizes they have been necessary, but are inadequate. Thyon's appropriation of his books does not, then, upend his world. Like the destruction of the library in the Unseen City, it becomes a catalyst for action rather than a barrier. Books are not the key—reading, interpreting, and retelling are. Like Tiffany and Lyra, he is as much storyteller as reader, reimagining the tales he has accumulated and absorbed. His reading does not limit his interpretation—or his imagination—but sets it free to imagine the truth about the Unseen City and to dream a relationship with Sarai across boundaries of time, space, and species.[19]

Tiffany Aching—protagonist of a subset of Terry Pratchett's Discworld series—is more like Deeba than Lazlo: a skeptical reader from the start. But the one book she has, the *Goode Childe's Booke of Faerie Tales*, operates like a sacred text nonetheless. It directs the behavior and belief of the people who burn down Mrs. Snapperly's cottage, and it furnishes at least some of the monsters deployed by the Fairy Queen in her incursions into Tiffany's world.[20] Her critical reading, then, involves accepting the truth—both metaphorical and literal—in the book. Her skepticism is well earned, however. When she sees her one-time rival, Letitia, looking like a princess, Tiffany remembers

reading the well-thumbed book of fairy stories that all her sisters had read before her. But she had seen what they had not seen; she had seen through it. It lied. No, well, not exactly lied, but told you truths that you did not want to know: that only blond and blue-eyed girls could get the prince and wear the glittering crown. ... if all you had was a rather mousy shade of brown hair, you were marked down to be a servant girl. (Pratchett 2010, 129)

[19] *Strange the Dreamer* is the first volume of a two-volume novel. It ends with Lazlo and Sarai's destinies unfulfilled.

[20] The townspeople who uncritically take in the tales and burn down Mrs. Snapperly's cottage offer the worst-case scenario counter-example to the heroines of the novels I discussed in Chapter 3 who model their lives on fairy-tales. Since Tiffany decides from the beginning that she is shut out from that option, she always reads more critically.

This moment echoes a passage at the beginning of the first Tiffany Aching novel, *The Wee Free Men*, when she reflects that "it was the blond people with blue eyes and the redheads with green eyes who got the stories. If you had brown hair you were probably just a servant or a woodcutter or something. Or a dairymaid" (Pratchett 2003, 35–36). But, three novels later, Tiffany learns that her earlier stance is at best a half-truth. She has realized that "you could be the witch! … You didn't have to be stuck in the story. You could change it, not just for yourself, but for other people" (Pratchett 2010, 130). The novels thus demonstrate how to reread the story critically: to question why the girl with the mousy brown hair cannot take control of the action, and to prove that she can.

I Shall Wear Midnight offers the series's most extensive exploration of the tension between skeptical and accepting readings. Like most of the novels I discuss in this chapter, *I Shall Wear Midnight* is not *about* reading or books. But the persistent undercurrent of both trusting and mistrusting books connects it to *Un Lun Dun* and to other novels in which readers engage with religious or prophetic texts. Tiffany reads intensively, more like the fundamentalist readers I treated earlier in this chapter than, for example, Lazlo Strange. And, like many sacred texts, *The Goode Childe's Booke of Faerie Tales*, seems to put limits on characters' agency, defining the boundaries of their experience. "It seemed to her that it tried to tell her what to do and what to think. Don't stray from the path, don't open the door, but hate the wicked witch because she is *wicked*. Oh, and believe that shoe size is a good way of choosing a wife" (Pratchett 2003, 66). In *I Shall Wear Midnight*, Tiffany learns that Letitia—the blond, blue-eyed "heroine"—has felt similarly constrained by the book. The novel demonstrates, however, that just as Tiffany can take control of the action, Letitia can be a witch. Both reinterpret and revise the stories they have been given.

Tiffany's (and, here, Letitia's) relationship to fairy-tales is thus different from that of the protagonists of the novels explored in Chapter 3 such as *Beastly*'s Linda, the sisters of *Sisters Red*, or even Mia of *The Princess Diaries*. While they all reinterpret their stories, the heroines I discussed in Chapter 3 embrace their status as fairy-tale heroines rather than taking the skeptical position that both Tiffany and Letitia do. Tiffany's more critical stance comes with a broader, more expansive view of the fairy-tale tradition, which is here not limited to the familiar, Disneyfied tales that influence the earlier-discussed novels.

While the earlier Tiffany Aching novels have fairy-tale villains who would not be out of place in *The Goode Childe's Booke*—the Fairy Queen, the hiver (a parasitic dreamer), and the Wintersmith—the villains in *I Shall Wear Midnight* are both more realistic and more dangerous. Mr. Petty, who beats his daughter and thereby kills his grandchild, is the kind of petty tyrant who populates many old folk tales—the fathers of "Cap O'Rushes" or "Catskin," the stepmother in "Snow White" or "Cinderella." Unlike those parental tyrants, however, Mr. Petty takes action that is recognizable from the "real" world outside of fairy-tales, and thus casts those tales into new light. While his daughter survives his tyranny, her child will not come back to life.

The Cunning Man, Tiffany's pursuer throughout the text, is the most dangerous villain Tiffany encounters in the series. A villain who would not be out of place in any number of historical contexts, he is "a witch-finder and a book burner and a torturer"—and the relationship among those three occupations is not, of course, accidental (Pratchett 2010, 156). The Cunning Man reads and writes literally, imposing his fear of witches onto a credulous community and insisting, as so many like him have done, that his personal rejection is a world-historical event and a danger that must be violently suppressed. As historically oriented fairy-tale critics have long reminded us, fairy-tale villains have their basis in lived experience.[21] Tiffany knows this, and while her skepticism never fully wanes, she learns to reread the tales that she and Letitia have both rejected and finds the truth within them. Eskarina Smith reminds her that "the world is made up of stories," and she must try to use the ones she reads to her advantage (Pratchett 2010, 156). Tiffany becomes like Lazlo, then: a more accepting reader and a storyteller, engaging with and reworking stories in order to reorder her society. And, like Lazlo, she must do so within community—whenever she takes too much upon herself, she fails.

Books become windows for Tiffany, literalizing the metaphor I drew on in Chapter 4: they become, as they are for so many others, "a way of getting from one world into another" (Pratchett 2010, 271).[22] Books teach Letitia magic, but, most importantly, a book is the source and the solution to the Cunning Man's villainy. *The Bonfire of the Witches*

---

[21] See especially Darnton (1984) and Zipes (1991) (among many others).

[22] See the discussion in Chapter 4 of Rudine Sims Bishop's "Windows, Mirrors, and Sliding-Glass Doors."

appears as another sacred text, a magical book that first contains and then releases the Cunning Man's hatred of witches into the world. As Tiffany says to Letitia, it is a "book that boils with evil, vindictive magic"—a book that cannot be reinterpreted or ignored but must simply be controlled. Or so it at first seems, when Tiffany and Letitia lock the book into a book press to keep it from opening itself and releasing its evil. But it is, finally, in acceding to the book's worst fears about witches that Tiffany is able to defeat its author.

In her final encounter with The Cunning Man, Tiffany reenacts an old saying—"*The hare runs into the fire*"—and repeats another one: "*Leap, knave! Jump, whore! … Be married now forever more!*" (Pratchett 2010, 189, 326). Running through fire—burning the witch—and embracing the uncontrolled sexuality of the witch (or at least the language associated with it) Tiffany reuses and reinterprets material directly out of both the *Good Childe's Booke* and the Cunning Man's tome. But she reenacts them not alone, but in community: with Letitia, Roland, Preston, and the Feegles, the Wee Free Men who have accompanied her throughout the series. Rhymes, stories, omens—they all turn out to have their place. Only by taking them out of context and into community, however, can Tiffany reread, retell, and reinvigorate the stories that are part of her destiny—and, in so doing, reclaim her future from the Cunning Man.

Un Lun Dun's Deeba Resham, like Tiffany, begins as a skeptical reader. Miéville clearly satirizes fundamentalist readings of sacred texts by including within his fantasy a speaking book, revered and interpreted by a priesthood of Propheseers. The prophetic Book speaks authoritatively on the coming of the Shwazzy (Choisi, or Chosen One) and outlines the multi-step quest that will lead to the salvation of UnLondon.[23] As with many quests, the tasks are obscure and the text requires interpretation: interpretation that takes place within the propheseers' limits.[24] When Deeba substitutes herself for Zanna, rejecting the Book's insistence on a single Shwazzy, and even more when she short-circuits the quest, going straight to the end, we may think that Miéville is simply poking fun at traditional fantasy, all the while making clear its quasi-religious adherence to literalism.

[23] To avoid confusion, the Book is capitalized here when referring to the character of the prophetic Book.

[24] As Resnick and Resnick suggest, the limitation of interpretation is one of the qualities of a sacred text.

But the text actually makes a more subtle, and discomfiting, point: while the Book is often wrong, it is sometimes, and in very important ways, right. And while Zanna is a failed Shwazzy, Deeba ably takes on her mantle and fulfills the destiny that the book has predicted for her, most crucially by reading the Book itself critically. While the propheseers seem to suggest that the Book can be read transparently—if only by them—it soon becomes apparent that their readings are unstable. As they explain to Zanna and Deeba, "there's always a difficulty of interpretation. But from careful reading—over generations!—we've learnt many things" (Miéville 2007, 88). Yet whenever Deeba asks for information, it is partial, confusing, or nonsensical.

In UnLondon, books—even unread books—are potentially salvific, and their destruction can seem like heresy as well as fascism. The Smog-Unstible's pleasure at consuming them is both to prevent others from learning and to absorb their knowledge himself: "*You will fire the libraries. ... And I will wait at the top and breathe the smoke of them all, and I will know* everything" (Miéville 2007, 205, emphasis in original). Books and other texts proliferate in the novel: from Obaday Fing's suits made from book pages, to the bookladders on which Deeba returns to UnLondon, to the Book itself that (creatively reinterpreted) guides their action. To complete a quest, then, is to be a reader—of books, signs, and symbols.[25] Deeba's skepticism and openness to interpretation make her, not Zanna, the quest hero.

The danger of reading is somewhat different in *Un Lun Dun* than in the other books I've looked at in this chapter. The Propheseers' control of the Book limits access to its meanings, and the Book itself contains both error and misinformation. Most egregiously, it identifies Deeba as "the funny sidekick" (Miéville 2007, 228). Here, Miéville's novel turns on itself, metafictionally calling the quest—and other quest narratives—into question. Defending the importance of the sidekick, for example, the Book suggests, "What about Digby? What about Ron and Robin? There's no shame..." (Miéville 2007, 228).[26] Deeba, however, objects:

[25] Justyna Deszcz-Tryhubczak, noting Deeba's multiliteracy, writes, "Interestingly, young as Deeba is, she may be seen as both a digital native and a critical reader of literature who is capable of interpreting information and using it constructively to reshape the world" (Deszcz-Tryhubczak 2013, 149).

[26] Digby is the sidekick to Dan Dare, a British comic hero popular in the 1950s and again in the 1970s (https://en.wikipedia.org/wiki/Dan_Dare). Ron is of course Ron Weasley of the Harry Potter series, and Robin is Batman's sidekick. Notably, all of them—like the heroes whom they accompany—are male. Miéville's quest narrative undoes most of the tropes of a quest, except the quest itself.

"No one is! [a sidekick]...To say they're just hangers-on to someone more *important*..." (Miéville 2007, 228, emphasis in original). Deeba's rejection of the sidekick is part of her larger rejection of the quest narrative—what the Book calls "the standard Chosen One deal" (Miéville 2007, 229). As Deeba realizes, the stages of the quest are, like the nonsensical prophecies in the Book, meaningless.

And yet of course there is also truth in the Book, as there is in the *Goode Childe's Booke of Faerie Tales*. There is a Shwazzy, it just isn't Zanna. And the crucial "misprint"—"nothing *and* the UnGun" for "nothing *but* the UnGun"—turns out to be accurate after all, as Deeba realizes: the Smog fears the UnGun when it shoots nothing, creating a vacuum that inhales it (Miéville 2007, 274, 409, emphasis added).

While Deeba is both a creative and a skeptical reader, she too requires a community of readers and storytellers to support her interpretations. The community of Propheseers is insular and ineffective (if not dangerous), but Deeba gathers around her a diverse assortment of unlikely allies who find ways to reinterpret and reuse (in the case of Obaday Fing) the words that make up the city of UnLondon. While nothing is as it seems in the city, it is also not the opposite of what it seems, as the "un" prefix would suggest. It is up to the community of readers to determine what is and isn't valuable in their reading. When they do, they become the authors of their own destiny.

If we first meet Tiffany and Deeba as skeptical readers, Lyra Belacqua of the *His Dark Materials* trilogy is not a reader at all. Characterized early on as a "coarse and greedy savage" who tries to elude her tutors in order to play in the claypits of Oxford, she is an unlikely emblem of critical reading (Pullman 1995, 36). Yet when she acquires the alethiometer, a "golden compass" or symbol reader that gives her access to truth—if she can both ask the right questions and interpret the answers—she slowly develops the skill. While adult readers of the device use books of symbols to help them both pose their questions and interpret the results, Lyra begins by using it intuitively, and then learns the meanings of the symbols as she goes. There is no such thing as a fundamentalist reading of the device. So her readings are stories, stories which give her access to truth. As she is first learning to read the device, for example, she explains to Farder Coram: "I can see what it says, but I must be misreading it. The thunderbolt I think is anger, and the child...I think it's me...I was getting a meaning for that lizard thing, but you talked to me, Farder Coram, and I lost it" (Pullman 1995, 152, ellipses in original). As she works with the alethiometer, she must question her intuitions, consider possibilities and context and decide whether to act on her own readings.

The alethiometer, then, functions something like a sacred text throughout Pullman's trilogy. Like the sacred texts I've discussed earlier in this chapter, it is both a repository of truth and a conundrum to be interpreted. Its meanings are constrained, and its interpretation—until Lyra acquires hers—controlled by an elite "priesthood" of readers. Lyra's ignorance of the readerly tradition of the alethiometer frees her and, at least initially, reading it alone does not seem to harm her as Benton and Cabot's solitary reading harms them. It would seem that Pullman has, in the alethiometer, created a sacred text for a secular age: providing access to truth without the trappings of religion. It is, in Robert Fuller's words, spiritual but not religious.[27]

Lyra's ability to read the alethiometer manifests itself almost as soon as she acquires it. Like Lazlo in *Strange the Dreamer*, she is a self-taught reader; like Deeba in *Un Lun Dun*, she is associated with a prophecy; like Tiffany Aching, she is more comfortable telling stories than reading them. Like all of them, she encounters unexpected dangers through her reading, but it is also her ability to read carefully and critically—and, finally, within a larger community—that allows her to take control of her story and evade the dangers she faces. Those dangers, unlike in the other fantasy novels discussed here, are explicitly religious: Pullman's version of Christianity, known here simply as the Church, functions as the ultimate threat to free thought.[28] It is a more all-encompassing, less flexible vision of what *The Hired Girl*'s Joan encounters in her lessons with Father Holst: a theocracy that limits both interpretation and action.

Although Lyra is self-taught in reading the alethiometer, Lyra's father, Lord Asriel, models a subtle kind of reading that may influence her own. In a discussion of the Fall story in Genesis, Asriel calls the story something "like an imaginary number, like the square root

[27] See Robert Fuller for a more thorough and nuanced description of this issue. Fuller differentiates between a European gap between "the relatively small number of religious persons [and] the nonreligious majority" and, in the US, a "gap between the churched and unchurched" which is not analogous to the European split: "In the United States ... only a small percentage of the population can be considered wholly without spiritual interests" (Fuller 2001, 171). Nonetheless, as a recent Pew Foundation survey confirms, many "religious" people are strikingly ignorant of their traditions (Pew Forum 2010).

[28] The threat in *I Shall Wear Midnight* also resembles a fundamentalist Christian objection to witchcraft, unlike any of the other dangers in the series.

of minus one: you can never see any concrete proof that it exists, but if you include it in your equations, you can calculate all manner of things that couldn't be imagined without it" (Pullman 1995, 372–373).[29] Asriel's use of the story makes it a metaphor in the sense that feminist theologian Sandra Schneiders has defined it: "Genuine metaphor is not primarily a rhetorical decoration or an abbreviated comparison. It is a proposition (explicit or implied) constituted by an irresolvable tension between what it affirms (which is somehow true) and what it necessarily denies (namely, the literal truth of the assertion) ... It forces the mind to reach toward meaning that exceeds or escapes effective literal expression" (Schneiders 1993, 38).[30]

Reading the alethiometer, like Asriel's reading of Genesis, is metaphorical reading. Lyra must turn symbols into stories, intuiting, through multiple possible layers of meaning, which one is most likely in the moment. Lyra understands metaphor intuitively, as we see when she reads the alethiometer with Farder Coram for the first time:

'I was thinking about Mr. de Ruyter, see....And I put together the serpent and the crucible and the beehive, to ask how he's getting on with his spying, and—'
'Why them three symbols?'
'Because I thought the serpent was cunning, like a spy ought to be, and the crucible could mean like knowledge, what you kind of distill, and the beehive was hard work, like bees are also working hard; so out of the hard work and the cunning comes the knowledge, see, and that's the spy's job; and I pointed to them and I thought the question in my mind, and the needle stopped at death....D'you think that could be really working, Farder Coram?'
'It's working all right, Lyra. What we don't know if whether we're reading it right. That's a subtle art.' (Pullman 1995, 143–144; ellipses in original)

---

[29] This is one of the many places where *The Golden Compass* revises a familiar story: Asriel's Genesis, while similar in many ways to the book of Genesis in the Hebrew and Christian Bibles, includes the dæmons, a central part of Pullman's mythology. Lyra, taught by Oxford's dons, has rejected biblical narrative as a "kind of fairy-tale" (*GC* 372). In an earlier essay, I have explored the way this reading of the story turns it into a metaphor (see Gruner 2011, 292).

[30] In an earlier essay, I have further explored the relationship between Pratchett and Pullman's metaphorical approach to sacred stories and feminist theology (See Gruner 2011).

Immediately after Coram speaks, a messenger comes with the news that de Ruyter is dead, confirming Lyra's reading of the device. Yet the knowledge that she can read it is not welcome: "she was not pleased or proud to be able to read the alethiometer—she was afraid" (Pullman 1995, 147). Lyra recognizes that she is dealing with an intelligence beyond her own and arriving at revelations of truths she could not otherwise access. While she hides the alethiometer from many, then, she does not read it alone. Rather, the small communities she finds herself in—the Gyptians, Iorek and Will, even the kidnapped children at Bolvanger—support and reinforce her reading, even if (as with the other children) they are not really aware of it.

Lyra's intuitive understanding of metaphor is echoed in the third volume of the trilogy, *The Amber Spyglass*, among the *mulefa*, the wheeled creatures among whom Mary Malone finds community. Referring to their creation story as a "make-like," the *mulefa* Atal also implies that it is a history, a history of a time thirty-three thousand years ago (Pullman 2000, 224).[31] Collapsing the distinction between empirical truth and myth, between fundamentalist and unfixed readings, both Atal and Lyra open up possibilities beyond what the Church has taught. It is, as Schneiders suggests, an emancipatory strategy, one that enables or even (especially in the case of the *mulefa*) represents both community and agency. Like the other readers discussed in this chapter, Lyra faces danger through her reading, but also moves toward freedom through the practice of interpretation.

Taken together, these novels suggest both the importance of sacred texts and their danger. Rather than simply—reactively—reject the concept of a sacred text, or even a sacred reading, these novels approach them with caution, encouraging their young readers to read in community, to refuse unitary or fundamentalist readings, reworking, and revising sacred narratives to authorize their own development. Their deep, communal reading is the key to their developing agency. In Chapter 2, we saw how communal reading can, in best-case scenarios, lead to the development of agency in some school stories, but its effects can be limited by both the institutional structure of the school and the concomitant failures of community. In the female-focused fairy-tale and

---

[31] I discuss both creation stories at greater length in an earlier essay (Gruner 2011, 279–280). Gooderham (2003) (whose reading has greatly influenced my own), Gray (2009), and Wood (2001) provide further discussion of these stories, but do not focus on reading.

romance revisions of Chapter 3, young readers developed empathy and agency when they were able to move away from informational to deeper, more interpretive readings of their foundational texts, but such readings were rare and deeply compromised by gender expectations. In the literacy narratives of Chapter 4, racialized minority readers who could find themselves in a literary canon—or begin to build their own—began to develop themselves not only as deep readers but storytellers and writers as well. Indeed, storytelling and writing have been the form of agency most common to all of the successful readers I've examined so far. The skeptical readers of this chapter continue that trend, reading in community to develop their own access to truth, their own stories. In the next chapter, I examine how all of these reading methods—communal reading, deep reading, empathetic reading, skeptical reading—combine to produce new stories of citizenship.

Works Cited

Armstrong, Karen. 2000. *The Battle for God*. New York: Knopf.

Bishop, Rudine Sims. 1990. Mirrors, Windows, and Sliding Glass Doors. *Perspectives* 6 (3): ix–xi.

Brande, Robin. 2007. *Evolution, Me, & Other Freaks of Nature*. New York: Knopf.

Briggs, Melody, and Richard S. Briggs. 2006. Stepping into the Gap: Contemporary Children's Fantasy Literature as a Doorway to Spirituality. In *Towards or Back to Human Values?* ed. Justyna Desczcz-Tyhubczak, and Marek Oziewicz, 30–47. Newcastle: Cambridge Scholars Press.

Darnton, Robert. 1984. *The Great Cat Massacre and Other Episodes in French Cultural History*. New York: Basic Books.

Day, Sara K. 2013. *Reading Like a Girl: Narrative Intimacy in Contemporary American Young Adult Literature*. Jackson: University Press of Mississippi.

Deszcz-Tryhubczak, Justyna. 2013. 'Minister,' Said the Girl, 'We Need to Talk': China Miéville's *Un Lun Dun* as Radical Fantasy for Children and Young Adults. In *Critical Insights on Contemporary Speculative Fiction*, ed. Booker M. Keith, 137–151. Ipswich, Salem, MA: Salem Press.

Fischer, Steven Roger. 2003. *A History of Reading*. London: Reaktion Books.

Fuller, Robert C. 2001. *Spiritual, But Not Religious*. New York: Oxford University Press.

Gooderham, David. 2003. Fantasizing It as It Is: Religious Language in Philip Pullman's Trilogy, His Dark Materials. *Children's Literature* 31: 155–75.

Gray, William. 2009. *Fantasy, Myth and the Measure of Truth: Tales of Pullman, Lewis, Tolkien, MacDonald and Hoffmann.* Basingstoke, England; New York: Palgrave Macmillan.

Gruner, Elisabeth Rose. 2011. Wrestling with Religion: Pullman, Pratchett, and the Uses of Story. *Children's Literature Association Quarterly* 36 (3): 276–95.

"Harry Potter and the Sacred Text." 2018. http://www.harrypottersacredtext.com/.

Jasper, David. 1989. *The Study of Literature and Religion.* Minneapolis: Fortress Press.

Miéville, China. 2007. *Un Lun Dun.* New York: Ballantine.

Pew Forum on Religion and Public Life. 2010. "U.S. Religious Knowledge Survey." Pew Forum on Religion & Public Life. November 1. http://pewforum.org/Other-Beliefs-and-Practices/U-S-Religious-Knowledge-Survey.aspx.

Pinsent, Pat. 2006. Revisioning Religion and Spirituality: Contemporary Fantasy for Young Readers. In *Towards or Back to Human Values? Spiritual and Moral Dimensions of Contemporary Fantasy,* ed. Justina Deszcz-Tryhubczak and Marek Oziewica. Newcastle: Cambridge Scholars Press.

Pratchett, Terry. 1991, 2002. *Witches Abroad.* New York: HarperTorch.

———. 2000. Imaginary Worlds, Real Stories. *Folklore* 111: 159–168.

———. 2003. *Wee Free Men.* New York: Harper Trophy.

———. 2004. *A Hat Full of Sky.* New York: Harper Trophy.

———. 2006. *Wintersmith.* New York: Harper Tempest.

———. 2010. *I Shall Wear Midnight.* New York: HarperCollins Children's Books.

Pullman, Philip. 1995. *The Golden Compass.* New York: Knopf.

———. 2000. *The Amber Spyglass.* New York: Knopf.

Resnick, Daniel P., and Lauren B. Resnick. 1989. Varieties of Literacy. In *Social History and Issues in Human Consciousness: Some Interdisciplinary Connections,* ed. Andrew E. Barnes and Peter N. Stearns, 171–196. New York: New York University Press.

Schlitz, Laura Amy. 2015. *The Hired Girl.* Somerville, MA: Candlewick.

Schneiders, Sandra M. 1993. The Bible and Feminism. In *Freeing Theology: The Essentials of Theology in Feminist Perspective,* ed. Catherine Mowry LaCugna, 31–57. San Francisco: Harper San Francisco.

Taylor, Laini. 2017. *Strange the Dreamer.* New York: Little, Brown.

Trites, Roberta Seelinger. 2000. *Disturbing the Universe: Power and Repression in Adolescent Literature.* Iowa City: University of Iowa Press.

Trousdale, Ann M. 2004. Black and White Fire: The Interplay of Stories, Imagination and Children's Spirituality. *International Journal of Children's Spirituality* 9 (2): 177–188.

Whaley, John Corey. 2011. *Where Things Come Back.* New York: Atheneum.

Wood, Naomi. 2001. Paradise Lost and Found: Obedience, Disobedience, and Storytelling in C. S. Lewis and Philip Pullman. *Children's Literature in Education* 32 (4): 237–259.

Zipes, Jack. 1991. *Spells of Enchantment: The Wondrous Fairy Tales of Western Culture*. New York: Viking.

CHAPTER 6

Reading, Resistance, and Political Agency

My memories of the summer of 1973 are firmly located in two distinct spots: the living room in my grandparents' old house, where a small black and white TV was uncharacteristically on most of the days, fuzzily displaying the Watergate hearings from morning until night, and my grandfather's pine grove, where future Christmas trees created "rooms" with their boughs, hiding me as I lay under them reading.

It's hard for me to associate that reading with the hearings, though I did spend a good bit of time with a collected Mark Twain, one of the few books in that old house that I found entertaining enough to keep me occupied in the hours I spent in those pine groves. Twain's caustic wit and cynical view on American institutions may have been reinforced by the hours of hearings I watched; all I know is that three years later, I was the only kid in my high school class to sport a green "Carter" button during the first presidential election I remember following.

Today's adolescents came to political consciousness in a vastly different environment. My media environment consisted at the time of four television stations (only three reliably received over the air in my grandparents' remote rural home), books that had been on their shelves since my mother's childhood, and a very rare excursion to the movies. (I remember seeing the first "Star Wars" movie in the summer of 1977, for example.) There was a local weekly paper and the daily *New York Times*, which might or might not make it to us on the date of issue. I listened to FM radio on a tiny red transistor and borrowed my

© The Author(s) 2019
E. R. Gruner, *Constructing the Adolescent Reader in Contemporary Young Adult Fiction*, Critical Approaches to Children's Literature,
https://doi.org/10.1057/978-1-137-53924-3_6

brother's LPs when he wasn't looking. Today's teens, of course, interact with innumerable media outlets, consuming and creating text, image, and sound in a dizzying array of formats, the most of important of which are often passé before adults fully acknowledge them. Recently in teaching Angie Thomas's *The Hate U Give*, I called attention to the main character's use of Tumblr to mourn her friend Khalil. My students, just a few years older than Starr, asserted that no one used Tumblr any more and, moreover, found it unlikely that Starr would have a Tumblr to begin with. Whether or not their assessment was fair or accurate, their larger point holds: contemporary teens interact with varieties of media that were unimaginable not even a generation ago, and that date so rapidly as to be almost obsolete before they catch up to their parents. As has been said many times before, this makes it hard to assume a common culture or set of references—but it even makes it hard to assume a common set of textual or literacy practices. And where my coming to political consciousness aligned with conventional mainstream political activity—supporting a candidate and, in time, voting—in the works that I discuss below, civic agency looks as different as the textual practices that surround it. A deep distrust of the institutions of government—one that may have its roots in those long-ago hearing rooms, but that has certainly accelerated in recent years—plays out in the novels I discuss in a variety of ways. Civic agency, then, may mean resisting an oppressive government, or harboring a fugitive; it may mean learning one's political history and acting on it, or refusing to conform to the status quo. It is also, at least as I see it, a function of a particular kind of literacy—indeed, Maryanne Wolf has argued that without what I am calling deep reading—"try[ing] on views that differ from one's own," and using our "analytical and reflective capacities"—"we will fail as a society" (Wolf 2018, 200–201).[1]

In the first two years of the new millennium, two events occurred that went on to shape the lives of most American children and young adults: the attacks on the World Trade Center and the signing of the No Child Left Behind bill. The first ushered in the "war on terror," which, as I write, continues unabated. The second recognized and firmly reinforced the American regime of educational testing and data collection.

---

[1] Wolf's argument, articulated in *Reader, Come Home*, is perhaps only the latest in a series of arguments and assertions linking reading and democratic practice. I work through several others in this line of thought below.

The two are connected in surprising ways. Philip Pullman was one of the first to connect the attack on the Towers and the Bush administration's implicit attitude toward education, particularly reading:

> One of the most extraordinary scenes I've ever watched ... occurs in the famous videotape of George W Bush receiving the news of the second strike on the World Trade Centre on 9/11. As the enemies of democracy hurl their aviation-fuel-laden thunderbolt at the second tower, their minds intoxicated by a fundamentalist reading of a religious text, the leader of the free world sits in a classroom reading a story with children. If only he'd been reading Maurice Sendak's *Where the Wild Things Are*, or Arnold Lobel's *Frog and Toad*, or a genuine fairy-tale! That would have been a scene to cheer. It would have illustrated values truly worth fighting to preserve. It would have embodied all the difference between democratic reading and totalitarian reading, between reading that nourishes the heart and the imagination and reading that starves them.

> But no. Thanks among other things to his own government's educational policy, the book Bush was reading was one of the most stupefyingly banal and witless things I've ever had the misfortune to see. *My Pet Goat* ... is a drearily functional piece of rubbish designed only to teach phonics.[2] You couldn't read it for pleasure, or for consolation, or for joy, or for wisdom, or for wonder, or for any other human feeling; it is empty, vapid, sterile. (Pullman 2004)

Pullman's association of the September 11 attacks with reading moves in several different directions. First, he identifies the attackers as bad readers, "intoxicated by a fundamentalist reading of a religious text." As we saw in the previous chapter, YA authors are keenly aware of the danger of fundamentalist or unitary readings, and Pullman similarly recognizes the danger of the authoritarian reading represented by the attackers.[3] But Pullman goes on to identify a second kind of dangerous reading—the "empty, vapid, sterile" book that President Bush reads in the famous clip. *My Pet Goat* stands in here for any kind of reading designed for its conformability to reading protocols: again, it is a single

---

[2] Pullman's use of "functional" here is distinguished from, for example, Resnick and Resnick's use of the term, which focuses on information gleaned from the text rather than the text's value for reading instruction (Resnick and Resnick 1989, 179).

[3] Chimamanda Ngozi Adichie's 2009 TED Talk, "The Danger of a Single Story," similarly focuses on authoritarian readings or unitary interpretations of events.

story, purpose-driven and, as Pullman says, "drearily functional" rather than entertaining, enlightening, or (in a humanistic sense) educational.

Which brings us to the second event. Less than six months later, Bush signed one of the signature pieces of legislation of his early presidency, the educational standards bill known as No Child Left Behind. At the signing ceremony, he made a somewhat remarkable comment. Gesturing toward the box that held the bill, he noted that not only had he not read it, but he did not intend to read it at all. It is of course unsurprising that he had not read the bill; presumably, he had legislative aides to do that. Moreover, the signing took place in January, 2002, when the world was facing a global threat that had, in the words of practically everyone, "changed everything." The NCLB legislation had passed both houses in what now feels like a rare spirit of bipartisanship, the summer before the 9/11 attacks, had gone through the reconciliation process soon after, and was being signed in a joyful ceremony at which these remarks were made. I point out the comment, however, because, as Pullman suggests, there is a historical relationship between the terror attacks that "changed everything" and a certain kind of outcomes-oriented education that precedes those attacks but that certainly gains momentum afterward. Both involve failures of imagination, of interpretation—of, in fact, reading. Bush's blithe confession reveals, I believe, a truth that the law he was signing is designed to obscure: that, contrary to years of educational theory and indeed to the language of the law itself, NCLB actually sought to delink political agency and reading.[4] In the chapter that follows, I will explicate the ways in which reading, in the post-9/11 era, fails to support political agency, and then how they can be reconnected, through multiliteracy, for a more open and democratic future.

Political agency has of course long been associated with reading, but a close examination of that linkage suggests that the connection may require further analysis. Founding father Benjamin Rush put it aphoristically: "Literature and liberty go hand in hand" (Neem 2017, 6).[5] Analysts of

---

[4] It may also suggest that, like *My Pet Goat*, the law is not, in fact, readable. Laws, like some educational reading materials, are understandably designed for "scanning" rather than engagement. Lissa Paul discusses this kind of reading in "The Naked Truth About Being Literate."

[5] Neem quotes Rush's *A Plan for the Establishment of Public Schools*, published in 1786. I mention American political theory explicitly here because the history of public education in the USA is directly associated with the development of citizenship in the early Republic,

empirical data on reading and political participation concur: "time spent reading is a significant predictor of political interest—even when other factors known to affect attention to politics are taken into account. The more time Americans spend reading, the more attentive they are to public affairs" (Bennett et al. 2000, 175). These experts suggest that reading itself makes better citizens. They argue that the link between literacy and political agency is not purely wishful. Reading, reading deeply, and reading carefully are, they claim, essential to democratic practice. Contextualizing the empirical data, Evangelos Intzidis and Eleni Karantzola note (citing Fairclough 1995) that "critical awareness about language and literacy is a prerequisite for effective democratic citizenship and should therefore be seen as an entitlement for citizens" (Intzidis and Karantzola 2008, 12).[6] But recent YA novels linking civic agency and literacy suggest that too often deep literacy is discouraged or simply ignored. Close attention to the texts, like Pullman's reading of the *My Pet Goat* scene, demonstrates that we need to focus on more than simple functional literacy. Both what and how one reads, these novels ultimately suggest, are crucial to the development of political agency. In the novels I discuss in this chapter, literacy is never just one thing. "Literacy" shatters into "literacies," in these novels—which then perhaps recombine into "multiliteracies" as the characters learn to read, in Paulo Freire's words, "the word and the world" around them. At times—perhaps most often—this fails, or develops into only a partial literacy, a reading that is limited only to certain readers, or to certain "texts." But when characters develop truly symbiotic multiliteracies, interacting with each other and their worlds in terms of parity rather than exploitation, they begin to demonstrate a kind of democratic citizenship that looks to the future with hope rather than despair.

Thus, in this chapter, I analyze a series of novels that relate literacy to democratic practice. In recent fantasy novels like Kristin Cashore's *Bitterblue* (2012; the third novel in the Graceling trilogy), Frances Hardinge's *Fly by Night* (2005; the first of two linked novels), and Shannon Hale's *Princess Academy* (2005; the first novel in a trilogy), literacy appears to be the key to an informed citizenship. These novels

making the literacy/citizenship link explicit in ways that are less apparent in nations with a more complex educational and political history. The US context, of course, owes a great deal to European Enlightenment theorists and was not without its own conflicts.

[6] These claims, of course, stand in for many others made over the years. See Introduction.

trace an arc from the suppression of literacy in tyrannical (or at least anti-democratic) regimes to the greater dissemination of literacy, creating (implicitly or explicitly) an informed citizenry. They connect literacy to political agency in a relatively uncomplicated way, building an arc from illiterate powerlessness to literate engagement through the material characters are able to read. The novels' female protagonists develop multiliteracies, moving beyond printed texts in their ability to read and interpret the world around them, and this expanded literacy is key to their political agency. While the novels didactically encourage reading as a means to political agency in their implied readers, however, the novels limit the acquisition of truly empowering multiliteracy to a select few. The demands of genre seem to trump those of democratic citizenship, as multiliteracy remains an elite skill unattainable by the vast majority. Metafictional novels set in a slightly more realistic world are also skeptical about the link between literacy and political empowerment. Thus in Markus Zusak's *The Book Thief* and Kiese Laymon's *Long Division*, literacy may be a path to agency, but it is a path fraught with ambivalence, especially for oppressed and/or minority protagonists. It is no accident that this latter novel involves an African-American protagonist: the history of suppressing the literacy of enslaved people, and of segregated schools and literacy tests, provides the context for its skeptical attitudes toward literacy.[7] Both what and how one reads are crucial components of this skepticism. Yet on the whole this novel is also a depiction of, and argument for, the importance of deep reading to citizenship. We see a similar trajectory in China Miéville's *Un Lun Dun*, though the latter offers both the most playful and the most critical approach to reading of these three texts. Finally in certain contemporary dystopian novels for teens, such as M.T. Anderson's *Feed* and Patrick Ness's *Chaos Walking* trilogy, active citizenship requires not only literacy, but resistance to being read, a form of deep critical literacy that is also aware of the literacies actually creating and controlling the protagonists' lives. These novels require a critical multiliteracy of both their implied readers and their protagonists.[8] They suggest that reading books—satisfying though

---

[7] Chapter 4 takes up race and reading more fully.

[8] Although I connect these novels to NCLB and the testing regime that it arises from and reinforces, only two of the novels treated in this chapter represent testing, even obliquely (*Princess Academy* and *Long Division*). The bill's importance lies in its justifications as much as its effects.

it may be—is not enough to develop young adults into political agents. Rather, they must develop interpretive skills in a variety of media, and do so collaboratively, creating a critical, communal multiliteracy in order to become civic actors.

Democratic (?) Fantasy

Fantasy fiction has often been deployed to conservative, if not reactionary ends, as the alternative worlds proposed so often return to an imagined past in which traditional hierarchies of, especially, gender and race, still hold sway.[9] And yet at the same time, of all genres, fantasy may have the greatest potential for suggesting ways of reshaping or reimagining history, relying as it so often does on an invented world in which new rules, new logics, may apply.[10] *Bitterblue, Princess Academy,* and *Fly by Night* embody this paradox. Each creates a setting that suggests a particular historical period: the medieval period for the high fantasy novels *Bitterblue* and *Princess Academy,* and the eighteenth century for *Fly by Night,* which draws on elements of both high and domestic fantasy. And while the high fantasy worlds of *Bitterblue* and *Princess Academy* have few connections to our own in terms of geography or particular concerns, *Fly by Night* seems directly to reference eighteenth-century London.[11] Yet in practice these settings, rather than reinforcing the values of the past, create a kind of anachronism, in that all three seem to move toward the position that widespread literacy is a path to social change through participatory citizenship, if not democracy. This change is figured as an obvious and unchallenged good (at least for the reader). That is, the novels import the values of the contemporary West to an alternative past. In doing so, however, they create only limited access to

[9] See Megan Isaac, "Re-animating Democracy in the World of Fantasy," 1–2, and Daniel Baker: "In the West, the vast majority of fantasy ... have been reflections, if not products, of conservative politics" (Baker 2012, 438). For an alternative view, see McKinley Valentine's blog post, "Is the Fantasy Genre Fundamentally Conservative?"

[10] Frederic Jameson may be the most relevant critic here—he writes in *The Political Unconscious,* for example, on fantasy's relationship to utopian thinking. See also Baker (2012).

[11] See Coats (2006) for *Fly by Night*; I base my claim about *Bitterblue* and *Princess Academy* primarily on the presence of an absolute monarchy as well as widespread illiteracy.

political agency for their characters: the limits of genre prevent the more liberatory outcomes the novels seem to be working toward.

In *Bitterblue*, the sequel to Kristin Cashore's *Graceling*, literacy is explicitly a means of resistance. In a kingdom until recently ruled by a man (King Leck) who can charm anyone, control their thoughts, and blur their memories, only written words can offer a source of resistance to his power, through the preservation of memory. The new queen Bitterblue, like others of her class, can read, but—as she discovers—the majority of her subjects cannot. Making friends with two city-dwellers as she roams the streets incognito, Bitterblue learns that there is an active resistance to her regime, manifest especially in secret publications and secret lessons in reading. Readers such as the printer Teddy and his friends, the librarian Death, the king's deceased wife Ashen, and Bitterblue herself—the latter two of whom are skilled not only at reading but at ciphering—are the keys to restoring the history that Leck's tyranny has erased.

Bitterblue's literacy encompasses not only print but the codes and ciphers that all the leaders of her realm use to protect their communications. And, even more importantly, it includes the embroidery that her mother sewed during her childhood, embroidery that tells stories through an enciphered system of symbols. Similarly, the wall hangings and statues in Leck's castle are representational rather than fantastic. When Bitterblue learns to "read" the artwork in the same way that she reads embroidery, ciphers, and traditional text, she begins to be able to piece together the history of Leck's tyranny that has been hidden from her and her citizens. Her multiliteracy is key to her increased political agency. The literacy that involves reading art, however, seems to be limited to those of Bitterblue's caste: even as she invites the townspeople to learn to read, some kinds of literacy will remain out of reach.

Nonetheless, as more truths of Leck's tyranny and cruelty are revealed through reading, storytelling, and the clues left in the palace art, Bitterblue considers how to create a more just, if not exactly more democratic, regime. She asks herself, "How will I teach everyone to think things through, and make their own decisions, and become real people again?" (Cashore 2012, 498). Literacy, along with reparations and historical records, turns out to be key to her solution. Indeed, the novel ends by invoking what might even be its own creation: "Bitterblue found a fresh piece of paper and wrote [her] memory down, to capture it, because it was part of her story" (Cashore 2012, 539). But while in context her characterization of her subjects as not yet "real people" may only suggest their illiteracy and inability to engage in political action, her language is telling. Perhaps inadvertently, Cashore here suggests that those who cannot (or perhaps even do not) read are somehow less than human.[12]

Princess Academy and *Fly by Night* are less overt in their association of reading with full humanity. In *Princess Academy*, as in *Bitterblue*, it seems as if literacy will be the means to developing democratic processes. However, both the demands of genre and the contemporary tradition of associating girls with reading[13] may actually simply substitute literacy education for democratizing processes. In *Bitterblue*, as we have seen, reading is directly associated with active citizenship, if not democracy: Bitterblue's people must learn to read in order to know their pasts, and to imagine an alternative future. *Princess Academy*, on the other hand, associates reading with the other skills (such as commerce and quarry speech) that Miri must develop in order to help her own people and to reject her possible future as a princess. At least at first, reading is simply part of the "princess academy," where Miri and the other candidates for princess are being trained in courtly, feminine behavior. Its usefulness is directly related, then, to class and to social assimilation.[14] Unlike the wealthy "lowlanders" of the novel, the people of Miri's territory are clearly working class and largely illiterate. Perfectly able to trade and to quarry, adept at singing, storytelling, and the mysterious quarry language that travels through the stone beneath their feet, they have not found reading necessary. Unlike the people of *Bitterblue*, then, traditional print literacy is not denied them but simply not (yet) relevant: they are literate in a variety of far more useful ways.

[12] In "Bewildering Education," Nathan Snaza notes the ways in which humanity is figured as both origin and telos of education for philosophers and theorists from Plato to the New London Group, Rousseau to Freire. While his focus is on the more capacious "education," context makes it clear that literacy is the largest component of this education.

[13] Although in the medieval period and through to at least the eighteenth century women and girls were far less likely to be literate than men and boys (Fischer 2003, 279), in those places with near-universal literacy late twentieth and early twenty-first century, they are far more associated with reading in general and pleasure reading in particular. See Chapter 3 on gender and reading.

[14] See Eldred and Mortensen's argument regarding "Pygmalion."

The girls of the princess academy, however, must learn to read in order to be eligible to become the prince's bride.[15] And in developing their literacy, they discover its value beyond the court. For Miri, reading is a way to reinforce and expand the knowledge presented in lectures, as when she reads that the linder rock her people quarry is worth far more than the traders have been giving them (Hale 2005, 101–103). But her literacy, like Bitterblue's, is not limited to print. Rather than visual art, as in *Bitterblue*, music supplements Miri's literacy and becomes an integral part of her ability to "read" and communicate in the world. The texts thereby illustrate Paolo Freire's assertion that "Reading does not consist of merely decoding the written word or language; rather, it is preceded by and intertwined with knowledge of the world" (Freire and Macedo 1987, 29). In these texts, "the world" includes artistic expression. Reading first appeals to Miri as a means of "fixing" or recalling stories from an oral tradition. While the content differs vastly, the function of textual reading here is thus not so dissimilar from that in *Bitterblue*: preserving memory. The most important element of Miri's reading, however, is the knowledge she gains from it. She learns not only the elements of courtly behavior that life as a princess would require (lessons she, for the most part, turns out not to need), but, more importantly, the rules of commerce that govern her community. With this knowledge—particularly of the value of the district's primary export, and of the difference between a trading economy and one based on the more symbolic use of money—Miri is able to empower the people of her village and resist the temptations of courtly life, a life in which she would have far less agency than in her home.

In Frances Hardinge's *Fly by Night*, as in *Bitterblue*, teaching reading is the dangerous but necessary means of resisting oppression. The secret schools of the city (the successor to "Ragged Schools," in a clear reference to eighteenth to nineteenth-century England) are a subversive and barely organized educational opportunity.[16] Reading, in the "Fractured Realm," is associated with not only political but also religious opposition—the theocracy that governs the realm prefers its citizens illiterate.

[15]The novel suggests a situation much like the TV reality show "The Bachelor," in which a group of girls is gathered from which one will be chosen as the prince's bride. The show debuted three years before the novel was published.

[16]The novel itself recalls children's primers by ordering the chapters alphabetically and naming them as if in primer fashion: "A is for ...," "B is for...," etc.

As Philip Pullman has noted, "theocracies don't know how to read, and democracies do" (Pullman 2004).[17]

But even though Mosca can read, she can still be deceived, still be manipulated—though, most often, by appearances or glib speakers, not by texts. Thus, for example, the multiple "Lady Tamarinds" she sees at court confuse her—and Lady Tamarind herself manipulates Mosca with her words of reassurance and intrigue (Hardinge 2005, 282–283). Again, as Pullman says, "democracies don't guarantee that real reading will happen. They just make it possible" (Pullman 2004). Yet in these three novels the opposite case is made: "real reading" is necessary for the establishment of more democratic governance. Reading precedes political change in all three—as is, of course, historically accurate as well. The rise of the printing press and mass literacy functioned as precursors to, not results of, increasing participatory democracy.[18]

It is also not enough. In all three texts, reading alone cannot change the political situation, though the more people who know how to read, the greater the resistance. The texts do not, however, romanticize reading or overstate its power—physical resistance is also inevitable. The "battle" at the princess academy is not, of course, against the regime— but it does come about because of the regime's failure to protect the girls at the school. In *Fly by Night*, many deaths precede the uneasy truce that ends the novel. In *Bitterblue*, similarly, many die before Bitterblue discerns the truth and restores a more generous order to her realm. Reading can help restore history after Leck's death, and both Bitterblue's reading of ciphers and Teddy and Saf's printing and teaching prepare the realm for greater participation—but, as in the other novels, not reading alone.

All three novels end with a hope for the future involving literacy. Mosca rejects the opportunity to stay in Mandelion, thinking to herself, "*I don't want a happy ending, I want more story*" (Hardinge 2005,

---

[17]Of course, as we saw in Chapter 5, they often do know how to read—but may eschew interpretation.

[18]Although Eagleton argues that reading's solitary nature militates against collective action (Eagleton 1983, 222), Steven Fischer nonetheless traces the clear route from the wider availability of print texts, and active reading of them, to the political movements that transformed Europe from the Renaissance through the nineteenth century. See also Alberto Manguel's claim that for most literate societies, "reading is at the beginning of the social contract" (Manguel 1996, 7).

482–483, emphasis in original). Miri, after returning to her village, will both go to the capital to "read all the books in the palace library" and "open an academy in the village where anyone can come learn" (Hale 2005, 311). Bitterblue imagines a "library where stories were kept" as part of her "Ministry of Stories and Truth" (Cashore 2012, 537–538), and the novel ends with Death, the librarian, giving her a note about his work. This note catalyzes her own memory of her escape from Leck, which she writes down, "to capture it, because it was part of her story" (Cashore 2012, 539). None of them, however, ends with the suggestion that the realm will be politically transformed. As Megan Isaac has noted, this may—at least in part—be a restriction of genre: high fantasy is so indebted to the "romance-quest pattern," which is itself a product of both monarchy and patriarchy, that full democracy is unlikely even (or perhaps especially) in an otherwise feminist novel.[19] But it may also be a result of an attention to transactional literacy rather than deep reading: the protagonists of these novels learn true things from reading, but those "true" things are rarely interrogated.[20] While the protagonists of these novels must become multiliterate, then, their reading and interpretation remain largely informational. While uncovering historical truth is the first step toward healing trauma—and all of these novels involve historical trauma—it is not enough. In more metafictional novels, we see the play with interpretation that may provoke a deeper reading and a clearer path to civic agency.

Breaking Frames: Metafiction and Civic Agency

Martin Zusak's *The Book Thief* has no debts to pay to high fantasy, and books are highly valued within its storyline. Indeed, in the novel books are tightly controlled and even burned, thus making reading, it seems, an obvious means of resistance. Because the Nazi regime prescribes only one book—*Mein Kampf*—as essential reading, rereading and revising themselves become at least nominally oppositional. For example, Max rewrites *Mein Kampf* as "The Standover Man," using the obliterated pages of Hitler's text as his own paper. But Liesel's theft of books—from her brother's gravesite, a book-burning, and the mayor—is also depicted

---

[19] See Isaac (2016, 1 and 8, especially).

[20] See also the discussion of reading in the Harry Potter series in the introduction.

as a kind of resistance. And her reading of the stolen texts offers solace to her neighbors huddling in bomb shelters, allowing them to return to their homes refreshed and restored.

Liesel's reading in *The Book Thief* begins as resistance simply to the fact of her brother's death. When she picks up *The Grave Digger's Handbook*, she can't even read it—the book is a talisman. Its meaning is twofold: "1. The last time she saw her brother./2. The last time she saw her mother" (Zusak 2005, 38). The contents of the book are opaque to her until later, when her foster father Hans Hubermann reads it to her. Other books that she steals also mean, mostly, love, because Hans reads them to her as well. They also mean guilt because they are acquired by theft.

But for all *The Book Thief* represents and endorses literacy, the content of the books Liesel reads and steals does not, initially, seem to matter. She is entranced by books, overcome with wonder when she first visits the library in the mayor's wife's house:

> Each wall was armed with overcrowded yet immaculate shelving. It was barely possible to see the paintwork. There were all different styles and sizes of lettering on the spines of the black, the red, the gray, the every-colored book. It was one of the most beautiful things Liesel Meminger had ever seen. (Zusak 2005, 134)

At first, Liesel does not even ask to read one of the books in the library; she merely gazes upon them. And even when, on returning, she begins to read some of them, the narrator, Death,[21] notes that "Later on, as an adolescent, when Liesel wrote about these books, she no longer remembered their titles" (Zusak 2005, 145). The books do have a metaphorical significance to Liesel's own story. After obtaining *The Grave Digger's Handbook*, she receives two books from her foster father, both seemingly children's books: *Faust the Dog* is written by "a man named Mattheus Ottleberg" and has pictures; *The Lighthouse* is longer than *Faust the Dog* and written by a woman (Zusak 2005, 88–89). The effort to protect her childhood through her reading vanishes quickly, however,

---

[21] The genre of *The Book Thief* is hard to determine. In many ways a straightforward historical novel, it is narrated by Death, whose occasional intrusions into the text make it seem more like a work of magical realism. I have settled on "metafiction," following Joe Sutliff Sanders, whose work on Miéville and Zusak I have found immensely helpful.

if it was not always already doomed. She begins to read *The Whistler* at the mayor's house and later receives it as a gift from the mayor's wife; after Liesel angrily returns it, Rudy pulls it from the river, and its suspenseful depiction of horrors far removed from their own seems to become a source of comfort when she reads it to her neighbors, huddled in an air-raid shelter (see esp. Zusak 2005, 213 and 323–324). *The Mud Men*, another gift, is "about a very strange father and son" (Zusak 2005, 222). *The Dream Carrier, A Song in the Dark, The Complete Duden Dictionary and Thesaurus*—their titles, taken together, begin to tell Liesel's story metaphorically. Combined with *Mein Kampf, The Standover Man, The Word-Shaker*, and Liesel's memoir, *The Book Thief* itself, these titles indicate Liesel's concerns and her development over the course of the novel. From *The Grave Digger's Handbook* to *The Shoulder Shrug, The Whistler* to *The Dream Carrier* to *The Last Human Stranger*, the books Liesel steals suggest her concerns, her conflicts, her life story.[22]

The books that Max writes for Liesel are a little more complex in their associations and meanings than the books she steals or is given by her foster father. *The Standover Man* is another act of resistance, written palimpsestically on the painted-over pages of *Mein Kampf*. The book that signifies his own oppression had held the key to the Hubermanns' house, thus already undoing its own central meaning. Similarly, *The Word-Shaker*, remade into its own parody, tells a story of opposition to the Hitler regime, suggesting that Liesel herself ("the Word-Shaker") is an agent of resistance through her reading and writing. Yet overall, Liesel—although she does indeed become a reader and a writer—is never depicted as an activist or a true political agent in the novel, despite her efforts to hide Max (in imitation of her foster father) and her thievery of books.

Joe Sutliff Sanders has argued that the brand of metafiction practiced in *The Book Thief* has "the potential to unsettle the reader and provoke the reader into an active role, but even as it prods, it provides a comfortable authority in whose wisdom the reader is told to rest," and the preceding claims about the specific uses of the books within the fiction would seem to confirm this (Sanders 2009a, 350–351). Yet, while this is

---

[22] Liesel's books (other than *Mein Kampf, The Complete Duden Dictionary and Thesaurus*, and, perhaps, *The Book Thief*) do not exist in the world of the reader, though a quick Google search suggests that young readers—and, no doubt, others—need to verify this.

arguably the case for Liesel, the implied reader must probe more deeply into her books to make meaning out of them—meaning that is both difficult to discern and, at times, profoundly discomfiting. *The Whistler*, a story about a serial-killer, becomes a bizarre form of comfort reading for Liesel's neighbors. While Hans Hubermann is shocked by the content of the book, its comfort may derive from the allegorical depiction of the madman who controls their lives. Or, it may simply provide the listeners escapist entertainment. Again, the implied reader must grapple with the meaning of the book in ways that the characters almost never do.

Most importantly, the idea that one could paint over *Mein Kampf* and thereby diminish its power, as is suggested by Max's writing in *The Standover Man* and, especially, *The Word-Shaker*, offers a comfort that the action of the book belies. No amount of rewriting can diminish the horror of the Nazi regime. The implied reader is expected to accept within the fiction not only what *cannot* be true in the world of fact (which is, after all, a characteristic of magical realism and fantasy), but, in a novel that makes no claims to alternate history, what *was* not true in the world of the past. In other words, although the book does not depict critical reading, it demands it of its implied reader. And the political agency that literacy seems to provide Liesel is a mirage.

Kiese Laymon's *Long Division*—like *The Book Thief*, a metafictional novel with a strong commitment to history—asserts the importance of both transactional and deep reading throughout.[23] Yet both within the text and for the implied reader, reading is difficult, at times distancing, and always discomfiting. Laymon has written that he "wanted to question traditional literary fictive trajectories by writing to folks (or sensibilities) who don't read for a living" (Laymon 2013a, loc. 51), and the action of the book affirms this goal. The main character of *Long Division*, ninth-grader Citoyen (City) Coldson, says of himself that "I'm known as the best boy writer in the history of the school" (Laymon 2013b, 8). In the tradition of that earlier YA classic, *The Outsiders*, as well as *The Book Thief*, at least one version of the novel we read is purportedly the writing of the protagonist—but City himself, like Laymon's intended audience, is not much of a reader. He later admits: "I can't even lie, though. I probably only finished two books in my whole life" (Laymon 2013b, 174). His uncle Relle puts the failure to read in

---

[23] See Chapter 4 for more on *Long Division*.

context: "Fuck a book. Ain't no one reading no books in 2013 unless you already a star or talking about some damn vampires and wolfmen" (Laymon 2013b, 100).

Amie E. Doughty has argued that children in fantasy literature must reject or move beyond books because they represent adult authority.[24] As we've already seen, this does not hold true even for all fantasy texts, and it is certainly too simplistic for metafictions like *Long Division*, despite its protagonist's claims about his own reading. When we first meet him, City does indeed reject reading. However, he receives his copy of *Long Division*, the book within the book that threads through the plot of the novel, from his school principal. She gives it to him with the warning that "some books can completely change how we see ourselves and everything else in the world. Keep your eyes on the prize" (Laymon 2013b, 19). It may come from adult authority, then, but this particular book becomes a symbol of empowerment and, quite literally, self-authoring.

At first, the book's value seems to be primarily content-based: City finds himself, or someone just like him, in the book. And reading *Long Division* does indeed change everyone, just as Principal Reeves had warned. The book thus becomes not only a talisman (though it does seem to be that) but also a book that seems to compel reading. The book's lack of an author, somewhat mysterious title, and close relationship to the events in the main characters' lives keep them all engaged. So, too, does its ability to give voice to their emotions:

> There was something wrong with *Long Division*, the book I'd borrowed from Principal Reeves's office. Even though the book was set in 1985, I didn't know what to do with the fact that the narrator was black like me, stout like me, in the ninth grade like me, and had the same first name as me. Plus, you hardly ever read books that were written like you actually thought. I had never read the words 'chunky vomit' in the first chapter of a book, for example, but when I thought about how I'd most want not to be treated, I thought about 'chunky vomit.' (Laymon 2013b, 29)

In Laymon's essay "How to Slowly Kill Yourself and Others in America," he describes *Long Division* as "about four kids from Mississippi who time-travel through a hole in the ground. The kids think time-travel is

---

[24]See Doughty (2013) (1–8) for a précis of argument.

the only way to make their state and their nation love itself and the kids coming after them" (Laymon 2013a, loc. 727). Laymon's focus here is on the kids' political agency, developed through empathy. Their insistence that they may indeed be able to "make their state and their nation love itself" is central to all three narratives, from 2013, 1985, and 1964, and to their efforts to read and write their way into and out of the stories they find themselves in.[25] How they read becomes almost as important as what they read: they begin to participate in the story and—especially—to write back to it.

One way City himself is first brought into his own text is—perhaps ironically, given his antipathy to reading—a quiz that he reads more than once. Principal Reeves asks 2013 City to complete a quiz as a punishment, and he later finds it on the desk at the Lerthon Coldson Civil Rights Museum. This quiz is key to how to read *Long Division* and what YA reading can provide for a reader like City. In eleven true/false questions, the quiz links reading and agency through both empathy and rereading: through the actual practice of reading, in other words, rather than the content or form of the text. Although the entire sequence of questions suggests the connection among empathy, citizenship, and reading, three of them are particularly germane:

3. You were brought to this country with the expectation of life, liberty, and the pursuit of happiness.
   True/<u>False</u>
6. Only those who can read, write, and love can move back or forward through time.
   <u>True</u>/False
8. If you haven't read or written or listened to something at least three times, you have never really read, written, or listened.
   <u>True</u>/False (Laymon 2013b, 256–257; City finds the quiz with the answers already marked).

---

[25] Laymon's novel owes a debt to Octavia Butler's *Kindred* (1979), a time-travel novel that takes a contemporary African-American woman back in time to the first part of the nineteenth century. Kenneth Kidd, following Kate Capshaw Smith, cites *Kindred* as one of a handful of important African-American novels that use time-travel to confront historical trauma (Kidd 2005, 133).

The text reinforces City's answers to these quiz questions (underlined above, as in the text). Throughout the novel, City and his friends are repeatedly reminded of their second-class status. The segregated water fountains of 1964 and the failure of post-Katrina reconstruction to reach Melahatchie, Mississippi, are only two among many reminders of their exclusion from the language of the Declaration of Independence. But City and his friends, in all three time periods, are motivated first of all by love—a love that forms the beginning of political agency. This love—or empathy—derives at least in part from City's experience of "finding himself" in *Long Division*. The surprise of finding his emotions expressed in language becomes the empathy of recognizing that he is not alone—which enables him to connect to those he formerly rejected, such as Evan Altshuler and LaVander Peeler. In 2013, City loves Shalaya Crump and—ultimately—LaVander Peeler and searches for the lost Baize Shephard as well. In 1985, he begins to think he might love Baize, and in 1964, he tries to save his grandfather from the Klan and realizes the meaning of the love he has for both Shalaya and Baize. As he says to LaVander Peeler in 2013, "It's the most real book ever, man. For real, it's about tomorrow and yesterday and the magic of love. I'm serious. A version of me is in the book and Baize Shephard is in there, too. You might be in there, too. I haven't finished it so I don't know" (Laymon 2013b, 199). And, indeed, LaVander is there as well: the novel ends after City has told LaVander he loves him, and the two boys sit together in the time-travel hole, reading *Long Division* together and writing a new conclusion. As City and the others read and reread various versions of *Long Division* throughout the novel, they time-travel both through its language and through the "hole in the ground." The hole seems both a metaphor for the Underground Railroad and, perhaps, for the solitariness of reading—a solitariness that LaVander and City overcome at the end, reading the novel together and writing its new, perhaps more hopeful, ending.

As both the implied reader and the various versions of City move through this recursive novel, readers are forced into readings and rereadings that are reminders of things they may have known, or dimly remembered. It is through these readings and rereadings that City moves from being a character in someone else's script—the figure in someone else's YouTube video—to a person with agency, reading and writing his way into his own recursive and complicated story. In the course of *Long Division*, City learns about his (various) times and selves through "reading" MTV, reading and rereading this quiz, Baize's raps that he finds on her computer, and other non-book texts, as well as the book itself. He also begins to listen to his grandmother's stories and to write his own down.

His activities correlate with those recognized in a 2010 Scholastic survey: teens queried in it were far more likely than their parents to recognize their engagement with alternative media as reading, including "looking for and finding information online" (54% of teens; 51% of parents); "looking through postings or comments on social networking sites like Facebook" (28% of teens; 15% of parents); and "texting back and forth with friends" (25% of teens; 8% of parents) (Scholastic 2010, 13). While the survey does not ask about all of the kinds of engagement depicted in the novel, it clearly demonstrates that reading is changing, and the novel both depicts and is part of that change.[26] Simply reading a book is not enough for City or for his companion and implied readers; they are reading, writing, and creating a variety of kinds of texts, all of which require interpretation.

The blank pages at the end of the different versions of *Long Division* depicted within the text suggest that the characters themselves must finish their story and must write their own endings. Rereading the novel, and rewriting it, as both versions of City do, allows the characters and the readers to "identify and clarify multiple points of view," construct knowledge, and fill in gaps, as Vicki Jacobs suggests the adolescent reader must learn to do (Jacobs 2008, 14 and 15). This kind of reading literally helps them develop their agency—to "make their state and their nation love itself and the kids coming after them." As 2013 City recognizes his love for LaVander—and 1985 City recognizes his for both his girlfriend/wife Shalaya and his daughter Baize—the novel ends, ambiguously but hopefully, going underground yet again.

Un Lun Dun is perhaps the most pointedly focused on political agency of these three texts. It is, after all, a novel in which the secret weapon is an Act of Parliament (the "Clinneract," or Clean Air Act), and in which accomplishing the quest requires learning recent political

---

[26]Although the Scholastic Corporation publishes their "Kids and Family Reading Report" biennially, these questions have not recurred since 2010. The International Reading Association's (2012) Position statement defines adolescent literacy as "the ability to read, write, understand and interpret, and discuss, multiple texts across multiple contexts" (2).

history. Joe Sutliff Sanders has argued that Miéville's only novel for young adults requires a more critical reading than does *The Book Thief*, and this requirement does indeed seem to correlate with a particular kind of political agency[27]: Deeba is able to effect a kind of change that is only suggested in the other novels discussed in this section. While all three encourage their implied readers to read critically, *Un Lun Dun* is the most successful at depicting the activity.

All of UnLondon is made of words—the city is defined by what it isn't (London) but also grown from language in unexpected ways. Like a post-structuralist fever dream, the novel depicts the ways that language begets language, as when Mr. Speaker's and Deeba's utterances become the "Utterlings." When the Utterlings revolt, it is because Deeba reminds Mr. Speaker—and the novel's implied readers—that "words don't always mean what we want them to" (Miéville 2007, 245). Her insight—that no two people hear the same words, interpret them the same way—translates into a rebellion among the words that Mr. Speaker has spoken into being, and some of them join Deeba and her comrades.

But words—trustworthy or not—are the stuff of UnLondon in more ways than one. From the "battlements of books" behind which Unstible sits in the prologue, to the suit of stories that Obaday Fing wears, from the puns that reveal hidden truths to the path into UnLondon through a mountain of books, the novel reveals the open secret of all fictions: that they are all made of words. Fing's suits include one made of *Moby Dick*, which he can never get to fit properly, and another made of *The Other Side of the Mountain*, which works better. The shift from "adult," philosophical literature to a children's adventure novel seems appropriate, as *Un Lun Dun* shares qualities of both (Miéville 2007, 42). Unstible's "piles of books like battlements" appear in the prologue, but fail to protect him (Miéville 2007, xiii). One of many "true" puns is "Webminster Abbey," literally built of spiderwebs (Miéville 2007, 278), while the route to UnLondon through bookstacks is predicted

---

[27] Sanders claims, for example, that "literature that encourages children to think for themselves and argue with authority comes to be identified as leftist" (Sanders 2009b, 295), and that *Un Lun Dun*, in particular, "reveals a model for children's metafiction that, whatever its limited potential for subversion, encourages critical reading" (Sanders 2009a, 355).

(unexpectedly accurately) by the page of the Book[28] that Fing fashions into a glove: "ENTER BY BOOKSTEPS ON STORYLADDERS" (Miéville 2007, 133).

The novel also provides the implied reader the comfort of recognizing a familiar genre and the thrill of undoing it. The Book explains that the Shwazzy's (Choisi's) role "was a sort of standard Chosen One deal. Seven tasks, and with each one she'd collect one of UnLondon's ancient treasures. Finally, she'd get the most powerful weapon in all the abcity—as powerful as the Klinneract...the UnGun" (Miéville 2007, 229). Deeba, who appears in the Book's index only as "the *funny sidekick*" (Miéville 2007, 228, emphasis in original), is able to circumvent the prophecy precisely because she is not the Chosen One.

Justyna Deszcz-Tryhubczak, like Joe Sutliff Sanders, has written convincingly of the radical potential[29] of *Un Lun Dun*, a potential that is most clearly figured through Deeba's critical literacy. Deeba explicitly rejects both the "sidekick" status that a conventional fantasy would assign to her, and—perhaps more importantly—the inerrancy of the Book, a prophetic text that speaks to the people of UnLondon with gnomic authority. Her ability to recognize the "Clinneract" as the "Clean Air Act," moreover, teaches her and the other UnLondoners that an Act of Parliament may be a weapon as powerful as a gun.

But critical reading, as *Un Lun Dun* presents it, requires more than simple questioning of the text. While the Book is wrong about most things—or, perhaps better, only partially right—Deeba is the only person who also recognizes when it actually is right, when the seeming typo is in fact accurate. The Book recounts the prophecy: "The Smog's afraid of nothing but the UnGun" (Miéville 2007, 274). Almost immediately, however, it revises the claim: "Well to be honest it actually says

---

[28] To prevent confusion between the novel *Un Lun Dun* and the prophetic Book within it, the latter is always capitalized here, as in the previous chapter.

[29] Deszcz-Tryhubczak claims that "in radical fantasy for young audiences, juvenile characters participate in abolishing the existing power structures and contribute to the formation of new networks of social and political relations. These revisionary practices occur in the context of the young protagonists' inner maturation, a typical interest in texts for children, but do not culminate in the integration of young people into the power structure of a given society. Rather, young characters consciously participate in collective efforts to overcome oppression" (Deszcz-Tryhubczak 2013, 141). These fantasies, then, are distinguished from the YA literature Trites analyzes by failing to depict the protagonists' reintegration into the status quo.

'nothing *and* the UnGun,' but we realized that must be a misprint" (Miéville 2007, 274, emphasis in original). At the moment, the Book's acknowledgment that there are misprints—or at least one misprint—in its pages serves only to validate Deeba's rejection of its prophetic status. But in the climactic encounter with the Smog, she realizes that the words are not a misprint: the Smog is afraid of "*Nothing* and *the UnGun*" (Miéville 2007, 408, emphasis in original). This rereading mirrors those she has done earlier, reversing and reflecting her earlier tendencies. Deeba's reading is both critical and deep: she returns repeatedly to the same language, considering multiple possibilities as interpretations shift in light of new information. Her empathy—in this case for the Book, despondent over its failed prophecies—also becomes central to her ability to read more deeply and fully.

Within the text of *Un Lun Dun*, the characters reject the quest fantasy genre, shifting the sidekick into hero mode, short-circuiting the series of heroic tasks, and rejecting the prophetic text. Yet the novel nonetheless participates in the genre by having its protagonist—Deeba, not Zanna—fulfill the quest and defeat the villain. Just as the Book both is and isn't truly prophetic, *Un Lun Dun* both is and isn't a quest fantasy. Holding these two opposed truths in their heads, characters and implied readers alike must read critically. Thus, the kind of political agency Deeba models is, at least implicitly, also available to the critical teen reader—or, perhaps better, readers.

Dystopian Futures

While all of the novels so far discussed clearly promote literacy, books, these books paradoxically demonstrate, are not the only or perhaps even the best sites of literacy today; teens in these novels challenge their status as non-citizens, or non-agents, in part by challenging the status of the book—and then reclaiming it along with other forms of reading for a new audience of readers.

Recent dystopian fiction for teens, far more than the novels so far discussed, suggests that reading books is not enough to form citizens. Indeed, reading itself operates in mutually exclusive ways, to help develop political agency and to diminish it, depending on who is reading, what they are reading, and how they are putting their reading to use. In the global war on terrorism, individual political agency is reduced as the government participates in a larger effort to reduce people to data. The two signature acts of the Bush administration, No Child Left Behind (passed in the summer of 2001 and signed into law in January 2002) and the Patriot Act (passed in the immediate aftermath of the September 11 attacks), share little else but a deep concern with data: with the collection, above all else, of vast amounts of data about American and, in the case of the Patriot Act, world citizens. This data must be read, and it is here that contemporary dystopian fiction intervenes, with deep concerns about literacy. While NCLB pays lip service to the importance of reading, the kinds of critical literacy that would contextualize that reading or, when necessary, enable resistance to being read (by corporations, by government data miners, by terrorists) are in fact not at the forefront of our current or projected educational systems. M.T. Anderson's *Feed* (2002) and Patrick Ness's *Chaos Walking* trilogy (2006–2008) depict worst-case scenarios of both universal data mining and functional illiteracy; only the development of new, multi-modal literacies can enable resistance to the oppressive state control that these novels envision.

One of the first things that happened in the USA after the 2001 terror attacks was, of course, the collection, sifting, and reading of information: as the government looked for signs to see what it could or should have known before the attacks, it also tried to render them legible. The USA Patriot and, later, USA Freedom Acts, which hand over to the government the "feeds" of information about US citizens that are their digital footprints, are one attempt to develop such legibility. The rationale, as most Americans remember, for the passage of such wide-ranging acts, was that "everything had changed." As Naomi Klein reminds us in *Shock Doctrine*, however, that mantra was used to ease the passage of numerous laws and doctrines that had their ideological roots in a pre-attack context. Most notably, the phrase was used to advance a host of "public-private partnerships in local infrastructure, social welfare services, and, of course, education" (Smith 2011, 159, citing Klein 2007, 289; see Klein 2007, "Introduction"). NCLB had been passed before the attacks (though not signed into law) but it became part of the regime of surveillance and legibility that increased afterward, just as Klein argues.

As Sara Schwebel notes, *Feed* is one of the earliest post-9/11 novels and in many ways still one of the most prescient, recognizing as it does the US status as both victim and perpetrator of political violence (see Schwebel 2014, 197). Anderson in fact began the novel before the 9/11 attacks and finished it afterward, and while it makes no direct reference to the attacks, it nonetheless clearly takes place in a world much like ours where terror attacks[30] and counter-terrorism have become a way of life, and where—as Schwebel notes—consumption has become most Americans' drug of choice for forgetting the aggression with which the nation is endlessly involved (Schwebel 2014, 206). At the same time, however, the novel had its genesis in a request for a story about literacy and reading (Anderson 2002, "A Conversation with M.T. Anderson," n.p.), and its main character Titus's inability to read and write is a central facet of his identity. So at its core, the novel is concerned with these two things: terrorism and reading.

Like many other writers, Anderson expressed a sense of the futility of writing in the immediate aftermath of the attacks, writing later that, "For several months afterward, I didn't do any writing, because it felt to me that writing was a silly thing to do when there was so much strife going on all around me" (Anderson 2008, 2–3). Many writers expressed similar anxieties in the immediate aftermath of the attacks. As Patrick Gray notes in *After the Fall: American Literature Since 9/11*, the terror attacks of that day seemed to suggest "that language itself [had] been invalidated, that the currency of the writer's trade [was] counterfeit and worthless … 'Nothing to say' became a refrain, a recurrent theme with writers, as they struggled to cope with something that seemed to be, quite literally, beyond words" (Gray 2011, 15). While Anderson of course did go on to finish the novel, he did so in a vernacular that calls into question the value of language, a debased and broken language that nonetheless paradoxically conveys both the necessity of literacy and its inevitable limits. While *Un Lun Dun* reminds readers that fictions are made of words, *Feed* represents the failure of a debased language to create anything of value.

Something similar can be said of Patrick Ness's *Chaos Walking* trilogy, published in three installments from 2008 to 2010. Set, like *Feed*, in a dystopian future, *Chaos Walking* focuses on war, terrorism, and colonialism, raising questions about humans' failed stewardship of the earth and every other place they have so far explored. The illiteracy of

---

[30]One important revision Anderson made after 9/11/2001 was to change the "terrorist" of his early draft to the "hacker" of the published novel. Another was to delete references to "unexplained violence in the Middle East" (Schwebel 2014, 205).

the main character, Todd, becomes a key issue in his ability to discern his position in relation to the various players. Like Titus, Todd is easily manipulated by voices in his head—in this case not from a consumerist feed but from a world in which such voices are, in part, the voices of the planet. As with Titus's feed, Todd's voices seem to make traditional print literacy obsolete or invalid. Thus like Titus, Todd cannot read—or cannot read well—and this inability makes him both more manipulable than more literate characters and, perhaps, more cautious.

But the novels do not posit a simple one-to-one relationship between literacy and resistance to oppression, however comfortable it might be to endorse such a relationship. Both Titus and Todd have companions—the similarly named Violet and Viola—who are literate, yet their resistance is no more effective than Titus and Todd's. This opposition is not terribly surprising: much of the contemporary public discourse about adolescent literacy in particular suggests that boys less likely than girls to develop into fluent, skilled readers.[31] Yet despite Violet and Viola's superior literacy skills, their outsider status in the societies they are navigating hampers them, rendering them at times, and in different ways, no more effective at resistance than Titus and Todd. Critical literacy must go beyond print, requiring a deep familiarity with all the ways in which not only information but entertainment, pleasure, consumption—finally, all of culture—is conveyed in a given society (see, e.g., Graff 2001). All four adolescents need to become critically and multiply literate in order to identify and resist the systems that oppress them. For Titus and Violet, resistance to the Feed and the oppressive consumer society it serves is finally futile, though their example may inspire their implied readers. For Todd and Viola, learning to use the Noise as the planet's indigenous people, known as the Land or as Spacks, do, provides greater hope for resistance to oppression. In both cases, however, the main characters must first learn to read the systems within which they are operating—systems which, as we shall see, are also always reading them. Their status as legible texts must direct their own reading.

---

[31] See Chapter 3 for more on gender and reading. See also, for example, Smith and Wilhelm (2002); but see Barrs (2000), Hateley (2012), and others for counter arguments and examples.

When President Bush signed No Child Left Behind into law, he explicitly linked its reading standards with the war on terror, saying:

> We've got large challenges here in America. There's no greater challenge than to make sure that every child—and all of us on this stage mean every child, not just a few children—(applause)—every single child, regardless of where they live, how they're raised, the income level of their family, every child receive a first-class education in America. (Applause)

> And as you know, we've got another challenge, and that's to protect America from evil ones. And I want to assure the seniors and juniors and sophomores here at Hamilton High School that the effort that this great country is engaged in, the effort to defend freedom and to defend our people, the effort to rout out terror wherever it exists, is noble and just and right, and your great country will prevail in this effort. (Applause) (Bush 2002)

He went on to note that "too many of our kids can't read. You know, a huge percentage of children in poverty can't read at grade level. That's not right in America. We're going to win the war overseas, and we need to win the war against illiteracy here at home, as well. And so this bill … this bill focuses on reading" (Bush 2002). The connection between fighting illiteracy and fighting terror was, of course, politically expedient: in January of 2002, the USA had been at war in Afghanistan for three months and the president was already trying to marshal support for an attack on Iraq, which would come only two months later. The language in his speech is striking as well for what it doesn't do, however: there is no effort at all to tie reading to peace or education to freedom. Rather, they are simply juxtaposed in his remarks, as if by associating one with the other, all will magically become parts of the same whole.

And they did. NCLB and the USA Patriot Act became the signature bipartisan legislative efforts of the Bush administration, as well as, arguably, the two most controversial pieces of legislation. Both of them morphed into new legislation (the Common Core standards and the USA Freedom Act) in the Obama administration. What they have in common is both rendering their citizens legible in new ways to data gatherers, policy-makers, and (not incidentally), large corporate interests, and requiring them therefore to develop ever more sophisticated reading techniques of their own.

In Anderson's world of the feed, traditional text reading has, as I've already noted, been rendered obsolete—or at least so it seems. The feed, originally conceived of as an educational tool, provides information instantaneously: "*encyclopedias at their fingertips, closer than their fingertips*" (Anderson 2002, 47). Fiction is also supplied through the feed in "feedcasts" such as "*Oh? Wow! Thing!*" which, as Titus explains, "has all these kids like us who do stuff but get all pouty, which is what the girls go crazy for, the poutiness" (Anderson 2002, 48). Games, films, music, news, and shopping all travel through the feed in one nearly undifferentiated stream. Titus and his friends are nearly passive recipients of the feed, uncritical and hardly able to differentiate the various streams that reach them. Violet, who received her feed later than most people do—at age 7 rather than at birth—and who is homeschooled by her professor father, is both able to read and a critical consumer of the feed; while these two are not necessarily causally linked, their coincidence does seem to suggest that her ability to read traditional print material improves her ability to analyze and ultimately to resist the consumerist feed as well.

Like Titus, Todd Hewitt of the *Chaos Walking* trilogy lives in a world where reading has been rendered obsolete—or so it at first seems. Todd lives in New World, an earth-like planet with one important difference: men (and animals) broadcast their thoughts at all times, in what the men call The Noise. This "Noise," though it seems to occur naturally, has strange affinities with the Feed—it enters the mind unbidden, and it conveys both unfiltered and directed information. At first we, like Todd, see it only as a confusing chaos of words and voices and pictures that Todd experiences as a nightmare, "like a flood let loose right at me, like a fire, like a monster the size of the sky come to get you cuz there's nowhere to run" (Ness 2008, 20). Titus's feed, too, seems like a flood, even if he experiences it as a benevolent one: "It came down on us like water. It came down like frickin' spring rains, and we were dancing in it" (Anderson 2002, 70).

Neither the Feed nor the Noise is simply a neutral presence that obviates traditional reading, however. Rather, reading has been rendered obsolete or undesirable by an oppressive regime that has then substituted—or simply denied—another form of information delivery and entertainment. This is most clear in *The Knife of Never Letting Go*:

> Before I was born, boys were taught by their ma at home and then when there were only boys and men left, we just got sat down in front of vids and learning modules till Mayor Prentiss outlawed such things as 'detrimental to the discipline of our minds' ... And then one day Mayor Prentiss decided to burn all the books, every single one of them, even the ones in men's homes, cuz apparently books were detrimental as well. (Ness 2008, 18)[32]

Later, we learn how even the seemingly unmediated Noise can in fact be controlled and manipulated by those in power, much like the Feed. Both, needless to say, seem to obviate reading. Student data, citizen data, and consumer data all become part of the noise from which various data miners are seeking various signals. While reading seems unnecessary to Titus and his friends, then, it is clear that those who control the interpretation of data—those who can and do read—actually control lives, such as Violet's. Titus fails to read Violet's stories, and the data miners reject them, but Anderson's novel presents them—and Titus's broken stories, the failed vernacular of a dying planet—for an implied readership that can still, perhaps, learn from their mistakes.

Thus, *Feed* suggests the dangers of being illiterate in a world where one is always being read. Political engagement is a joke: news of political protests comes sandwiched between sitcoms and ads and the President is an incoherent boob (Anderson 2002, 71, 85, and 119). Resistance is not only futile but, in the case of both the hacker and Violet, fatal. Ness's trilogy suggests a way out of this despair, in the cooperation and mutuality of both readers and read. As Todd and Viola learn to read their worlds, and as they increasingly learn how best to be read—not to resist being read, but to read together—they suggest new possibilities for growth, and even new literacies. As the *Chaos Walking* trilogy ends, the old order is defeated: Mistress Coyle, the suicide bomber, has killed herself and some of the colonists; the oppressive Mayor Prentiss is also dead, another suicide; the Land and the newer colonists are beginning to cooperate; and Viola is reading the words of Todd's mother's diary to Todd in an effort to bring him back from a near-fatal wound. That the novel ends with this reading suggests that even in this utopian vision of communal communication, shared speech, the written and read word

---

[32] The book-burning here, of course, recalls that of Nazi Germany, represented in *The Book Thief*, as well as the destruction of reading materials in *Fly by Night*, *Bitterblue*, and *Un Lun Dun*.

matters. The multi-modal literacy that Todd is beginning to develop before the end, that Viola has begun to perfect, that Ben and the Land and others in this new world are, in different ways, starting to develop, both represents and derives from the characters' political agency: new literacies create a new order.

It is a tenuous and imperfect order, however. In the most hopeful of these scenarios—in texts like *Un Lun Dun, Long Division, Chaos Walking*, and even, perhaps, *Bitterblue*, the ability to read and interpret a variety of materials—multiliteracy—is the key not only to a possible future political agency, but also to the recovery of a historical trauma. When the trauma goes unaddressed, as in *Feed*, or the literacy is too limited, as in most of the texts, agency itself is also constrained. At best, then, YA authors encourage their implied readers to develop skills beyond the text. Only then, they suggest, is the kind of political agency Deeba or Violet or City or even Bitterblue models also available to the critical teen reader. In these texts, and in varying ways, reading changes lives. Perhaps it can change the lives of the novels' readers as well.

Works Cited

Adichie, Chimamanda Ngozi. 2009. The Danger of a Single Story. TED Talk, July. https://www.ted.com/talks/chimamanda_adichie_the_danger_of_a_single_story.

Anderson, M.T. 2002. *Feed*. Cambridge, MA: Candlewick.

———. 2008. Letter to Half Hills High Students, May 19. http://www.halfhollowhills.k12.ny.us/uploaded/User_Folders/english/MT_Anderson_Letter.pdf.

Baker, Daniel. 2012. Why We Need Dragons: The Progressive Potential of Fantasy. *Journal of the Fantastic in the Arts* 23 (3): 437–459.

Barrs, Myra. 2000. Gendered Literacy? *Language Arts* 77 (4) (En-genderings): 287–293.

Bennett, Stephen Earl, Staci L. Rhine, and Richard S. Flickinger. 2000. Reading's Impact on Democratic Citizenship in America. *Political Behavior* 22 (3): 167–195.

Bush, George W. 2002. Remarks on Signing NCLB. http://georgewbush-whitehouse.archives.gov/news/releases/2002/01/20020108-1.html.

Cashore, Kristen. 2012. *Bitterblue*. New York: Dial.

Coats, Karen. 2006. *Fly by Night* (Review). *Bulletin of the Center for Children's Books* 60 (1): 17.

Deszcz-Tryhubczak, Justyna. 2013. 'Minister,' Said the Girl, 'We Need to Talk': China Miéville's *Un Lun Dun* as Radical Fantasy for Children and Young Adults. In *Critical Insights on Contemporary Speculative Fiction*, ed. Booker M. Keith, 137–151. Ipswich, Salem, MA: Salem Press.

Doughty, Amie A. 2013. *"Throw the Book Away": Reading Versus Experience in Children's Fantasy*. Jefferson, NC: McFarland.

Eagleton, Terry. 1983, 1996. *Literary Theory: An Introduction*. Minneapolis, MN: University of Minnesota Press.

Eldred, Janet Carey, and Peter Mortensen. 1992. Reading Literacy Narratives. *College English* 54 (5): 512–539.

Fairclough, Norman. 1995. *Critical Discourse Analysis: The Critical Study of Language*. London: Longman.

Fischer, Steven Roger. 2003. *A History of Reading*. London: Reaktion Books.

Freire, Paulo, and Donaldo Macedo. 1987. *Literacy: Reading the Word and the World*. Westport, CT: Bergin & Garvey.

Graff, Harvey J. 2001. Literacy's Myths and Legacies: From Lessons from the History of Literacy, to the Question of Critical Literacy. In *Difference, Silence, and Textual Practice: Studies in Critical Literacy*, ed. Peter Freebody, Sandy Muspratt, and Bronwyn Dwyer, 1–29. Cresskill, NJ: Hampton Press.

Gray, Richard. 2011. *After the Fall: American Literature Since 9/11*. Malden, MA and Oxford: Wiley-Blackwell.

Hale, Shannon. 2005. *Princess Academy*. New York: Bloomsbury.

Hardinge, Frances. 2005. *Fly by Night*. New York: Harper Trophy.

Hateley, Erica. 2012. 'In the Hands of the Receivers': The Politics of Literacy in *The Savage* by David Almond and Dave McKean. *Children's Literature in Education* 43: 170–180.

International Reading Association. 2012. *Adolescent Literacy*. Position Statement, rev. 2012 ed. Newark, DE. https://www.literacyworldwide.org/docs/default-source/where-we-stand/adolescent-literacy-position-statement.pdf.

Intzidis, Evangelos, and Eleni Karantzola. 2008. Literacies for Active Citizenships. *Literacy and the Promotion of Citizenship: Discourses and Effective Practices*. United Nations Educational, Scientific and Cultural Organization (UNESCO) Institute for Lifelong Learning.

Isaac, Megan. 2016. Re-animating Democracy in the World of Fantasy. Unpublished Talk, Children's Literature Association Annual Convention, Columbus, OH.

Jacobs, Vicki A. 2008. Adolescent Literacy: Putting the Crisis in Context. *Harvard Educational Review* 78 (1): 7–39.

Jameson, Frederic. 1981. *The Political Unconscious: Narrative as a Socially Symbolic Act*. Ithaca: Cornell University Press.

Kidd, Kenneth. 2005. 'A' is for Auschwitz: Psychoanalysis, Trauma Theory, and the 'Children's Literature of Atrocity'. *Children's Literature* 33: 120–149.

Klein, Naomi. 2007. *The Shock Doctrine: The Rise of Disaster Capitalism*. New York: Picador.

Laymon, Kiese. 2013a. *How to Slowly Kill Yourself and Others in America*. Chicago: Bolden (E-pub).

———. 2013b. *Long Division*. Chicago: Bolden Books.

Manguel, Alberto. 1996. *A History of Reading*. New York: Viking.

Miéville, China. 2007. *Un Lun Dun*. New York: Ballantine.

Neem, Johann M. 2017. *Democracy's Schools: The Rise of Public Education in America*. Baltimore: Johns Hopkins University Press.

Ness, Patrick. 2008. *The Knife of Never Letting Go*. Cambridge, MA: Candlewick.

———. 2010. *Monsters of Men*. Cambridge, MA: Candlewick.

Paul, Lissa. 2000. The Naked Truth About Being Literate. *Language Arts* 77 (4) (En-genderings): 335–342.

Pullman, Philip. 2004. The War on Words. *The Guardian*, November 5. https://www.theguardian.com/books/2004/nov/06/usa.politics.

Resnick, Daniel P., and Lauren B. Resnick. 1989. Varieties of Literacy. In *Social History and Issues in Human Consciousness: Some Interdisciplinary Connections*, ed. Andrew E. Barnes and Peter N. Stearns, 171–196. New York: New York University Press.

Sanders, Joe Sutliff. 2009a. The Critical Reader in Children's Metafiction. *The Lion and the Unicorn* 33 (3): 349–361.

———. 2009b. Reinventing Subjectivity: China Miéville's *Un Lun Dun* and the Child Reader. *Extrapolation* 50 (2): 293–306.

Scholastic Kids and Family Reading Report. 2010. *Turning the Page in the Digital Age*. http://mediaroom.scholastic.com/files/KFRR_2010.pdf.

Schwebel, Sara L. 2014. Reading 9/11 from the American Revolution to US Annexation of the Moon: M.T. Anderson's *Feed* and Octavian *Nothing*. *Children's Literature* 42: 197–223.

Smith, Michael W., and Jeffrey D. Wilhelm. 2002. *Reading Don't Fix No Chevys: Literacy in the Lives of Young Men*. Portsmouth, NH: Heinemann.

Smith, Rachel Greenwald. 2011. Organic Shrapnel: Affect and Aesthetics in September 11 Fiction. *American Literature* 83 (1): 153–174.

Snaza, Nathan. 2013. Bewildering Education. *Journal of Curriculum and Pedagogy* 10 (1): 38–54.

Valentine, McKinley. 2012. Is the Fantasy Genre Fundamentally Conservative? Blog Post, October 11. https://mckinleyvalentine.com/2012/10/11/is-the-fantasy-genre-fundamentally-conservative/.

Wolf, Maryanne. 2018. *Reader, Come Home: The Reading Brain in a Digital World*. New York: HarperCollins.

Zusak, Markus. 2005. *The Book Thief*. New York: Knopf.

CHAPTER 7

Epilogue: Reading Reading in *Harry Potter and the Deathly Hallows*

This book, like so many academic books, has taken a long time to write, and over the course of its long gestation I have told many origin stories about it. I have even done so in the pages of this book. But this is the true one. I wrote this book because I was angry at J.K. Rowling.

"Angry" might not be quite the right word. "Confused," perhaps? "Frustrated"? The story I have told goes like this: since about the year 2000, I've had students in my classes who were Harry Potter fans. But by 2009 or thereabouts things changed. I had students for the first time who were not only fans, but who credited the series with making readers of them. These were not always my best students—though some were—but they were all enthusiastic, even voracious, readers. They might have started with Rowling's series, but they hadn't stopped there. They had proved to themselves that they were readers by making it through the over 4000 pages of the series, and moved on to other fantasy literature, or to realistic YA, or to whatever was assigned in their English classes. Whatever they were reading, they asserted, they had become readers because of Harry Potter.[1]

---

[1] In a recent *Paris Review* blog post, Frankie Thomas tells a lovely origin story of close reading and Harry Potter. In her version, the "secret gay love story" of Sirius Black and Remus Lupin in *Harry Potter and the Prisoner of Azkhaban* made close readers of the series' queer fans: "In those days, we were Talmudic scholars and she [J.K. Rowling] was God" (Thomas 2018).

© The Author(s) 2019
E. R. Gruner, *Constructing the Adolescent Reader in Contemporary Young Adult Fiction*, Critical Approaches to Children's Literature,
https://doi.org/10.1057/978-1-137-53924-3_7

And yet in these novels that so encourage reading in their adolescent audience—novels that both individually and taken together comprise a revisionary school story, in which we might expect to find some focus on reading[2]—reading actually plays a surprisingly minor role. While the children and later young adults of the Harry Potter series do buy and use books, magazines, and newspapers, and while letters, spells, and incantations (not to mention pranks) all play a part in the series, the act of reading receives little attention—until the series' end, when it suddenly becomes central. As I come to the end of this book, I return, then, to the Harry Potter series as a synecdoche for contemporary YA literature and its construction of the adolescent reader. In the series, as in the literature I've been discussing throughout this book, reading—especially deep, critical reading, and reading together—is first taken for granted, ignored, and even mocked, but then becomes the surprising key to an engaged adolescent agency.

For the first six books of the Harry Potter series—the books that comprise the actual "school story," since in book seven the protagonists must leave Hogwarts—we see nothing remotely resembling a literature class. While analogs of mathematics, science, history, and even foreign language study occupy Hogwarts students throughout their seven years at the school, imaginative literature of any sort plays no part in their education. Writing is measured by the foot and reading by the page, but interpretation and explication are entirely absent—at least from the formal curriculum. Literacy is, then, purely transactional—the students seem only to read for immediate use or future information, which will be tested in the wizarding equivalent of "O" or "A" levels.

Other critics have found in the Harry Potter series a celebration of reading. See, for example, Seth Lerer's claim that "Books are everywhere in these stories. The wizard children live in libraries; they prepare their potions out of written recipes; and whenever children are in danger, fall ill, or are set a task of bravery, it is the book that saves them. *Harry Potter* ... is a story about reading, an argument for literacy as a key to the imagination" (Lerer 2006, 640). Lerer cites a single scene in support of this broad claim: the scene with which *Harry Potter and the Prisoner of Azkaban* opens. As he notes, Harry is in bed, reading by flashlight—a scene Lerer reads, like other such scenes in other texts, as a scene

---

[2] See Chapter 2 for a discussion of reading and school stories.

of healing, a scene of immersion in literature that provides the young character and the young reader with comfort, security, and imaginative development. Here I believe Lerer makes the same mistake so many humanists do in discussing reading, the error I discussed especially in Chapter 2: he confuses the informational literacy transaction with true literary reading.

So it's worth looking at that scene from *Azkaban* more closely. Harry is, indeed, reading in bed, as his guardians the Dursleys have forbidden him access to his school materials over the summer, and he has a paper to write. He is hiding his reading from them because they fear it—as they fear all magic and, it is fair to say, all evidence of imaginative engagement. So far Lerer seems right enough. But Harry is reading rather strategically here: he is actually "look[ing] for something that would help him write his essay" on witch-burning in the sixteenth century (Rowling 1999, 1–2). And the book he is reading is one of the most frequently referenced imaginary books in the HP canon: Bathilda Bagshot's *A History of Magic*. What we are witnessing is thus, as so often in the early books of the Harry Potter series, an informational literacy transaction rather than any kind of deep or critical reading. Harry is a student doing an assignment, just as Melinda is when she tries to break the code of *The Scarlet Letter* or Tom Henderson is when he mines *The Catcher in the Rye* for vocabulary words. Informational literacy transactions, as I noted earlier in this book, are necessary and even valuable—but they are not what humanists generally mean when they talk about the value of reading.

Harry is, in fact, hardly a book lover. Just ten pages after this idyllic scene of reading in bed, he opens birthday presents that have arrived by owl. As he contemplates the package from Hermione, the narrator—focalizing Harry—remarks: "Knowing Hermione, he was sure it would be a large book full of very difficult spells—but it wasn't. His heart gave a huge bound as he ripped back the paper and saw"—that it wasn't a book at all, but a broom care kit (Rowling 1999, 12). A few pages later he does receive a book as a gift, from Hagrid, and it tries to bite him.

Of course, Lerer is right that the children at Hogwarts consult books frequently. Harry, however, rarely returns to Bagshot's magnum opus—almost every reference to the text in *Harry Potter and the Deathly Hallows* (in which both Bathilda herself and the book feature prominently) is a reminder that he hasn't read it (see, e.g., Rowling 2007, 158 and 318). The children do frequently inhabit the library, as Lerer says, but almost always in search of specific information. In *Harry Potter and the Sorcerer's Stone*, for example, they haunt the stacks in search of information about Nicholas Flamel—information that they ultimately find on a wizard trading card rather than in a history book. The significant exception here is, of course, the children's storybook that Dumbledore leaves to Hermione, *The Tales of Beedle the Bard*: though even in this case, it seems at first that he leaves her a school assignment—the deciphering and translation of the runes—rather than a bedtime story.

Like the deluminator and the snitch that Dumbledore bequeaths to Ron and Harry, *The Tales of Beedle the Bard* is at first a puzzling bequest. Scrimgeour's assessment is not too far off when he suspects it contains "codes, or any means of passing secret messages" (Rowling 2007, 126)—but even though Hermione and her fellows suspect a coded message, it does not yield up its secrets easily. Even when Hermione deciphers the runes in which it is written, the meaning of the bequest—and of the tales within—is still obscure. Ron complains that "reading kids' stories" isn't "useful," and for long stretches of the novel, his assessment seems accurate (Rowling 2007, 202). Indeed, it is only in the context of another text that *The Tales* begin to make sense to the friends. When Hermione notices the mark ("Grindlewald's mark") in Rita Skeeter's quasi-factual *The Lives and Lies of Albus Dumbledore*, she narrows her focus from the *Tales* as a whole to the "Tale of the Three Brothers," in which the mark first appears, and there uncovers the secret of the hallows. Thus far it seems that the *Tales*, like so many other books in the series, exist primarily as a source of information, simply a clue to the existence of the Hallows. Hermione, like Tom Henderson in *King Dork*, seems to become simply a code-breaker, interested in a book for the secrets it can yield up about something else, something true that exists outside of the text.

Indeed, "The Tale of the Three Brothers" makes clear what might otherwise have gone unnoticed: *Harry Potter and the Deathly Hallows* is, above all, a story about deep reading, about interpretation—like other YA novels I've discussed in this book, though unlike its predecessors in the Harry Potter series. Not only *The Tales of Beedle the Bard*, but Rita Skeeter's *The Lives and Lies of Albus Dumbledore*, Xenophilus Lovegood's *The Quibbler*, and texts as various as Kendra and Ariana Dumbledore's headstone and Lily Potter's incomplete letter are suggestive, mysterious, central to unraveling the mysteries of the novel, and also in need of critical interpretation. Even after Harry makes the decision to seek out

Horcruxes rather than Hallows, "he felt that he was still groping in the dark; he had chosen his path but kept looking back, wondering whether he had misread the signs, whether he should not have taken the other way" (Rowling 2007, 503). Like Tom Henderson in *King Dork*, when Harry gives up code-breaking, rejecting the Hallows for Horcruxes, he actually becomes a deeper reader. He and his companions ultimately develop the kind of reading Maryanne Wolf extols in *Reader, Come Home*: analytical, reflective, inferential—and collective (see Wolf 2017, 199–201).

It is something of a mystery how Harry becomes as skilled a reader of the signs as he does, since the most intense training he's had in interpretation during his time at Hogwarts has been the almost comically worthless course on Divination. Although David Steege calls the course the one "most like a literature seminar" in the Hogwarts curriculum, it is a satirically bad one, suggesting that interpretation is arbitrary and entirely subjective (Steege 2002, 153–154; see Gruner 2009, 221).[3] Hermione—the student who most resists Trelawney's methods—becomes the trio's most accomplished reader, pointing out to Harry, for example, that "wizarding history often skates over what wizards have done to other magical races" (*Hallows* 517).[4] Hermione, that is, realizes that truths can be partial, histories slanted, and texts in need of interpretation—though, crucially, such interpretation should not be utterly subjective or relative, but grounded in something beyond mere whim. Without Hermione's more attentive, resistant, reading, Harry might not be able to interpret the signs that are most important to him. Deep reading, in other words, is also communal reading.

---

[3] Trelawney's Divination seminar and Hairwoman's efforts to teach the students in *Speak* to interpret Hawthorne have much in common, it seems to me, not least their insistence that there is one right answer.

[4] Hermione's empathetic reading may remind us both of the gendered reading analyzed in Chapter 3 and the reading methods of marginalized youth discussed in Chapter 4. As a "Mudblood" or Muggle-born wizard, Hermione faces discrimination that her friends do not, which seems to sensitize her to the fates of other magical races, as noted above. The irony of her position is that she is, as a Muggle-born, unfamiliar with the fairy-tales in *The Tales of Beedle the Bard*. While the girl readers of Chapter 3 ground their reading practices in their familiarity with fairy-tales and romances, Hermione has to acquaint herself as a teenager with texts that Ron, for example, has known since childhood. Rowling's play with gender norms here is unusual in a text and series that often relies rather heavily on gender stereotypes.

According to J.K. Rowling, *The Tales of Beedle the Bard* was never intended to be published as a standalone text. When it was, it was as a means to an end—in this case, funding for "the Children's High Level Group, which works to benefit children in desperate need of a voice" (Rowling 2008, xii).[5] Associating literacy with a voice once again, as with *Speak*, takes it beyond the purely informational and didactic purposes for reading and connects it to the development of agency, a development that takes place most fully in the final book of the series, as Harry makes one after another leap of understanding: that, for example, Draco, not Snape, had mastered the Elder Wand; that the Snitch will open for him as he walks to face his death. Another of the *Tales*, "The Fountain of Fair Fortune," provides a further example of the need for interpretation—as the companions learn to read the signs of the fountain they also realize that only one of them truly needs it.[6] Despite the abuse and neglect he suffers as a child, and the in many ways inadequate education he receives at Hogwarts, Harry develops into the kind of reader who does indeed have agency and a voice. His story—and stories like the ones in *The Tales of Beedle the Bard*—thus has the capacity to make better readers of his audience, who are invited to join in the interpretive community, to add their voices to the voices already in play.

THE TALES IN CONSENSUS REALITY

Most of the novels I have discussed in this work are metafictions in that they focus our attention on reading and readers, even if they do not explicitly call our attention to the texts as fictions. *The Tales of Beedle the Bard* works differently, but also metafictionally. The imaginary text cited within the pages of the novel took on concrete form when it was published first as a collector's edition and later as a standalone text sold only on Amazon.com—"translated" by Hermione Granger and "with commentary by" Albus Dumbledore. The entire enterprise was designed to benefit a literacy organization, the Children's High Level Group, founded by J.K. Rowling. Published as a standalone text, the *Tales* come wrapped in the sort of apparatus that might seem to invite critical

---

[5] *The Tales* was the first of the many spinoff texts generated by the series.

[6] In *Proust and the Squid* Maryanne Wolf makes similar connections between literacy, empathy, and agency: as Wolf notes, "the three major jobs of the reading brain are recognizing patterns, planning strategy, and feeling" (Wolf 2007, 140).

reading: notes (by Rowling) and commentary typically invite interpretation, after all. But the content of this material, starting with Rowling's introduction, almost immediately appears to close down interpretation, pointing readers exclusively to moralistic readings of the tales. A few examples will suffice:

> Beedle's stories resemble our fairy-tales in many respects: for instance, virtue is usually rewarded, and wickedness punished. (Rowling 2008, vii)

> In *The Tales of Beedle the Bard* ... we meet heroes and heroines who can perform magic themselves, and yet find it just as hard to solve their problems as we do. Beedle's stories have helped generations of Wizarding parents to explain this painful fact of life to their young children: that magic causes as much trouble as it cures. (Rowling 2008, viii)

> Asha, Altheda, Amata, and Babbitty Rabbitty are all witches who take their fates into their own hands, rather than taking a prolonged nap or waiting for someone to return a lost shoe. (Rowling 2008, ix)

> The heroes and heroines who triumph in his stories are not those with the most powerful magic, but rather those who demonstrate the most kindness, common sense, and ingenuity. (Rowling 2008, x)[7]

These comments direct a reader's interpretation narrowly, turning the stories into moral tales for the young. However, like similar defenses of "our" fairy-tales—and, for that matter, of fantasy literature and the Harry Potter canon itself—the claims fall somewhat flat. After all, "our fairy tales," as Rowling terms them, often reward wickedness (such as theft—see: Jack the Giant-Killer, Puss in Boots, and Hansel & Gretel, for example), and few fairy-tale heroes could be termed "virtuous." Rather, as in the tales she implicitly cites (Sleeping Beauty, Snow White, and Cinderella) he is often simply in the right place at the right time, while she—the heroine—is either asleep or simply waiting. Similarly, while it's clear that Harry and his friends demonstrate kindness, common sense, and ingenuity—like, for example, Babbitty Rabbitty—they are not

---

[7] As Yung-Hsing Wu notes, "most fans agreed that the Tales represented an extension of the lessons about friendship, self-reliance, and perseverance the novels teach and, therefore, offered another opportunity to foster that moral education through reading" (Wu 2010, 200).

above an occasional cheat or even an unforgivable curse. Rowling's comments—whether we take them in defense of Beedle's *Tales* or, indeed, of her entire series—can only take us so far in interpreting, and finding value in, imaginative literature.

More complicated are "Dumbledore's" comments on, for example, "The Wizard and the Hopping Pot." He writes in his notes, underscoring Rowling's didactic introduction, that "the young wizard's conscience awakes" when the pot's noise becomes too loud for him to bear (Rowling 2008, 11). An attentive reader might beg to differ with this assessment, however; perhaps the young wizard is simply bullied by the pot, which "filled to the brim with salt water, and slopped tears all over the floor as it hopped, and brayed, and groaned, and sprouted . . . warts" when he refuses to help the neighbors (Rowling 2008, 7). Indeed, the pleasure of the tale is in the excesses of the hopping pot, which is the most active character in the tale. As the young wizard continues to deny help to his neighbors, the pot's excesses grow, until we find it "choking and retching, crying like a baby, whining like a dog, and spewing out bad cheese and sour milk and a plague of hungry slugs" (Rowling 2008, 7). Disgusting—and, like the Weasley twins' Puking Pastilles, Nosebleed Nougats, and Ton-Tongue Toffees, utterly enjoyable as long as it's not happening to you. If "spewing out bad cheese" is what it takes to awaken a conscience, then the Weasley twins' Wizard Wheezes are a public service. More likely, however, like many of "our" fairy-tales, this tale simply revels in the pleasures of absurdity and excess. Dumbledore's commentary is, then, a misdirection, a sop to an overly scrupulous reader.[8]

At the same time that Dumbledore's commentary (mis)directs a reader's interpretation, however, it also acknowledges alternate readings. In a commentary almost as long as the tale itself, the headmaster goes on to provide not one but two alternate versions. The first is a non-Muggle-loving version in which the pot "protects an innocent wizard from his torch-bearing, pitchfork-toting neighbors by chasing them away from the wizard's cottage, catching them, and swallowing them whole" (Rowling 2008, 13–14). This version, of course, manages to retain the

---

[8] Karen Coats, in her review of the Tales, suggests that "the commentary would serve as a teachable introduction for older students to the kinds of essays and topics one might take up in writing about stories" (Coats 2009, 295); while it is better than Sybil Trelawney's "gloomy overinterpretation," however, one might take such a suggestion with a grain of salt (Steege 2002, 153–154).

pleasurable aspects of the tale—the grotesque excesses of the hopping pot—while providing a moral diametrically opposed to that of the "original." Even more interesting is the bowdlerized version produced by one Beatrice Bloxam, who—like certain critics of fairy-tales and fantasy from the eighteenth century to the present—objects to the tales' "unhealthy preoccupation with the most horrid subjects, such as death, disease, bloodshed, wicked magic, unwholesome characters, and bodily effusions and eruptions of the most disgusting kind" (Rowling 2008, 17).[9] We get only a brief sample: "*Then the little golden pot danced with delight— hippitty hoppitty hop!—on its tiny rosy toes!*" (18). Dumbledore's commentary concludes: "Mrs. Bloxam's tale has met the same response from generations of Wizarding children: uncontrollable retching, followed by an immediate demand to have the book taken from them and mashed into pulp" (Rowling 2008, 19). Dumbledore's commentary, then, serves several functions simultaneously: it directs the reader into the "correct" or authorized interpretation of the tale, it acknowledges that other readings have prevailed in the past, and it gives readers the additional pleasure of rejecting at least one "official" version.

The pleasure—and perhaps even the purpose—of the tales, it turns out, is not in uncovering their rather obvious didactic morals, but in the metafictional play to which they invite a reader—a metafictional play which is, it turns out, true critical literacy. If metafiction is, as Patricia Waugh claims, "a term given to fictional writing which self-consciously and systematically draws attention to its status as an artefact," then *The Tales of Beedle the Bard* is clearly, especially in its standalone context, a metafiction (Waugh 1984, 2). The text of the *Tales* transgresses the boundaries between the fictional universe of the HP saga and the "real world" by joining J.K. Rowling, Hermione Granger, and Albus Dumbledore on a single fictional plane (see González de la Llana Fernández 2010). This blurring of the fictional and "real" is the quintessence of metafiction, and allows the young reader, already thoroughly versed in the Potter saga, to delight in the continued fiction that Rowling's tales actually did take place, somewhere, somehow.

Waugh goes on to claim that writers of metafiction "explore a *theory* of writing fiction" in their metafictions; Rowling, however, seems

---

[9] Here we may hear prefiguring echoes of Megan Cox Gurdon's "Darkness Too Visible," cited in the introduction—one of many articles objecting to fictional depictions of "damage, brutality and losses of the most horrendous kinds" in YA literature.

to me to explore a theory of reading rather than a theory of writing (Waugh 1984, 2, emphasis in original). Here is where the form and the content of the text are perhaps at odds: the playfulness of the form (with its footnotes, illustrations, and commentary) is undercut by the content of the notes and commentary themselves, which are, as we've already seen, almost painfully earnest, didactic, and directive to their assumed young readers. Indeed, they seem to betray a certain distrust of the reader, a desire to make sure the reader gets the "right" message from the text.[10] Yet we might rather claim that they are there much as many of the rules at Hogwarts are—to be resisted, questioned, challenged: to make their readers better.

While *The Tales of Beedle the Bard* demonstrates on one level a supreme distrust of its readers, leading them by the hand to a pre-ordained interpretation, the metafictive play with interpretation that they demonstrate reopens them to critical interrogation. The teenagers who populate the novel must become critical readers, suspecting the adult authority that tells them that children's stories can't possibly be true, or important. Thus, too, readers of the standalone tales may find more value in resisting the overt moralizing of their apparatus.

As Claudia Nelson has written of other metafictions for young readers, reading "promises an alternative to and an escape from adult hegemony" (Nelson 2006, 233). This is the true importance of the tales, not the overt lessons of morality and fair play that they contain (which could, after all, be conveyed in innumerable ways). Harry's final question to Dumbledore in the King's Cross chapter of *Harry Potter and the Deathly Hallows* is perhaps, then, the most telling validation of all: when Harry asks whether their encounter is "real" or "happening inside [his] head," Dumbledore proclaims, "Of course it is happening inside your head, Harry, but why on earth should that mean that it is not real?" (Rowling 2007, 723). As the readers we have examined throughout this book demonstrate, it is precisely what happens inside our heads that is the most real: by reading we—and they—build the future.

---

[10] In a 2009 talk at Oxford University, Diane Purkiss claimed that this is Rowling's method throughout; she particularly cited the [over]use of adverbs as a way of signposting interpretations to the unskilled reader, for example.

WORKS CITED

Coats, Karen. 2009. The Tales of Beedle the Bard (Review). *Bulletin of the Center for Children's Books* 62 (7): 295.

González de la Llana Fernández, Natalia. 2010. Metaficción en *The Tales of Beedle the Bard* de J.K. Rowling. *Espéculo. Revista de estudios literarios,* 44. http://www.ucm.es/info/especulo/numero44/metarowl.html.

Gruner, Elisabeth Rose. 2009. Teach the Children: Education and Knowledge in Recent Children's Fantasy. *Children's Literature* 37: 216–235.

Gurdon, Meghan Cox. 2011 Darkness Too Visible; Contemporary Fiction for Teens Is Rife with Explicit Abuse, Violence and Depravity. Why Is This Considered a Good Idea? *Wall Street Journal,* June 4. http://newman.richmond.edu:2048/login?url=https://search.proquest.com/docview/870051663?accountid=14731. Last updated November 18, 2017.

Lerer, Seth. 2006. "Thy Life to Mend, This Book Attend": Reading and Healing in the Arc of Children's Literature. *New Literary History* 37 (3): 631–642.

Nelson, Claudia. 2006. Writing the Reader: The Literary Child in and Beyond the Book. *Children's Literature Association Quarterly* 31 (3): 222–236.

Purkiss, Diane. 2009. Not Wild About Harry? Harry Potter and the Eco-witches. Lecture given for British Studies at Oxford, July 14. St. John's College, Oxford.

Rowling, J.K. 1999. *Harry Potter and the Prisoner of Azkaban.* New York: Arthur A. Levine.

———. 2007. *Harry Potter and the Deathly Hallows.* New York: Arthur A. Levine.

———. 2008. *The Tales of Beedle the Bard.* London: Children's High Level Group.

Steege, David K. 2002. Harry Potter, Tom Brown, and the British School Story: Lost in Transit? In *The Ivory Tower and Harry Potter: Perspectives on a Literary Phenomenon,* ed. Lana A. Whited, 140–156. Columbia: University of Missouri Press.

Thomas, Frankie. 2018. Harry Potter and the Secret Gay Love Story. *The Paris Review,* December 10. https://www.theparisreview.org/blog/2018/12/10/harry-potter-and-the-secret-gay-love-story/.

Waugh, Patricia. 1984. *Metafiction: The Theory and Practice of Self-Conscious Fiction.* London: Methuen.

Wolf, Maryanne. 2007. *Proust and the Squid: The Story and Science of the Reading Brain.* New York: Harper Perennial.

———. 2017. *Reader, Come Home: The Reading Brain in a Digital World.* New York: HarperCollins.

Wu, Yung-Hsing. 2010. The Magical Matter of Books: Amazon.com and *The Tales of Beedle the Bard.* *Children's Literature Association Quarterly* 35 (2): 190–207.

INDEX

© The Editor(s) (if applicable) and The Author(s) 2019
E. R. Gruner, *Constructing the Adolescent Reader in Contemporary
Young Adult Fiction*, Critical Approaches to Children's Literature,
https://doi.org/10.1057/978-1-137-53924-3

Printed by Printforce, the Netherlands